Children of the Womb

All are Precious in God's Sight

By

Curt Blattman

To thm Manasés my fad richy blers yu [signature]

This book is a work of fiction. Places, events, and situations in this story are purely fictional. Any resemblance to actual persons, living or dead, is coincidental.

ISBN: 1-4140-3553-5 (e-book)
ISBN: 1-4140-3552-7 (Paperback)

This book is printed on acid-free paper.

Scripture quotations identified *KJV* are from the *King James Version* of the Bible.

1stBooks – rev. 12/17/03

Dedicated:

To Beth, for all her common sense advice

To Desirae, for all her vast potential that one day I hope she fully
realizes

&

To the millions of "Children of the Womb," whom one day I pray
won't need to worry
which womb they happen to be conceived in.

1

One Unforgettable Summer

When my father tried to keep me from reading my statement to the entire nation on network television, just three days after the city of Palmerville, New York became the talk of the country, I told him that I wasn't going to compound the terrible mistake I had made by trying to hide what I had done. And yet, I could never have guessed that those words, words shared from my heart nearly two years ago, would set in motion the most important fight for life in the history of America.

I guess the best place to start my story is right at the beginning. It was on a warm and muggy summer day back on August 7, 1982, or so my mom told me, that a six lb. five oz. bundle of joy named Louise Ann Jordan was born. My parents were thrilled to have me and when my little brother Don was born five years later all our many friends in our little city of 3,207 thought we were the perfect family.

Our family was a textbook one: two kids, a stay home mom and a dad who worked hard as the owner of Jordan's Hardware. School, friends and church on Sunday mornings were the things Don and I enjoyed the most about growing up in Palmerville. I loved hanging out with my friends after school and Mom enjoyed having my girlfriends sleep over. My Barbie doll collection was the envy of the neighborhood, although when my dad bought me my seventy-fourth doll for my tenth birthday, I felt that it was time to call it quits.

At our sixth grade graduation ceremony, I received the award as the best math student in Palmerville Elementary, as my parents sat watching proudly in the audience.

Up until this time, the most traumatic thing I can remember happening to me in my very sheltered life was the time I fell off of my bike and broke my arm. I was seven at the time and loved my blue Raleigh almost as much as my Barbie doll collection. The doctor at Memorial General was just wonderful. He said I wouldn't be riding my bike for the next couple of months, but that once my arm had healed, I would be as good as new. Dr. Johnson was so gentle and kind and full of compassion that I told Mom, when I came home from the emergency room, that I wanted to become a doctor or nurse one day and help people get better just like he did.

At twelve I had to get eight stitches to close a bad cut on my leg when I fell on our driveway trying to run for a ball that Don and I were just throwing around. Again Mom was there to bring me to the emergency room where Dr. Peters patched me up. He was great. He was just like Dr. Johnson. He knew how to make you feel better even though the pain was real. I guess these two experiences with doctors made me believe that people in the medical field were always there to help and heal.

By the time my thirteenth birthday had rolled by, I had begun to be interested in boys like so many other young girls my age. I loved going with my girlfriends to see romantic movies whenever they came to the local movie house. It was at about this time that my mom sat me down and explained what all of these physical changes I was experiencing were all about. We spent a long time talking about boys and the dangers of having sex before being married because my parents believed that sex should only take place then. They believed in the Bible and they told me premarital sex was a great sin in the eyes of God.

I trusted my parents and knew how much they loved me. And I believed what they said but, at the same time I saw what men and women did in the movies and on TV and I wondered what was so wrong about kissing and having sex if two people really cared for one another as long as they weren't hurting anyone.

I had just turned fifteen, and as a new freshman at Palmerville High, I was both nervous and excited. It was during my second week at high school that I met Jason. He was also fifteen and the best looking guy in school. I wanted to go out with him even though my parents said that I wouldn't be allowed to go out with boys until I turned sixteen. I guess that, like most young teens, I was torn between wanting to please my parents and wanting to go out with boys, and because of that, I began to tell little white lies. For example, I once used my mom's lipstick and forgot to put it back. Later, when she couldn't find it, I pretended not to know where it was. But I felt so bad that later I confessed to her. And, of course, as usual, she understood. Another time I was late coming home from school and told my dad that we had had to stay late to finish up a project. That time I stopped at Jill's house to try my first cigarette. Fortunately it made me feel sick and I never smoked another one. But the point is that I never lied about anything important. Until I reached high school.

I enjoyed everything about high school. All of my classes were interesting but the one I enjoyed the most was my seventh period history class probably because Jason was in it and I just couldn't keep my eyes off him. Then one day, out of the clear blue, he came up to me and asked me if I would like to go to the movies with him the following Saturday. Despite the fact that I wasn't allowed to go to the movies except with my girlfriends, I told him yes right on the spot.

My conscience bothered me for the rest of the week since I knew I would have to make up a story in order to keep my movie date that weekend but, just then, I wanted to be with Jason more than anything else. My folks really trusted me so when I asked them if I could go to the movies that Saturday with a few of my girlfriends they gave me their blessing and off I went.

It felt so exciting to be going on my first date and with - of all guys - my dream man. Jason seemed like the perfect gentleman. We ate popcorn, drank sodas and, best of all, he held my hand during the film. Later we took a long walk and by seven that evening after a long goodbye kiss, my first real kiss, I went home, determined not to tell my parents what had happened knowing that if I did that I would probably never have a chance to go out with Jason again. As it was, during the next month I must have seen him five or six more times without my parents ever suspecting a thing. By then I had become a pro at deceiving my mom and dad. I wasn't proud of it but my infatuation with Jason had become more important than obeying my parent's wishes. Besides, I reasoned, I was only spending time with a great guy who was a real gentleman. I will admit that by now we were kissing and hugging one another whenever we were alone. He even put his hands on my breast once, but he stopped as soon as I asked him to.

Even though Jason was only fifteen, he was very mature for his age. Since his dad was a banker and his mom a nurse at a hospital in the town of Appleton, which was about a thirty-minute drive from Palmerville, he was often left alone after school. One day after school Jason asked me to come to his house to hang out, adding that his dad had gone on business to Boston and that his mom wouldn't be home until six that night. I had never been alone in a house with a boy before, except, of course, with my little brother Don, and I was a little nervous. But, as I said, I knew that Jason was a gentleman and, after all, what could happen in one or two hours? I called home and told my mom I had to stay late at school for some tutoring in English and that I would catch a late bus.

Being alone with Jason made me feel like an adult for the first time in my life. We were both sitting on the sofa, hugging and kissing when, all of a sudden, I felt his hand on my breast. I told him to stop but this time he said that he loved me, and that if I loved him I wouldn't be so prudish. I didn't know what to do. Within a split second all kinds of thoughts began to cross my mind. I remembered everything my mom had told me, that I wasn't suppose to date or even have a boyfriend until I was sixteen and that any type of sex was wrong unless I was married. Oh, I remembered a lot of things, including what our youth leader at church had said several weeks ago about heavy petting being sinful.

At the same time a host of other voices were beginning to say that if I said no, Jason might want to stop seeing me. Even worse, if I said no maybe it would mean I didn't really love him. And I did love him. I did. And, after all, this felt so good and it was so exciting. I told myself that this wasn't really having sex. Before I knew what had happened Jason began to unloosen my pants and touched me in a way I had never dreamed he would.

Jason was like me. He had never had sex with anyone before. We were both so excited by now that we couldn't stop. He put a condom on and then it happened. And it felt so good. But at the same time I felt so guilty and ashamed. When it was all over I felt cheap and used.

As I returned home we were just about ready to have dinner. Dad offered up a word of prayer for the food and Mom asked me how my day at school had been. I told her everything was fine but deep inside I knew that I had done something terribly wrong in the eyes of Mom, Dad and God.

Over the next few weeks I began to feel dirty inside. Even though we kept on seeing one another, Jason wasn't special anymore. Although it wasn't all his fault, I felt violated. I knew I should have kept my virginity, that it was something special.

By mid-June I was beginning to be excited because school was just about over for the year and I had all kinds of exciting plans for my summer vacation. Staying up late, sleeping over at my girlfriend's houses, shopping at the mall and spending two weeks in Florida with my grandparents were all ahead of me. Of course, in a way I would miss school, but although I did well in all my subjects, I wasn't in love with homework. But I had several projects to complete and a lot of books to read. All in all, summer was going to be a lot of fun.

I couldn't wait to travel to Florida to spend two weeks with my grandparents. But during my first week at Tampa where Grandpa Bob and Grandma Sally lived I began to feel very nauseous and by the end of my second week, I was feeling homesick as well as just plain sick, and just wanted to fly home to Palmerville.

When I arrived at the airport it was great to see my dad, mom and Don waiting to meet me. Mom had been worried because she knew that I hadn't been feeling very well in Florida but I told her just getting home made me feel much better. But the truth was that I didn't know what was happening to me because I had missed two of my periods. What if the unthinkable had happened?

My best friend Sarah's big sister Joan had just graduated from Palmerville High that year and she was the one almost grown-up person with whom I knew I could share anything and not have it get back to my parents.

I will never forget that Wednesday night at the Burger King when I met Joan and told her about missing my periods and feeling sick. When I had finished describing my symptoms, she asked me the one question I didn't want to hear.

"Louise," she said. "Have you ever had sex before?"

"Yes," I admitted. "But it only happened once."

"Well I don't want to alarm you but I think you might be pregnant," she told me.

Joan leaned across the table toward me so that she could keep her voice low. She was blond and beautiful and right now her eyes were sad as they met mine.

"How is that possible," I protested. "We used a condom. There is just no way I can be pregnant."

"Condoms don't always work and from what I read just recently they have a failure rate of over 13% of the time."[1]

Joan was clearly doing her best to keep me from being embarrassed by talking to me in a very matter-of-fact way. I was glad I had told her. This was a lot better than listening to my mom cry and my dad yell.

I still was not willing to believe that just having sex once and using what I thought was sure protection could result in my becoming pregnant. Summer was almost over and school was now only three weeks away. I knew that if I was pregnant, my life was over. In a panic I asked Joan what in the world should I do. To my surprise she had an immediate answer.

"Last year an organization called Planned Parenthood came to Palmerville High and gave out all kinds of information about birth control, safe sex, and told us that all of their services were strictly confidential," she said. "They even told us that you could make an appointment to see them and not have to tell your parents."

"But if it's too late and I'm pregnant, what kind of advice can they offer me?"

Joan shrugged and looked away at the front counter where people were placing their orders.

"One of the options they said young people should consider if they get pregnant was abortion," she told me in a low voice.

The word "abortion" was something I really didn't think much about until now. And the mere mention of it caused my heart to race and my mind to panic. I was really scared but I knew I needed to consider all of my options.

Joan bought one of those kits to help detect if you're pregnant. When the test came back positive, reality began to truly set in. I was in major trouble.

Joan recommended that I get an abortion and not tell my parents anything. The nearest Planned Parenthood clinic was over an hour away, in Dalton but after talking with some of the people in the office there, she was able to find out that there was an abortion clinic only fifteen minutes from Palmerville in the town of Mayfield. Everything was happening so quickly that I felt terrified and so unsure about what to do. Joan, however, helped me sum up the courage to make an appointment the following week and even offered to take me there. She told me that they could definitely tell me if I was pregnant and how far along I was. I began to pray that the pregnancy test was not accurate. And yet I didn't test myself again. I guess I was holding on hard to the hope that this was all a bad dream.

Telling my parents was an option I considered but chose not to go there. If they knew there was even a chance I was pregnant, they would flip and if they knew I was thinking about getting an abortion they would make sure that didn't happen. And it wouldn't be necessary for me to ever tell them because Joan had found out that, according to New York State law, you didn't have to tell your parents or get their permission to get an abortion. By now I had become an expert in deceiving them. It was easy to make up another story about going with my friends to the movies in order to be free to keep my appointment with the abortion clinic.

When it was time to go to my appointment I was full of all kinds of emotions. Of course I was nervous but the guilt I was feeling knowing that abortion was wrong was something I couldn't get rid of.

As we drove to the abortion clinic, Joan and I began to talk about what abortion was all about. I quickly found out that while I knew almost nothing, Joan knew almost as little as I did.

"Basically abortion is just ending an unwanted pregnancy, Louise," she said as we drove by the Burger King where we first discussed the possibility I might be pregnant. "I have a friend who had an abortion several months ago and it went fine. She told me that it was definitely the right thing to do."

"How old is your friend?" I asked her. "Did she say much about how the abortion went?"

It helped to keep talking. I was afraid that if I let myself think, I might tell Joan to turn around and drive home.

"Jackie is sixteen," Joan said. "She knew if she decided to have her baby all her future plans for college and a career would have been ruined. And there was nothing to it. She was able to go home in less than an hour after it was all over."

"Less than an hour? Wow! I guess she must have been relieved."

Joan turned to grin at my reaction. While I was still nervous it was clear that she was taking this pretty much for granted.

"And the best thing was that her parents never even found out," she said.

As we approached Mayfield, Joan's assurances began to make me feel better. Slowly I began to think that if all went well I might be able to pull off the whole thing and if I could, my life just might be able to return to normal. In my heart, however, I kept hoping the pregnancy test was wrong. I quickly found out it wasn't.

We drove up to the clinic around four in the afternoon and Joan told me that she would go in with me. The receptionist was very nice and made me feel a little better than when I first stepped foot in the clinic when all I wanted to do was turn around and leave. Dr. Foote examined me and told me I was definitely pregnant. He said that I was twelve weeks along and based on the fact that I had just turned sixteen, strongly recommended I get an abortion. He reminded me of Dr. Peters. He told me to get dressed and the nurse would explain everything I needed to know about the procedure and that I could ask her any questions I might have.

When I asked Nurse Patterson if Joan could stay by me as I shared my questions she smiled and nodded her head. She was a white-haired, motherly looking woman, someone I knew I could trust.

"Is an abortion painful?" I wanted to know. "And what does a twelve-week baby look like?"

"The procedure is very simple and it doesn't take more than ten minutes," she told me. "Most people are in and out of the clinic in no time and you should only feel some mild discomfort. And remember, Louise what Dr. Foote will be removing is not a baby but a fetus."

"Just exactly what is a fetus?"

"A fetus is just another name for the 'birth matter' before it becomes a baby," she told me with a shrug. "That's the way you should think of it, just a mass of tissue."

When she said it that way, it made me feel more confident about what I was thinking of doing. If it were a tumor I would have it taken out without a moment's thought. A mass of tissue or a tumor, what was the difference, really?

"Louise when would like to schedule your appointment for the procedure?"

"Can I go home and think about it for a few days?" I asked her.

"Well, of course you can, dear, but I must tell you that the longer you wait the more expensive the procedure becomes and the greater the chance you might experience pain."

As we continued to talk she began to explain that if I didn't have the abortion I would find it almost impossible to raise a child while in high school with no job and no money and that my entire social life would be ruined. She told both of us that the abortion would cost $400.

I took Joan aside to a room that overlooked the garden. We sat close together for a while, silently holding hands. And then we began to talk. We listed the reasons why I should go through with it. And then we talked for a long while about what would happen if I didn't. I knew I couldn't face that – my parent's anger, the humiliation.

"I'll bring you back next week if you decide to do it," Joan told me.

In a strange way, that was what made up my mind. It would be easy. I made the appointment for September 5th, two days before school was due to begin.

As we drove home that day I began to share with Joan that the key factor that convinced me to go through with the abortion was the fact that my parents would never find out about it. It was bad enough that I felt deeply ashamed. However, I just couldn't put my mom and dad through the entire shame and disgrace of having everyone in Palmerville know that the Jordan girl was pregnant.

2

A Town in Turmoil

The next problem was money. I had to figure out a way to come up with $400 before September 5th and still make sure my parents stayed in the dark. It's strange how things happen in life. I had just had my birthday a month before and I had received almost that exact amount in cash from my friends and family. Since I spent about $130 on new school clothes, I still had $270 left. Little had I realized when I turned sixteen that I would be using part of my birthday money to prevent my daughter from ever having her first birthday. When I told Joan that I didn't know how to come up with the rest of the money, she told me that she would lend it to me and that I could pay her back whenever I was able to. Then, with $400 in hand, all I had to do was to wait for the "big" day.

On the morning of September 5th I took one last look in the mirror before leaving my house for the clinic and what I saw was a girl who over the last few months had made up one lie after another in order to satisfy her feelings at the expense of her parents loving care and advice. I didn't like what I saw in that mirror but it was now time to go and finish what I knew I had to do. Joan stopped by at noon and we both told my mom that we were going to visit one of Joan's friends in the town of Stockton. With that we were off to see Dr. Foote.

We arrived at the clinic a half hour early and drove around the block once or twice before I summoned the courage to go in. As we reached the front door, Joan could see the panic in my eyes. She told me that it would be all over soon and to stay strong. Stay strong! All I wanted to do was run away and hide. As we walked through the door I knew in my heart that this was my last chance to turn back. But instead of turning back, I turned numb. I guess in a way that was good because if I continued thinking about what I was prepared to do I would have probably called the whole thing off.

I'll never forget how I felt as I stood at the desk in the outer office and Nurse Patterson presented me with the consent form.

"It's just a formality," she said smiling. "Your parents don't need to be consulted, you know. That's why you have to sign this."

And, even though it was all so reasonable, I still felt as though I had done something that was more – I guess you'd say final than anything I had ever done before.

As I entered the procedure room, I told God that I was sorry for what I was about to do and hoped that he would understand that, under the circumstances, I felt that I had no other choice.

The room where my abortion was performed looked clean and actually peaceful. The walls were painted a light blue and I can still remember the painting of an old log cabin hanging on the wall.

During the entire procedure, I kept my eyes closed. I just couldn't believe I was actually going ahead with it. But I was. And at that moment I was too frightened to cry. All I could remember was that horrible sound of what I was later told was something like a very powerful vacuum cleaner that was designed to suck up all of the "birth matter" that was inside of me. I guess I was too scared to look or not prepared to see what was being sucked out of me. After it was all over both Nurse Patterson and Dr. Foote said that I was a model patient and that everything had gone perfectly.

"Just lie here and relax," Dr. Foote told me.

But it was hard to relax, although I was greatly relieved. All seemed to have gone quite well. There had practically been no pain. My problem was gone. Best of all my folks never needed to know what had happened. But, deep inside, I knew that I had done something that could never be undone. And that troubled me.

"Here's a coke," Nurse Patterson said, coming into the examination room with a paper cup in her hand. "Go ahead. Drink up. And after that you can get dressed and go. Don't look so worried, dear. You can go ahead and pick up your life now. You know that, don't you?"

As Joan and I left the clinic I felt for the first time in several weeks like my life had been given back to me. Little could I have known that my entire world was about to be changed forever.

As Joan and I crossed the street to the lot where she had parked her blue Chevy, a young woman wearing a stylish suit joined us.

"Here's some information you ought to read," she said, handing us some material. "I certainly hope that neither one of you actually had an abortion because, after you read this, you may very well feel differently about what you've done."

Perhaps I should have known enough to refuse to take the brochures. Because I *had* had an abortion, hadn't I? But a lot had happened to me in such a little time that I wasn't thinking clearly and I expect that was true of Joan, too.

Once we were in the car, I opened the brochure and, as it happened, the first page I turned to showed the picture of a thirteen-week fetus. When I saw that it was a tiny but unmistakably perfectly formed real baby, I let out a scream that must have reached almost into the next county. And then, for the first time in my entire life, I became totally hysterical, laughing and crying at the same time, unable to stop until finally, Joan, who was clearly frightened, began to shake me. As I handed her the brochure she looked at the picture and immediately knew what must have been taking place in my mind and with my emotions.

"Louise, I'm so sorry," Joan told me. And I saw that she was crying, too. "I can't believe what we just did. I just didn't know what was in your body."

During the last few months I had been spinning one lie after another and now I was glad that Joan didn't try to put her own spin on what both of us had seen. I had just done the unthinkable to my baby and the last thing I needed now was for someone to try to keep me out of touch with reality. I desperately needed to acknowledge what I had done and not try to cover up another mess I had gotten into. I didn't need more deception to help rationalize that it was only "birth matter." The time for lies and cover-ups were now over. I realized that it was time now to find some way to heal myself even though the tiny life within me could never be brought back.

I needed time to think. As we drove home, I began to come up with an idea that I thought just might help me face up to what I had done, as well as let our entire community know what was going on behind the doors at 247 Bolton Road. When I told Joan what I was thinking about, she suggested that I phone my mom from her house and that we talk my plan over with Sarah. My mom even said I could spend the night there if I liked. So after we had finished our dinner that evening, the three of us went up to Sarah's room to discuss my crazy idea.

Sarah already knew that I was pregnant but she had no idea that I got an abortion until I told her that night. Like Joan and me, she knew next to nothing about abortion. When I showed her the picture of what my little baby had probably looked like, she couldn't believe it.

"But that looks just like a real baby," she protested. "You can even count the ten fingers in the picture. How could that doctor and nurse call your baby just some type of 'birth matter?'"

"If only I had seen that picture before I went into the clinic I would never have gotten the abortion," I told her.

The tears came once again as the three of us sat on Sarah's bed, holding one another. And then we began to talk. I had been too shaken after seeing that picture to read the brochure. But Joan had. And now she began to tell us things I didn't know if I could bear to hear.

"You won't believe what is already going on inside the body of a thirteen-week-old fetus," she said as Sarah and I dried our eyes. "At thirteen weeks this so-called fetus is a rapidly forming, complete little person. By three weeks the heart is already pumping blood[2] at over 130 beats a minute."

One part of me didn't want to listen to her but I knew that I had to be practical. And I knew, too, that in an odd way, it would keep me from falling into emotional bits and pieces. I asked Sarah if I could borrow her calculator.

"Sarah, Joan. Just do the math," I explained. "Thirteen weeks is equal to ninety-one days. Ninety-one days less three weeks means that my baby's heart had been beating for seventy days. Multiplying seventy days times twenty-four hours times sixty minutes times 130 beats per minute means that, at the time she died, my little baby's heart had beat 13,104,000 times."

As I thought about that large number my heart started beating a little faster itself. All three of us seemed shocked that at three months the heart was even beating at all.

"Did you know that a preborn begins to suck his or her thumb by nine weeks?"[3]

"Are you for real?" Sarah asked her sister. "Our little cousin Jerry is six and is still sucking his thumb."

"According to the brochure it is simply amazing just how quickly a baby grows," Joan went on, engrossed in what she was reading. "By eight weeks every organ and every body system in a preborn is present."[4]

It was then that I knew I was a murderer. I forced myself to say the word.

"Don't say that, Louise," Joan told me. "Dr. Foote and Nurse Patterson are the murderers, not you. They must have known that your baby wasn't a blob of tissue."

By now I was also feeling very uncomfortable with that New York State law that states a minor doesn't need to notify their parents or need their consent for an abortion. At first I thought this was a great law that would help me hide my problem from my parents. As the three of us discussed this law, we all began to realize that such a law made minors parents for a day. It sounds crazy. I had to get my parents permission to sleep over Sarah and Joan's house but I didn't need their permission to get an abortion. The law said I had to be at least sixteen to get my belly button pierced without parental consent but I could get my baby sucked out of my belly at thirteen, fourteen or fifteen without my parent's permission!

Sarah ran downstairs to get the telephone directory and when she came back, her mother was with her, with a tray of hot chocolate and cookies for us. It made me shiver inside when I thought about how she might feel about me when I had carried out my plan. But then I told myself that how people felt about me wasn't the most important thing. What was important was that I save other girls from what had happened to me.

When we opened the yellow pages to see if the clinic had an ad we were shocked to see that it took up almost a half of a page and that it was in full color. But what was most disturbing was the phrase right in the middle of the advertisement that said in capital letters, MINORS WELLCOME. Suddenly I began to cry again as I remembered how welcome Dr. Foote and his clinic had made me feel when they took my $400 and my baby.

I was so full of guilt that I just knew I had to come clean with the truth. I had deceived my parents and now I had been deceived, as well. In an attempt to get myself out of a very difficult situation I had had to lie to my parents and destroy a tiny innocent life. I knew I had to tell my folks what I had done or I could never get a good night's sleep again.

I had recognized a lot of things in a very small space of time. Now I knew that I had to share what I had learned to help prevent thousands of other teenage girls from making the same mistake I had made. My baby was now gone forever but I wanted to find a way to let those thousand's of girls see the pictures of these tiny babies before they enter these clinics and not after, as I had.

And where, I thought, was my baby now? Had it been thrown out like garbage? And then I remembered that Joan had mentioned to us that the brochure stated that abortion clinics often throw these unborn little children out like trash. The idea that my baby could be in a garbage dumpster right behind the clinic was one of the most heartbreaking things I could ever imagine. And that was when my plan of action was born.

"Listen," I said. "I know that this may sound crazy to you, but I want to go back to the clinic tonight."

At first they were shocked. I think that Joan, in particular, thought that I had come up with this mad idea because I had been emotionally unbalanced by the experience. And perhaps she was right. I only knew that it was something I felt I had to do and I think she and Sarah realized that I would do it without them if I had to.

"This is crazy," Joan said. "But if you are really set on returning tonight, I certainly am not going to let you go by yourself."

And with her assurance I was ready to return to Mayfield.

My plan was to drive over to the clinic late that night and try to climb into those garbage bins. We had seen several of these big dumpsters behind the clinic and I was willing to bet I would find what remained of my baby or some of the other babies that might share the same grisly grave as my baby.

But there was more to my plan and I didn't tell them that until later on. We were all expected to give a five minute report on some aspect of our summer vacation in our English class on our second day back in school which was this coming Friday. What I found in that dumpster would be the centerpiece of my report. I knew that such a presentation would probably get me in a lot of trouble with the school and my parents but there are just some things one has to do and I knew for certain that this was one of them.

By ten-thirty that night we had found a parking space about a block from the clinic. It was very warm but a powerful chill kept going through my body and I began to wonder what in the world was I getting myself into. I was so scared but even more than that, I was determined. With Sarah and Joan as my lookouts and with flashlight in hand I quietly made my way to the back of the Women's Health Services Center where I found myself face to face with a big steel green garbage bin.

As I opened the lid to the bin I began to feel a deeply eerie sensation in my body. I wasn't sure what I was going to find in that big green garbage bin but I knew that there was no turning back now. I had to hold my breath as I climbed in because the smell was so horrible. The hot muggy air only made the smells worse but I continued to rummage through the discarded bottles, cans, cigarette butts and medical items in search of life or should I say death.

Then out of the corner of my eye I spotted an unopened plastic bag. As I began to open it, I knew in my heart that my search was about to end. I had gone to horror movies before but I never thought that I was now going to be a part of one. Tiny arms and legs. Two crushed skulls. A tiny hand. And then, as I reached further into the bag I pulled out what I swore was my seventy-fifth Barbie doll. It was a real baby. It was delicate and was not mutilated like the other babies. It looked like a girl and she had both of her arms and legs, a tiny mouth and the smallest nose I had ever seen. Suddenly the horror overcame me. Somehow I made my way out of the container, closed the lid and ran back to Sarah and Joan as fast as I could.

I told them to get in the car and drive away as fast as they could. As we made our escape, I was in a state of total shock. All I could remember telling Sarah and Joan was that I had been to hell and back. They could see I needed time to compose myself and that I was in no condition to go home and so after driving around the county for about twenty minutes, we pulled over to talk. I asked both of my friends if they were prepared to see what I had discovered in the trash behind the clinic. They didn't seem very eager to want to know but they were now as much a part of my plan as I was. I told them to brace themselves before I opened my bag. Both girls had the same reaction that I had. Horror, disbelief and vomit were quickly manifest as they looked at the butchered remains of a life that never had a chance to be lived.

By the time we pulled into Joan's driveway it was just past midnight. It was late but we were not ready to go to sleep. Instead we began to plan for my big day that Friday at Palmerville High School.

Even though I was only going to have five minutes to share on one of my summer experiences we were up till almost five in the morning discussing what I was going to say and show to my sophomore English class. I was no longer as concerned about what might happen to me as to what I had done to my baby. For the sake of convenience I had already thrown away the rest of my birthday money, betrayed the trust of my parents and decided to play God by destroying a tiny innocent life. Those five minutes were going to have to make an impact and I was willing to face whatever consequences came my way. After four hours of going back and forth we all finally agreed that my presentation was ready and powerful.

"Louise, Sarah and I love you very much," Joan said. "But you have to consider what may happen. We know you're speaking from your heart but—-"

"I can't back off now," I interrupted her. "My conscience is clear that this is what God would want me to do. Since I have to tell my parents what I did anyway, I want them to know that, while I can't undo my mistake, I just might be able to keep other girls from following in my footsteps."

"Go with your convictions and share what's in your heart, Lou," Sarah told me as she nervously played with her dark brown hair and continued to pace the floor of her room. "Joanie and I are ready to stand behind you a hundred percent."

"Thanks for your support, Sarah," I told her. "I'm scared to death but if I don't go through with it I'll never be able to live with myself."

"Somehow everything is going to turn out OK but you - or should I say all of us - may have to travel on a wild ride to get there," Joan added.

I was grateful that I had one more day before school started since I was both emotionally and physically exhausted. I knew I wouldn't be able to relax on my final day off, but at least I could try my best to compose myself before my big presentation. Having to hide the bag with the baby parts and the tiny body in my closet that night had made sleeping in my room almost impossible. I kept waking up in a cold sweat, wondering when this nightmare would ever end.

Thursday, our first day back to school, normally should have been a day full of excitement. But under the circumstances, the sight of seeing so many familiar faces did little to change my somber mood.

I started my day in homeroom, and as soon as I took my seat, I said a little prayer to calm my nerves. As second period English class began I slowly walked through the door and took a seat near the back of the classroom.

Mrs. Sterling was about forty years old and couldn't have been more than five feet three inches tall. She had long blond hair and a beautiful smile but, after about ten minutes into the class, I could see she was very conservative and formal. I knew my presentation would probably give her a heart attack but there was no turning back now. When she told us to be prepared to give our summer experience presentations on either Friday or Monday I went into a panic. I had forgotten that everyone in the class had to give a presentation and didn't realize that we might not have time to finish them all in one day. I wanted to get it over with as soon as possible and couldn't bear to wait the whole weekend to give mine. She looked in her attendance book and said that those students with last names beginning with "A" through "K" would go on Friday and the rest on Monday. Needless to say I was greatly relieved that Louise Ann Jordan was still on track for Friday.

To the surprise of everyone Mrs. Sterling took the last few minutes of her class to share one of her summer experiences, telling us about a trip she and her entire family had made to Disney World in Florida. Apparently her three children had had a wonderful time and her youngest son, Barry who was five had fallen in love with Mickey Mouse. Just then the bell sounded and it was time to move on to US History.

After what had happened just two days before, it was difficult for me to mingle with my friends as though nothing had changed and I was especially glad that Jason was not going to Palmerville High this year. His dad had gotten a transfer to the Boston headquarters of his bank and Jason had just moved two weeks before with his family to Boston. Over the last month of the summer we had begun to lose interest in one another and his move was actually a welcomed relief to me.

Having Sarah in my English class was a powerful moral support to me. I had all but memorized what I intended to say and I spent my last night before the big day in asking God to help me stay strong. I had carefully hidden the baby parts and my newest baby Barbie doll in my closet. If my parents ever found them it would be curtains for me. Right before bed I carefully placed everything in my backpack and shoved my bag under my bed. I was up early the next morning and right after breakfast I kissed my mom good-bye, told her I loved her, and headed for the school bus.

The bell for Math had just rung to signal it was time to move on to our next class. As I made the long walk down the hall to Mrs. Sterling's class I caught up with Sarah and the two of us nervously entered our English class. Since the reports would be given in alphabetical order, Sarah, whose last name was Peters would be speaking on Monday. As for me, I figured I would be near the end of the group today.

Bob Benson went first and spoke about his trip to Georgia. Jerry Carter talked about all the fun he had had flying his kites. Julie Finney's story was the most interesting. She had gone, with her family on a safari to Kenya, and she told the class how a lion had almost attacked her. Several of the other stories were not too inspiring. When it was finally my turn, I slowly walked up to the front of the class and placed my backpack on a table in the front of the room.

I began by saying that I had felt strangely compelled one night earlier this week to travel to a medical clinic in the nearby city of Mayfield where, earlier that same day, I had had some minor surgery done.

"You see," I told them, "the doctor had removed something from me that day, something that I wanted back." By now the class was spellbound wondering what could I be talking about. I told my classmates that, after about ten minutes of searching on the clinic grounds, I had found what I had been looking for.

It was now time to share my dark secret, to show the evidence. Opening my backpack I quickly took out two covered trays and placed them on the table, saying, "This past Tuesday, I murdered my baby. The contents of these two trays represent all that remain of several other babies who were killed at the abortion clinic I went to."

With that I took off the covers. I knew that the sight of these severed little arms and legs, tiny hands, one ripped open chest cavity and several crushed skulls, alongside the body of the intact complete baby, would bring about a reaction, but I could never in a million years have imagined its magnitude.

Two of my friends, Jean and Heather, ran out of the room. Jane and two other girls began to vomit. Several of the guys came up for a closer look and Steven ran for the door shouting, "I'm going to get Principal Foster." As for Mrs. Sterling, she was in a state of shock. "Louise," she screamed, "what in the world is going on and have you gone mad?"

Just then the bell sounded to end class and students from all over the building began to pour into our English room, dozens of students and several teachers crowding around the baby parts to get a closer look. Panic and chaos had engulfed Palmerville High. It was almost as if a chain reaction had begun.

As I found out later that because my friend Jessica thought that my Barbie baby was still alive and might need medical help, she ran to the attendance office where they dialed "911" to request an ambulance. By the time Principal Foster had arrived the entire classroom was in a state of bedlam. When Jessica tried to tell the

"911" operator that one of the students had murdered her baby the operator not only dispatched an ambulance but the police.

People were coming at me from every direction. I quickly ran to the window to get some air. As I looked out I heard the sound of sirens. I also saw a news truck with cameras pulling up in front of school. Apparently Jeremy Penny had ran to his locker and called his dad, who was editor of the largest newspaper in the county, from his cell phone. Dean Simmons called out my name on the intercom and told me that my mother was called and was on her way to the school. By now something inside of me was saying that the town of Palmerville would never be the same again. And, certainly, neither would I.

3

Mr. Eliott's Words of Wisdom

"Mrs. Sterling, can you tell us what happened in your class this morning?"

The room was full of reporters now and cameras were everywhere.

"One of my students said she had just murdered her baby," she said, clearly nervous and confused. "She brought these baby parts back from the abortion clinic she went to."

"She what!"

"She said she had had an abortion and killed her baby in the process. You see, each student had to do a short presentation on one of the highlights of their summer vacation. And God knows why, Louise chose to talk about her abortion."

As she continued to try to explain what had taken place, my mom appeared wearing her favorite pink dress, and obviously frightened by the crowd of people. "Are you Louise's mother?" Mrs. Sterling demanded. Immediately the reporters crowded around my mom asking her how she could let her daughter get an abortion then come to school and show off these so called "end products."

Suddenly my mom fainted. Clearly the shock of hearing her daughter had had an abortion was too much for her to take in all at once, particularly since she hadn't had any idea I was even pregnant.

23

After about two minutes I knelt on the floor beside her. When she came to, she began to cry.

"Is it true you had an abortion, Louise?" she asked me. By now the two of us were both crying and holding on to one another. Just then one of the reporters held a microphone right in front of us.

"Young lady," he said. "Do you mean to tell me that your mom has just found out that you got an abortion?"

My plan had been to educate my class about the evils of abortion and perhaps get the whole school involved. But I began to see that I had a chance to make a statement that might even make tonight's local news. The microphones and cameras made me nervous but this was the chance I wanted. I also needed to confess and ask for forgiveness for the evil I had committed.

For the next ten minutes I told Mr. Jansen from WRRM news, my mom and the rest of the teachers and students in my crowded English classroom about the events that had led up to the chaos that was just now taking place at Palmerville High. While the cameras rolled, I apologized to my mom for the double life I had led and for all the lies I had told to cover up my secret. I said that I should have gone to my parents right away when I discovered I was pregnant but I had been too ashamed. Question after question was hurled my way and I answered all of them as honestly as I could.

"Louise," Mr. Jansen said, "do you feel that the abortion clinic gave you the proper counseling and information about the entire procedure?"

Looking right at the camera I began to lash out at Dr. Foote and Nurse Patterson.

"I was lied to," I said as calmly as I could. "They told me that since I was only thirteen weeks along they were just going to remove some 'birth matter' from my belly."

Quickly I ran and grabbed my little dead baby from the second tray and placed it right in front of the camera. "Does this look like 'birth matter' to you," I blurted out angrily, "or does it look like a baby?"

After the police questioned us as to what had happened Principal Foster decided to close the school for the rest of the day. Mom called Dad and slowly explained in detail all that she knew. Within twenty minutes, he was by my side and to my surprise and shock he didn't yell at me. Instead he gave me a big hug and told me he loved me. When all the interviews and questions were over, and Dad and Mom were ready to take me home, Mr. Jansen told us that my story might be on the local six o'clock news.

Just as we were walking down the hall to leave the building Principal Foster called my mom, dad and me into his office. I was ready to hear him read me the riot act right in front of my parents but instead he said, "Mr. and Mrs. Jordan, you have a very brave and courageous young daughter. I am very much against abortion. I consider it the killing of innocent life. While I certainly am not pleased that Louise got an abortion, she has helped me to understand how abortion clinics lie and distort the truth to deceive their patients into giving them their business."

"There's still no way for me to defend my actions," I said in a low voice.

Everything that had happened had shaken me. The night I had gone back to the clinic, the night I had made my plan seemed as vivid as though it had just happened. But I had already moved down a path that seemed, somehow, as if it had always been waiting for me. And I could be strong enough, I knew, to admit my own guilt.

"You're just one of thousands of young girls who made a serious mistake based on wrong information," the principal told me, as he leaned forward in his black leather chair smiling as if to indicate he knew just how bad I felt.

"But I still lied to my mom and dad and caused all of this commotion at Palmerville High," I protested.

"Louise, you are one of those rare young people who admit their mistake and try to do whatever they can to make it right," he assured me. "While your approach to making it right was, to say the least, highly unorthodox, I think you have definitely been able to make a statement about the evils of abortion."

"Thanks so much for understanding all of this craziness," my father said, holding out his hand. "Our family needs time to try to piece all of this together."

"Everything is going to be OK," Principal Foster said, smiling again. "My office is always open if ever you need to talk. Louise, remember that!"

With that we exchanged good-bye's and I gave my principal a big hug, and all during the car ride home, I tried to let my parents know how deeply sorry I was for hiding everything that had gone on in my life during the past six months.

"Louise, did we go wrong somewhere in raising you?" my mother asked. Her color had almost returned to normal by now but the look in her eyes clearly revealed a sadness I had rarely seen. "What else could have caused you to lie and deceive us the way you did?"

"You're wonderful parents," I told them. "I guess I took for granted all of the good things you taught me over the years. And then I gave in to my feelings and temporarily forgot all the positive lessons you guys taught me. While I can't change the past, I do want to start over. I guess I had to learn the hard way."

Word sure travels fast in a small town. Just then we turned the corner onto our street and found that our home had several visitors waiting for our return. By the time my dad had parked our car and put the key in our front door several TV cameras were recording our every move and questions were being fired at us from every direction. Two people from a local Right to Life organization asked if they could speak to me. Finally Dad, who is an ex-Marine, began to shout that he wanted everyone to leave. He told the reporters that in an hour or two he would come out and make a statement. With that said, he told my mom and me to go inside. We did and he quickly followed closing our front door behind him.

During the next hour I told my mom and dad about all the events that had led up to what had happened at Palmerville High today. Mom was clearly amazed. In fact, she looked at me as though she had never seen me before. But only just at first, only until she really understood what had happened.

Dad, on the other hand, while in shock, focused on my dramatic presentation in class. It was as though he understood that I had done it in order to tell everyone what had taken place in the most dramatic way possible. It was such a relief to share everything that was in my heart with them. By this time dad asked me to please go to my room. He needed some time in private to talk with my mom about all of these events.

During the next sixty minutes I could hear my dad and mom doing a lot of talking and I was certain that, knowing my father, he was trying to figure out how we as a family should address the media, which by now had literally camped out in front of our home. As we turned on the set to WRRM, our local news station, Roger Topaz, the news anchor, was opening the newscast with these words: "A sixteen-year-old high school student, Louise Ann Jordan, from Palmerville High, claimed today that she had murdered her baby." As he spoke, the camera zoomed in on the tiny aborted baby I had brought with me to class. Next Mr. Jansen, the man who interviewed me at school today, explained that this had not been a real murder but rather an abortion. I hadn't realized until I saw the tape, that I had been so emotional, so full of determination to be heard. But that was what came across. And this was the tape that I would soon learn was destined to make just about every major newscast around the country during the next two days.

Later it seemed that just about everyone in Palmerville saw and heard me on the local news. And the quote that made such a lasting impression on so many was now being repeated over and over again. Within the next twenty-four hours virtually all of America would be watching me place my dead baby right in front of their eyes and ask, "Does this look like 'birth matter' to you or does it look like a baby?"

Dad had not seen any of my interview until now and just could not believe how forceful a statement I had made in support of the pro-life cause. Since he was strongly against abortion, he felt that this entire experience might be able to do some good in opening people's eyes to just what abortion is all about. After the news report was aired, Mom manned our phone which had begun to ring non-stop, and Dad took me into his study to discuss what I wanted to say to the ever-increasing crowd that was gathering minute by minute outside of our home.

"Dad," I told him. "I don't know much about abortion. All I know is that it is very wrong because it kills babies."

It was hard for me to say words like "kill." Something inside me seemed to die inside each time it happened. But I knew I had to talk about what had really happened.

"You're certainly right about that," he replied. "All abortions have one thing in common – innocent babies are put to death."

Innocent babies! That chilling thought was something I just couldn't get out of my mind. My aborted baby was indeed very innocent and yet at the time I never looked at it that way.

"One thing for sure, I want everyone to know how sorry I am for having my abortion," I said, "And I also need to let other girls in my situation know that the people at Dr. Foote's clinic lie to their patients – at least they did to me."

"That's fine," he replied, picking up a rubber ball and squeezing it, something he always did when he was tense. "But before you make any statement, don't you think you should learn a bit more on the subject of abortion?"

I agreed to take a day or two to read up on abortion and to write down what I wanted to say. And then I intended to let him see it.

Fortunately during my freshman year at Palmerville High, I had joined the debating team. I really enjoy debating, no matter what the topic, because it forced me to study all sides of the subject. Our team coach, Mr. Nardelli said, that considering my age, I was already a skilled debater and at the end of our freshman year, he told our entire team that the skills we were developing in preparing and participating in our debates would prove invaluable, no matter what career we chose to go into. Little did I realize that I was soon going to put those skills to use in ways I could never have dreamed possible.

"I need to study the issue first," I told my father. "It should be as though I were preparing for a debate, shouldn't it? Because a lot of people don't understand and it's up to me to make them."

"That's just the approach I hoped you take," my dad told me, as he stood up and started to walk across the room.

"I have just the right book. If you come with me to my study I think I know where I can find it."

I had always loved my dad's study with bookcase upon bookcase surrounding his big oak desk. My father loved to read and his two thousand plus books were proof enough. After scanning one of the bookcases behind his desk dad grabbed a paperback book from the top shelf and handed it to me. "This book has a wealth of information about abortion," he told me. "If you read this book, it will help prepare you for what you want to share."

As I took the book dad told me something, I guess, I desperately needed to hear.

"Your mom and I are clearly disappointed in you because of what you did, but we are also very proud that you were willing to confess to your mistake," he said, hugging me close. "And we are equally proud that you have decided to try to help others not repeat what you had to go through. We love you, Louise, very much."

Tears began to well up in my eyes as I realized just how lucky I was to have parents who loved me no matter what.

By now it was almost eight in the evening and my dad went outside and told the entire crowd that had gathered, waiting to hear me speak, that I would not be giving any statements this evening. He added that I was going to take the weekend to prepare my thoughts and that I would probably make a statement on Monday night.

The book was titled *Why Can't We Love Them Both* by Dr. & Mrs. J. C. Willke.[5] I quickly turned to the back where pictures of tiny eight, eleven and fourteen-week-old fetuses were shown.[6] These pictures were remarkably similar to the ones I had seen in the pamphlet I had received this past Tuesday. If a picture is worth a thousand words then I knew a thousand times in my heart I must have killed my baby.

But just then the thought crossed my mind that perhaps all of these pictures were taken with trick photography. Perhaps these were not real babies but dolls made to look like them or perhaps plastic models. After all, I remember reading in a magazine article last year that some people believe we never really landed on the moon, that it was all a NASA publicity scheme and that trick photography and special lighting had been used to make you think that we landed there when, in fact, it had all happened behind closed doors in a studio.

But unfortunately, thanks to my experience, I knew that this was far from being an example of trick photography because I had seen and touched the real thing. There had been no cameras in the dumpster, only the gruesome end products of another day's work at Dr. Foote's clinic. The only trick that had been played this week was my being told that what was growing inside of my body was just "birth matter."

Well, I started to read that Friday night and I just couldn't put Dr. Willke's book down. Except for eating my meals, I spent the entire weekend reading page after page on every facet of the abortion issue. Before I made a public statement about why I had had an abortion and what had made me give such an extraordinary classroom presentation, I wanted to know the facts behind what abortion really was. By Sunday evening I had finished the entire book and I now knew for certain that I had, in fact, murdered my baby. Despite what anyone else might say, the word "murder" was not too strong.

After grabbing something to drink and a snack from the kitchen I joined my parents in the living room and began to discuss some of the new things I had just discovered.

I knew from my eighth grade history class that slavery had been legal in America during the first half of the nineteenth century. But what I hadn't known until now was that in 1857 the U. S. Supreme Court had ruled that black people were not legal "persons" according to the U. S. Constitution. What that meant was that blacks could be bought, sold, traded and even killed at the discretion of their owner. If a slave married and had children, those children, were automatically the property of their owner. And this meant that the slave owner could take these children and sell them. Not only that but the slave owner didn't need to keep families together and often he didn't. How could the highest court in America, practicing law in the freest country on the face of the earth, condone one of the most evil practices in the history of mankind! History has since recorded this U. S. Supreme Court case as one of the most monumentally wrong decisions ever made.

116 years after our highest court had spoken out in favor of slavery, our U. S. Supreme court in an eerie parallel decision spoke out again. This time they declared a different entire class of people, "the unborn," not legal "persons" according to the U. S. Constitution. In the famous *Roe v. Wade* decision our U. S. Supreme Court ruled that the unborn were not considered persons and therefore could be killed at the discretion of their owner, the mother. In both the slavery and abortion rulings the court voted seven to two in favor of legalization. I didn't know much about the field of law but there was one thing I knew for sure and that was that a thirteen-week-old pre-born was just as much a baby as a thirteen-week-old live birth. The only difference was that one baby was nine months older than the other and about seventeen pounds heavier.

I also could see that there was something very bizarre with these U. S. Supreme Court decisions.

"Dad," I said, now saying each word slowly and clearly, "according to the way I see it, back in 1857 it was illegal to abort a white unborn child but perfectly legal to kill a black slave if you decided you didn't want him anymore. But today it is perfectly legal to kill a white unborn baby but it's murder to kill a black person of any age."

"I never looked at it the way you have, Louise," he replied, looking stunned at the comparison I had just made. "But I see your point. Here we have a group of nine brilliant Americans living over 100 years apart, changing their minds on which class of people can live and which class may not."

As we continued to talk I was relieved to see that my mom seemed more relaxed. Her cheeks were their usually shiny red again and her eyes sparkled. When I asked her what she knew about how babies develop in the womb, she admitted that she didn't know much. So I told her about some of the things I had been reading in Dr. Willke's book.

"Mom," I said, "if we were living 100 years ago, science could only have told us that it took nine months for a baby to be born because there was little or no information about what was going on inside a woman's body."

By now Mom was all ears and wanted to know what had gone on inside of her body sixteen years ago when I was in the development stage. I picked up dad's *Why Can't We Love Them Both* book and began to share some of my underlined passages on how a baby develops inside a mother's womb.

"If I represented an average pre-born," I told her, sitting down on a footstool close to her chair, "then at twenty-one days my heart was formed and it was already pumping blood.[7] My eyes, ears and respiratory system began to form only four weeks after fertilization.[8] If they had decided to try to record my brain waves, they would have been able to do so at forty days with an Electroencephalogram.[9] And if they had taken a picture of my nine-week-old tiny hand, they would have been able to see me sucking my thumb.[10] At nine to ten weeks I could squint, swallow, and move my tongue.[11] And Mom, if you had put a pencil in the palm of my hand at nine weeks I could have bent my fingers around it."[12]

"Louise, how in heaven's name can 'birth matter' grasp an object in its hand?"

"Modern science has made it so simple that even a child could tell what I was at thirteen weeks old. Mom if I went into my old second grade class where Mrs. Roberts still teaches and asked her students what has a heart, a brain, ten fingers, ten toes, sucks its thumb and right now is hiding in Mrs. Roberts's belly, I bet you I would get the same answer from one hundred percent of the class. I feel quite confident they all would say a baby."

Perhaps it was just because I needed to be distracted from what had happened to me, but I was so excited that I had to get up and pace the floor. My mind was whirling with thoughts.

Another thing that really disturbed me concerned Grandma Jenny, I said. Dad's mom was almost seventy years old and hadn't been well for a long time. Finally she got so sick that my father had to place her in a nursing home in the town of Stevens Junction, ten miles north of Palmerville. I loved Grandma Jenny but I hated to visit her now because she didn't even recognize who I was anymore. She was almost like a vegetable, just sitting in her wheelchair and mumbling some words every now and then when only a few years ago we used to make chocolate chip cookies together and watch my favorite shows on TV. Even though I still loved my Grandma it seemed kind of sad to spend all that money to keep her alive. But she was still my Grandma and I felt that God still had a plan for her life even though I couldn't figure out what it might be.

All of a sudden I began to cry. "Louise, what's the matter?" Dad gently asked as he saw tears rolling down my face.

"I was just thinking that, while I can't imagine what plan God could possibly have with Grandma, I know for certain that God had a wonderful plan for my baby before I murdered it."

Dad was silent for a long time as he held me in his arms. He usually had words of comfort to share with me whenever I would cry; but this time he just held me and told me he loved me. Because of him, I felt strong enough to go back to my reading. It was so important that I be prepared to make my case.

From first page to last, Dr. Willke's book made me realize that I knew very little about what abortion was really all about, but when I had finished, I knew with absolute certainty that abortion was the act of killing a tiny human being. Every page documented the preciousness of the unborn. In my ninth-grade science class Mr. Eliott taught us that theories were OK to discuss and debate but scientific facts were the only truths we should place our trust in. The avalanche of scientific evidence that my thirteen-week-old pre-born was a real little person was so overwhelming that anyone who tried to deny it had to be living in a fantasy world.

After sharing a few more of my observations, I asked my parents a question that had been on my mind ever since I realized what a horrible thing I had done just a few days earlier.

"Dad," I said, with tears beginning to form in my eyes, "how can a doctor, trained to heal and save lives use his skills to kill and destroy life? According to what I've just read, doctors today are performing surgery on babies that are still inside the womb. I don't know for sure but I bet you if surgery is performed on a fetus while it's still inside a woman's body, the doctor's bill probably is for medical treatment on a second patient. And if there *is* a second patient then isn't the doctor saying that the unborn is clearly a 'person?' Why did my doctor lie to me, Dad? Why did he take my money and then kill my baby?"

Grief came flooding over me in a great wave but I knew that I could not give in to the tears. Not now. Not when there was still so much left to do.

"Sweetheart, Before I try to answer your question I need to ask you a question. How can you see things that we adults often can't?"

I paused for a minute. I knew what I wanted to tell him but it was so difficult to put into words.

"I guess my heart is still like the heart of a child. I just let my heart do the thinking for me. If after thirteen million heartbeats, I still didn't realize that I had another human life growing inside of me, then how could I ever know what reality really is?"

I could see that my father didn't want to answer my question but apparently Mom did.

"Some doctors are in it just for the money," she said, and it was clear that she was choosing her words very carefully. "And from what I understand abortions can be quite profitable. Sadly some doctors actually believe they are providing a vital service to women by helping them eliminate a big problem."

Mom's answer made sense but whatever drove these abortionists to destroy innocent life still had to come up against Mr. Eliott's law of scientific facts. They either had to deny the facts or rationalize them away. Either way Mr. Eliott's law stills holds true. Abortion kills a live human being!

By now we had been talking for hours and I knew I needed to spend the next day writing down what I wanted to say to the TV audience. Dad knew that meant missing a day of school but he agreed that school could wait another day. In fact, Dad said that he was only going to work a half day because he wanted to get home early to review what I was going to read later that evening.

It was so strange and wonderful at the same time. I had expected that he and Mom would be so angry with me, and, as it turned out, they had been so supportive.

By now I was exhausted. It had been an incredible week and my bed looked very inviting. As I put my head on my pillow and closed my eyes, I wondered what surprises tomorrow might bring.

4

The National Spotlight

On Saturday dad had several discussions with people from the news media regarding when I would give my statement as well as to which news station I might give an interview. Dad suggested that the best forum for me might be to hold a news conference at which I would read my statement and then take questions from the news media. Just the thought of facing a lot of people with my story made shivers run up and down my back but I felt that it would give me the freedom to share my message with the widest possible audience. I also knew that I had better get use to having questions thrown at me since dad had already informed me that I was probably going to be in the spotlight for the next few days. As far as location, I told my parents I wanted to hold my news conference right outside Dr. Foote's abortion clinic on Monday evening at seven.

Dad spoke to the head of the news department at WRRM who agreed to make all the arrangements for the news conference. All that remained was for me to prepare the written statement I would read on Monday evening. I had always enjoyed writing essays in school but this had to be something very special. I was up early that Monday morning and by noon felt as if I had put down the words I wanted to read. The night before I had called Sarah and Jenny Woods, a girl whose judgment I really trusted, and asked them if they could come over right after school to listen to what I had written. They would be my first audience and I hoped they would give me the go ahead.

As I began to read, they sat very quietly on my bed listening to each and every word. Sarah timed my statement and told me that it had taken six minutes.

"If you want your statement to be controversial," Jenny told me, giving me the thumbs up sign, "then I think what you've just read us is guaranteed to accomplish that goal."

"I think it's great, Lou," Sarah added, hugging me. "People need to know what a horrible thing abortion is. They need to realize that every day thousands of tiny innocent lives are destroyed."

"Do you think it will offend a lot of people since I use some pretty strong language?" I asked them.

"Yes," Sarah said. "But so what? I am already offended that Dr. Foote lied to my best friend and took the life of your baby. Somebody has to speak up for the babies. They certainly can't do it themselves."

"You're the perfect person to tell everyone what's really happening," Jenny chimed in. "Sarah and I are behind you and your speech one hundred percent. And if you back down now we both are going to be very upset with you."

"Thanks for the encouragement," I said. "But I still need the go ahead from a much tougher critic – my dad."

Normally my father wouldn't have come home until around seven. But today, he arrived home by mid afternoon to listen to what I had written. Dad listened intently, and as I concluded my remarks, rose from his leather chair and took my speech away from me.

"Louise, this is your speech and I promised myself that if you feel comfortable with it then I would give my blessing. However, I don't think you realize the powerful pro-choice forces that will come against our family if you read this statement. It's dynamite alright but it may cause too big an explosion for the Jordan family to handle."

"Dad, I can't wimp out now," I protested. "Either I expose what happened at the clinic this past Tuesday or else I might as well downplay the whole thing."

I had already exposed myself to ridicule and shame by making my classroom presentation. This was no time to hold back on my words. I had been lied to and because of that my daughter was now dead. I guess somehow, in my heart, I believed all along that my baby would have been a girl. Was I now angry? You bet. But I was also determined to let everyone know exactly how I felt about what had happened to me.

My father was a man of his word and even though he felt I should tone down my words he gave his blessing when he saw how important this was to me.

That night we all had an early supper, after which we were on the road to 247 Bolton Road. When we arrived at the clinic, I could hardly believe my eyes when I saw that there were already several thousand people surrounding the building. There were police all over the place and news trucks and cameras were everywhere. In my wildest dreams I could never have imagined that my high school presentation could have caused such a commotion. Apparently, when dad told the news station the time and the place for my news conference this past Saturday, word had immediately traveled all over the country. During the past few days my story was becoming the single most galvanizing event in the abortion debate since the famous *Roe v. Wade* decision back in 1973, a decision that had legalized abortion in America.

Police barricades were set up right in front of the clinic. On one side the pro-choice group was loudly demanding that my statement not be read. They kept shouting, "Let Women Choose," and "Keep Abortion Legal," as well as several other pro-choice phrases. On the other side of the street was a large group of people of all ages shouting my name and carrying pro-life signs. One sign that really touched my heart said, "Abortion Stops a Beating Heart." Although Dad and Mom were just as unprepared for this immense crowd as I was, they kept telling me to stay strong and go with my conscience.

Mr. Hanson, the head of WRRM, came over and introduced himself to us before taking us over to a makeshift stage area directly across the street from the abortion clinic. He told us that Roger Topaz, the same News anchor who had opened the Friday newscast with my story, would open this special news conference by briefly discussing the events that had taken place the last few days as a result of my classroom presentation. After a brief introduction, he planned to introduce me and announce that I had prepared a written statement that I wanted to read. And finally, after my statement, he would open up the conference for questions from the assembled news media. Mr. Topaz told me to try to stay calm and relax. He could see that I was very nervous but he had such a gentle tone in his voice that for the first time all day I began to calm myself down.

At seven sharp the cameras started to roll and Roger Topaz took center stage. It was destined to be a night that I would never forget.

"Good evening," he said in his deep baritone voice. "Tonight we bring you a special news story that has taken America by storm. It was only three short days ago that a small town tenth grader, sixteen-year-old Louise Ann Jordan made national news by claiming that she had murdered her baby. The picture of her holding a tiny aborted baby has become one of the most famous pictures in the history of television."

With that the television monitors began to show a replay of the pictures taken in Mrs. Sterling's classroom last Friday. Mr. Topaz went on to describe how the pro-life and pro-choice forces had either come to my defense, applauding my courageousness or lashed out at me discrediting what they called a cheap publicity stunt.

"Regardless of which side of the abortion issue you might be on," he continued, "it's now time to allow Louise Jordan to tell her story in her own words."

As I slowly walked up to the podium there must have been at least ten microphones staring me right in the eye. I took a deep breath and said a short prayer. I was ready to share and I hoped my audience was ready to receive.

"My name is Louise Ann Jordan," I began. "I am sixteen years old and in live in the city of Palmerville, New York. This past Tuesday I entered the building you see right behind me in order to participate in an unspeakable crime by willingly giving my consent to an execution style murder, a murder that the government of the United States of America sanctioned. I was a willing participant to an event that happens over four thousand times a day in America, a surgical abortion. However, while I was a willing participant in this monstrous act, I was at the same time, the victim of a monstrous deception, one that creates the illusion that all that an abortion does is to remove the 'products of pregnancy,' 'pregnancy tissue,' or 'birth matter.'"

All of a sudden a hush came over the crowd. Stunned faces began staring at me as if they couldn't believe what they were hearing.

"Let me explain how all this came about. Several months ago I made a major mistake – I had sex with my boyfriend. It happened only once. But unfortunately, just that one time was enough to cause me to become pregnant. Once I became certain of my pregnancy my world began to crumble right before my eyes. I thought that if I gave birth to my baby as a tenth grade high school sophomore my life would be ruined. And then I found out that New York State had an amazing law that said I could get an abortion without my parents having to consent to it or even be notified.

"I thought that this was my ticket out of my problem," I continued. "I could quickly get an abortion, my parents would never find out, and I could just as quickly return to a normal life. While I didn't know anything about abortion I was willing to let it be my vehicle of escape. What really clinched the deal was when Nurse Patterson told me that an abortion of a thirteen-week fetus was little more than removing 'birth matter' from my belly. The law was on my side since my parents would never have to know. And medicine was on my side too since an abortion was a simple procedure to remove some unwanted tissue."

I went on to tell them everything that had happened from getting the four hundred dollars that I needed for the abortion to meeting the woman who had given me the brochure in which I had seen that terrible picture. I also explained how I had made my way back to the clinic and described my gruesome discovery. By now I was feeling a surge of adrenaline as I began to conclude my statement.

"Every day in clinics like these all across this great land of ours four thousand perfectly formed tiny human beating hearts become forever silent. Every day in clinics like these all across this great land of ours four thousand tiny unsuspecting human beings have their skulls crushed, their arms and legs literally torn from their sockets and their lifeless remains disposed of like everyday household garbage, all in the name of convenience. And every day in clinics like these all across this great land of ours four thousand precious little bundles of joy are exterminated from the face of this planet as a result of a decision made back in 1973 when seven out of nine U.S. Supreme Court justices decided to play God and doom millions of our most defenseless citizens to live out their small life spans on death row. Unlike you or me, they have no chance to claim their innocence, no chance for a trial by jury and no chance for even a stay of execution. Back in 1857 our U.S. Supreme Court decided that the color of your skin determined if you could be slave or free. Today this same highest court in America has decided that life begins when they say it does!!!"

I had one more paragraph to go. That initial nervousness I was experiencing was totally gone. In its place was an incredible flood of energy and excitement that I had never felt before.

"The time has come for all of us to take a good look at what is going on every day in clinics like these all across this great land of ours. Please look at the pictures of these tiny precious pre-borns at thirteen and sixteen weeks old, tucked away safely in their mother's wombs, and then look into the mirror of your soul and tell me what you see. These are tiny human beings. If we deny their humanity, I dare say we must question our own. I thank you all for this opportunity to share with you my story."

As I spoke my last few words, I began to hear a thunderous round of applause that continued for almost five minutes. When this extraordinary response died down, Roger Topaz took back the microphone.

"Louise," he said, "it is obvious that you have thought out the pro-life position you are now championing very carefully. In all my years of reporting the news I have never seen a young person give so forceful a speech. I know that we have a lot of people waiting to ask you what may be some very personal questions. I hope that you will give us a little more of your time to field a few of them."

I smiled at him. Now that I knew that so many people in the crowd supported me, I was full of confidence and was more than ready to answer any questions that came my way. I had just disclosed some of my most intimate personal experiences. But if I could tell them more, I would. I knew that this was my chance to share with perhaps millions of people the reasons abortion was such a horrible evil. Although I had never done anything like this before I was ready to give it my best try.

Roger Topaz took the first question from a very pretty young lady who introduced herself on one of the portable mikes that were being handed around as Julia Davis, a TV reporter from Houston.

"Louise," she said. "It's hard for me to believe that in a little under a weeks' time you have become an expert on such a complex subject as abortion, especially since you told us that you knew nothing about this subject before this past Tuesday. Don't you think you lose some credibility?"

I was taken aback by this attack on my credibility but I knew that if I wanted to continue to be a defender of the unborn I had to come up with an answer. I paused for a few seconds before I spoke. My heart was pounding.

"You're correct that a week ago I knew very little about what an abortion was Miss Davis," I said. "And if it were up to this clinic we are standing in front of I would still know next to nothing about it today. But when I saw a picture of what a thirteen-week-old fetus looks like and when I held in my hands a tiny dead fetus probably not more than a few weeks older than my baby, I became an expert on the subject."

Mr. Santee, a heavyset reporter who introduced himself as representing the largest newspaper in Atlanta, asked the next question. "You have hurled some pretty harsh words at our U.S. Supreme Court," he said in a somewhat angry tone of voice. "Don't you realize that these nine U.S. Justices spent a lot of time analyzing the abortion issue from all sides before they decided in favor of legalization in *Roe v. Wade*? What makes you so certain that they are wrong and you are right?"

"I am sure that you are right and that they did analyze a lot of information before they made their final decision," I told him. "Unfortunately their decision suffered from two major flaws. If we use my aborted thirteen-week-old baby as an example, the U.S. Supreme Court Justices failed to consider two very fundamental factors. First, science has documented that my baby, before I took its life, already had experienced over thirteen million healthy and vibrant heartbeats. Every schoolboy knows that, when a person's heart stops beating, death is the result. If a human life ends when its heart stops functioning, then it goes without saying that a human life must be present if it is pumping blood through its perfectly functioning heart.

Science tells us a human heart begins to beat twenty-one days after conception."

For a moment I began to wonder if my schoolboy analogy had insulted Mr. Santee. But then I realized that my answers were not intended to make friends but save lives.

"The second fundamental problem with the legalization of abortion," I went on, "is that never once has the defendant, the unborn on trial, ever been able to state his case to a jury of his peers. Instead the U. S. Supreme Court has stood in as proxy for the unborn and by the very fact of its decision, struck down all appeals. It is my understanding that when a death row inmate is put to death by a lethal injection, his heart soon stops to beat and he dies. In a surgical abortion the unborn also has its heart stopped, and as a result, it, too, dies. However, at least the death row inmate had a trial by his peers. No such option is currently available to four thousand of our youngest U. S. citizens every day in America."

Next Walter Jones, a newspaper reporter from a Seattle paper had a question for my dad. "Mr. Jordan," he said. "I guess that all of the events during the past week must have come as quite a shock. Maybe you can give us some insight on what you make of this entire experience."

As I watched my father approach the mike, I felt relieved to be able to take a break from all the tough questions I had to answer.

"Mr. Jones, thanks for asking me this question and for giving me the opportunity to share my thoughts about what has happened during these past few days," my father said. His voice sounded calm but I was certain he must have been quite nervous. "Both my wife and I are conservative and believe that sex outside of marriage is wrong and sinful. My daughter knew that our rule was that she was not able to even start dating until she turned sixteen. Obviously to find out that she had had a secret boyfriend at fifteen, had sex, gotten pregnant, and had an abortion were ideas that were almost impossible to take in all at once. When I found out all of this in the span of a few minutes this past Friday I, too, was in a state of shock."

By this point I was beginning to be concerned where Dad was going with his response. He had already told all America that I had disobeyed his rules. I wondered what else he was planning to reveal.

"As an ex-Marine," he continued, "I have learned the importance of obeying your superior officers. Rules and regulations in the military, as well as in other areas of life, are designed for our protection as well as to train us to function more efficiently. A failure to obey important military regulations will brand you as a rebel. And rebels under the heat of real battle often can cause major problems to the success of a mission."

Dad went on to talk about rules and how sorry I was to have broken them. He spoke about my deception and how upset he was when he realized he would never be able to hold his first grandchild. He then put his arm around me before he went on and I pressed myself close to him, feeling much as I had when I was a little girl and had gone to him for protection. I remembered how much I had always depended on him. And I could still do it now. He finished answering the question by explaining why I had done what I had done when I had made my classroom presentation. It was wonderful how well he understood me.

Mr. Jones had one other question for my dad. "Mr. Jordan," he said and I could see from the expression on his face that he felt uncomfortable asking it. "Could you comment on the New York State law that your daughter said was a key to her decision to go ahead with her abortion?"

I knew that this was a sore point with my dad. He immediately proceeded to blast New York State's no parental notification/consent laws as outrageous.

He began to explain, "When Louise got pregnant this law made her the parent, since it was now up to her to decide whether any dialogue would ensue about her decision to keep her baby, give it up for adoption or abort it. Normally you would hope that your daughter would want to come to you on her own to discuss such a difficult decision. However, in many cases a young person with such a big problem, when given absolute decision making authority by law, will often take the quick and easy way out.

"Sadly, when organizations like Planned Parenthood, this abortion clinic behind me and the news media like you strongly support and encourage abortion, what do you think a young sixteen-year-old very frightened young girl will do? When the law allows a sixteen-year-old girl to take her parents totally out of the decision making equation on so crucial a life and death issue as abortion, we as a nation need to take a good close look at this very slippery slope we are going down."

Judging from the loud round of applause my dad's response received as he took his seat and the big smiles beaming from the faces of Mom and my little brother Don this was certainly shaping up as a very successful news conference for our cause.

A very interesting question came from a newspaper reporter from Chicago. A Miss Sharon Brolly asked me, "Louise, what right do you have to impose your morality on women who still want to have an abortion even after they have seen the pictures of thirteen-week-old fetuses?"

I looked at Miss Brolly who appeared to be in her mid to late thirties but sadly had only one hand. I guess she either had a serious accident or was born with a birth defect. I felt uncomfortable with what I was about to say but decided I had to do it.

"Miss Brolly," I began. "When you refer to morality I'm sure you're talking about issues of right and wrong conduct. Abortion, however, is not a matter of conduct. All abortions involve the death of an innocent life. And when life and death are at stake the morality argument becomes a very weak one. With all due respect these tiny babies at thirteen weeks old all have ten tiny fingers and *two* perfectly formed hands while you only have *one*."

Instead of applause or boos, there was an eerie silence after I gave this response. But I knew I had to tie my personal comment to Miss Brolly to the issue of morality. I'm sure by now I had made her upset but this was my chance to really bring home my point in a dramatic way.

"From this perspective Miss Brolly, you have a greater handicap than these tiny unborn babies. And as you know the pro-choice camp uses the handicap argument as one of their main reasons for keeping abortion legal. But in this particular instance, morally speaking, how can we justify taking the life of a fetus with two perfect hands but allow you to live when you only have one?"

I couldn't believe what I had just said and judging from the deafening silent neither could the crowd.

I answered several more questions and Roger Topaz who opened the news conference said that we only had time for one more question which came from a white-haired gentleman with a thin, inquisitive face who must have been in his late seventies. Mr. Harding wrote for a Mississippi newspaper and his question made me sad. "Miss Jordan," he asked, "did you ever consider having your baby and putting it up for adoption rather than aborting it?"

This last question brought tears to my eyes. For the first time I felt as though I were losing my composure. I had tried so hard to depend on reasonable arguments alone but now his question had brought back those feelings of guilt once again.

"When the abortion clinic confirmed that I was pregnant," I said, my voice trembling, "Dr. Foote said without hesitation that I should get an abortion. He told me that at sixteen I wasn't prepared to raise a child, physically, emotionally or financially. He also said that having a baby as a sixteen-year-old unwed mother would be a very cruel thing to put my baby through. Nurse Patterson added that the baby would ruin my life and I would miss out on the rest of my teenage years having to raise a child. That was the basic extent of my counseling. I was given one option – abortion. The word adoption never came up and I guess at the time I was too scared to know what to think. My parents would have been glad to share with me all the options available, but I obviously never gave them the chance to participate in my decision."

I knew that this was no time to let my guilt get the better of me. I needed to pull myself together. If my parents could forgive me for what I did then I knew that somehow I could forgive myself. And with that thought the trembling in my voice began to subside.

"I relied on the counsel I received from a profession," I continued, "that I had the highest regard for. And that's the medical profession. Over this past weekend a read a wonderful book that said that adoption was a great alternative to abortion. I have since learned that I could have had my baby and if I felt I couldn't provide her with a good upbringing there were over one and a half million couples in America that would gladly have agreed to keep my baby, raise it, and shower her with lots of love.[13] My big problem was actually the solution to a big problem that so many couples in America face – the inability to have children on their own. How I wish I had considered adoption as a viable option, before consenting to my abortion. I believe that most abortion clinics will not tell you about adoption because a decision to adopt is a lost sale for the abortionist."

I told them that I realized now I had had three options – keeping the baby and bringing it up with the help of my parents, giving her up for adoption, or submitting to an abortion. I told them that the choice I had made was the worst I would ever make. But at the time, it seemed to be my only choice.

"I just want to thank everyone," I began to conclude, "for giving me this opportunity to share some of the things I have learned about why abortion is such a great destroyer of life. If I could leave you with one thing to remember it would be that any way you choose to view abortion the one inevitable conclusion is that it kills a tiny human being."

For the next few minutes, as I listened to another loud round of applause and shouts of approval, I slowly began to realize that God might just have a special calling on my life. As the crowd noise finally subsided Roger Topaz, with an excited look on his face, came forward to bring this memorable evening to a close.

"Ladies and Gentlemen," he said, "you have just witnessed one of the most amazing news conferences I have ever been a part of. I think it is safe to say that the pro-life movement in America has its newest and youngest spokesperson. Louise Ann Jordan is clearly a young woman with a powerful story to tell. I know that we have not heard the last of her or the message she brings forth with such eloquence and conviction."

My dad and mom put their arms around me and then gave me the biggest hug I can ever remember getting from them. Dad once again let me know how much he loved me and that this was the proudest day of his life. However, he also left me with an ominous warning:

"This indeed was by and large a very friendly crowd, Louise," he said as we hurried to the car, "but in the days ahead be prepared for the fight of your life."

I was soon to learn that my dad knew exactly what he was talking about.

5

Back to School

As we drove home that night Mom kept telling me that she, like Dad, was very proud of the way I answered all the questions that were thrown at me.

"But now I hope that things can settle down and our lives return to normal," she added, pulling her sweater close around her shoulders.

"I doubt that will ever happen in the near future, honey," my father told her. "Given the nature of this controversy, the incredible national media attention and Louise's charismatic performance this evening, I think all of us should be prepared for a major disruption in our way of life."

"I think you're right, Dad!" I exclaimed. "Look what's waiting for us in front of our house."

As we approached our driveway I could count six news trucks and at least twenty people waiting at our front door to talk with us upon our arrival home. And it was now that I saw the marine in him come out. Dad could see that I was not ready to have more questions shot out at me. Telling my mom, Don and I to go straight inside, he said that he would talk to the media. I went upstairs to my room and opened the window which faced the front entrance to our home. Dad was definitely barking out the rules he expected the news media to adhere to in the future.

"Palmerville is a very small town and we're not use to having so many unannounced visitors at one time," he said. "I'll be happy to talk with you and allow my daughter to talk with you as long as you give us some space to breathe. I understand that Louise has taken away a certain amount of our family privacy by virtue of her outspoken stance on the abortion issue. However, we still demand a certain level of time to ourselves and as long as you are willing to give us that we will be able to work together. If not I am afraid our interviews will be cut to a minimum."

Dad's voice was so loud and clear that even if my window had been shut tight I would have heard everything he said. When one of the reporters asked if it would be OK if they came back tomorrow to ask a few questions, Dad said they would have to wait until tomorrow evening.

"After I close my store, eat dinner and have some time with my family," he said, "we'll be happy to field your questions."

With that the news media packed up their gear and sped off into the night. It appeared that dad had made his point and at least for tonight quiet had returned to the Jordan household.

Although it was now almost ten, it was time for a family meeting. My mom told both Don and me to come downstairs to the living room. She said that our father felt he wanted to talk with all of us because he sensed that our family was about to undergo some major changes to the way we lived our lives. Up until this point my little brother Don hadn't been consulted at all on all of the events of this past week. All he knew was that his big sister was a big splash in town and that she was on TV twice in the last week. Yes, he knew that I had an abortion but I'm sure he didn't fully understand everything that surrounded the whole ordeal.

Don may have been only eleven and the youngest member of our family but he was just as important to my mom and dad as I was. My father felt it was important to let him know what was going on and to get his input on the changes that were about to hit us. After all, whether Don liked it or not, he was going to have his life impacted by the activities that were already beginning to surround the entire Jordan family.

"We haven't paid enough attention to you, son," Dad said as he settled down on the sofa with Don close beside him. Although it was well past his bedtime, my brother was wide-awake, still excited by all that had happened. His blue eyes sparkled as Dad began stroking his blond hair. "What do you think of all this?" he asked.

Don was not use to being the center of attention but here he was being asked to give his opinion to the three older members of his family. I was very interested to know what my brother knew and what he thought about what I had done. We always had a good relationship but I really had no idea what he was going to say; however, I was eager to hear.

It seemed that Don had looked the word "abortion" up in the dictionary. And that had meant looking up "pregnancy" and "fetus," too.

"When I put it all together," he told us, "it meant that Louise had an 'unborn young,' in her belly. That means it was a baby, doesn't it? Louise really did kill her baby. And I'll bet she would have been my little sister and we would have named her Sally."

When he said that, I felt as though my world was collapsing about me. I burst into tears and so did Don. We hugged one another tight and I told Don how very sorry I was for what I had done. Just then I could feel the strong arms of my father engulfing Don, Mom and me completing the circle. I will never forget that moment when our family mourned the death of little Sally.

Dad told my mom, that for the rest of the week, he wanted her to drive both Don and me to and from school instead of taking the bus because he wanted to make sure that we arrived safely without the news media trying to sneak an interview with me on the way. I had no objections to this change in transportation and I would soon see how my dad had the uncanny ability to predict the future. I was by now totally exhausted and knew I needed some sleep if I wanted to make it to school tomorrow. As I climbed into my bed I couldn't help but wonder what type of reception I was going to receive when I returned to Palmerville High. I prayed that Mrs. Sterling had recovered from last Friday and that my classmates would understand why I had done what I did.

As soon as Mom and I drove up to Palmerville High, after leaving Don off, I knew that this would not be a normal day of high school for me. I spotted three TV news vans and was greeted at the front door by Principal Foster who asked if he could speak with us for a few minutes. Mom agreed and the three of us slowly made our way to his office.

"Mrs. Jordan, I can't tell you how proud I am of Louise," he told us, looking happier than I had ever seen him before. "She was absolutely wonderful on TV last night. My wife and I couldn't believe how mature Louise came across and how powerful her arguments were. I just wanted you to know that I completely support your desire to defend the lives of these precious children before they are aborted."

His kind words were exactly what I needed to start my school day. And for the first time I began to view my principal not just as the head of our school but as a friend.

"But not everyone at Palmerville High or in our little town will be as friendly as the crowd you spoke in front us last night," he went on. "For example, I happen to know that your science teacher, Miss Ventura is very pro-choice. Yesterday I had a meeting with the entire faculty and let them know that I didn't want any more disruptions to class due to issues relating to what happened here last Friday. If anyone tries to bother you or if anyone makes you feel uncomfortable for the stance you have taken, I want you to let me know, Louise. Mrs. Jordan, I can assure you that I will do everything in my power to allow Louise to tend to her studies with minimal disruption."

We thanked him and Mom went on her way. By now homeroom had ended and the halls were swarming with kids. Principal Foster walked with me to my math class and told me to have a nice day. I was so relieved that, so far, everything seemed to be going just fine. Mom had gotten me to school safe and sound and Principal Foster was one hundred percent on my side. I hoped that my classmates and teachers would be as supportive as our principal was, but something told me that not all of them would be.

Math class went really well. Mr. Hunter, my geometry teacher, was able to keep the entire topic of discussion on math. The only mention of abortion came up when the bell rang ending class and Bobby Baker came up to me and said his big sister had had an abortion and that he felt I was wrong for condemning everyone who believed abortion was a necessary option. Walking the long school halls to my second period English class proved quite an amazing experience. It seemed that just about everyone had an opinion or comment to share with me. Best of all, most of them were supportive.

Joel Tucker said that I was without a doubt the most famous person in the history of Palmerville, New York and asked for my autograph. Another girl named Mary, whose last name I didn't know, said her mother's best friend who worked for Planned Parenthood had called to say that my news conference was full of lies.

"But I agree with you," Mary told me. "I think that abortion is wrong and I got into a big argument with my mother about it. She thinks it's a private matter and that only the mother should decide. That's what she said, at least."

I thought for a moment before I replied. I didn't want to cause trouble between Mary and her mother but I knew now that there were some things I couldn't leave unsaid.

"When you talk about this again," I said, "perhaps you ought to tell her that the very fact that she says it's a mother's choice means that what is being aborted is already a child. When I took the life of my baby, I was already a mother. Tell her that, Mary. Just tell her that."

Right before I was ready to enter English class, a big clumsy looking guy named Jerry asked me if he could speak with me. He seemed quite shy but really sweet. Since the bell sounded to start class just then, I told Jerry that after English class he could ask me his question. As I took my seat, I noticed that Mrs. Sterling was sitting at her desk looking at a book. After about a minute of silence, she stood up and addressed our class.

"I am glad that Louise is back with us today," she said. "I hope that we can all concentrate on our subject for today – the works of Mark Twain."

It was amazing that only last Friday our English classroom had been in a state of total chaos and yet today we were going to calmly talk about Tom Sawyer and Huckleberry Finn.

After an uneventful discussion, class came to an end. But as I was getting ready to move on to my U. S. History class, Mrs. Sterling asked if she could speak with me for one minute.

"Do you want me to stay with you, Louise?" Sarah whispered, clutching her books tight, a look of concern on her face.

"No," I whispered back. "I'll meet you for lunch in the cafeteria."

When everyone had gone, Mrs. Sterling picked up the book she had been looking at before class started and asked me to take a look at the page she had open. As it turned out it was a photo album and the picture she showed me was of a young little boy talking with Mickey Mouse.

"Is that your son?" I asked her, remembering what she had told the class about her recent vacation to Disney World in Florida.

"Yes," she said, smiling. "It's Barry. He's five. But that's not what I wanted to talk to you about, Louise."

She pointed to one of the desks close to hers and gestured for me to sit down.

"Last Friday I felt – well, I felt so humiliated because it seemed to me that my class had turned into a circus. It just wasn't the way to start off a new year, at least not for someone who loves to teach as much as I do. I'm going to be honest with you, Louise. I thought you were trying to impose your morality on all of us. But that night, when my husband and I watched your interview on TV, Barry walked into the room just as they were showing that tape of your holding up your baby and I ..."

Clearly she was finding it difficult to go on. But I waited without saying anything because I guessed this was something she had to say.

"Well," she told me, and her voice was unsteady, "my heart broke when my five-year-old calmly turned from looking at the TV and said, 'Mommy, look at the tiny cute baby.' It was obvious he saw something I hadn't been able to see."

She then went on to tell me that later that same night while everyone was asleep she went downstairs to take another look at her vacation photo album. As soon as she saw the picture of Barry and Mickey, she silently started crying as she thought of the millions of little children like the one I had aborted who would never have the opportunity to meet Mickey Mouse like her son Barry had.

All of a sudden tears began to well up in both Mrs. Sterling's eyes and mine and we hugged one another. From that moment on a special bond of friendship began to form between us. It's strange how often it takes the innocence of a child to open our eyes to the truth.

History class went by quickly, and when the bell sounded, it was off to the cafeteria. As Sarah and I stood on line to get our lunch I saw Jerry.

"Hi, Jerry," I called out. "Join Sarah and I for lunch."

His face lit up and he excitedly accepted my invitation.

Jerry must have been over six feet and he walked with a slight limp. As we sat down and began to eat, he started to tell us a little about himself. His full name was Gerald Thomas Bedford and as it turned out his family had just moved into Palmerville back in the beginning of August. As Sarah and I soon found out, for someone who appeared so shy, Jerry liked to talk.

He told us that, sixteen years ago, his dad and mom had found out that they were going to have their first child. They were so excited until Jerry's mom went for her four-month check-up. It was then, he said, that the doctor told them that something was wrong and that there was a very good chance if they decided to keep their baby it would be born with a severe handicap.

Jerry stopped and tried to get out the words.

"Do you mean Down's Syndrome," I asked him.

"That's it," he said gratefully. "The doctor said it would be hard for them, having a baby like that. That's when my mom was going to do what he recommended and what you did."

"You mean have an abortion?" I asked him, covering one of his hands with mine.

He slowly nodded his head and then went on to tell us how his parents, just before they were about to enter the abortion clinic, met a young woman who explained to them what was growing inside his mom's body. They became so shaken by what they heard that they immediately realized they just couldn't abort their own child.

"And that child was me," Jerry said proudly. "I was that little baby, Gerald Thomas Bedford. Thanks, Louise for speaking out against abortion. If my parents hadn't changed their minds and listened to their doctor I wouldn't be hear to tell you how much I value my life. Louise, can I be your friend?"

Sarah and I were touched and showed it. Jerry was such a warm, open person that we fell in love with him right from the start.

"My mom saw you on TV," Jerry said, pulling a book out of his book bag. "She said that perhaps you'd read the passage she's marked here. Will you?"

"On the one hand," I began to read, "we provide special parking and elevators for the handicapped. We talk tenderly about those poster children with MS, spina bifida, and leukemia. We are touched when we see the telethons, the March of Dimes, the United Way ads. We sponsor the Special Olympics and cheer on the Down's syndrome competitors, speaking of the joy and inspiration they bring us. We look with admiration at a television series that stars a Down's syndrome young man. But when we hear a woman is carrying one of these very children, we say, 'kill it before it is born.'" [14]

As lunch period ended, I realized that God often allows us meet people like Jerry so they can teach us valuable lessons about life that we couldn't learn in any other way.

Mrs. Sterling and Jerry were a source of great encouragement to me and boy did I need that since my science teacher Miss Ventura was about to let me know that not everyone appreciated my pro-life stance. In fact as I was soon to find out millions of others considered me a very evil influence on the entire women's movement in America.

Principal Foster had already warned me that my science teacher, Miss Ventura, was someone who stood at the opposite end of the spectrum from me on the issue of abortion. I hoped that she had been at the meeting with Principal Foster when he told all the teachers not to allow any disruptions regarding the abortion controversy to interfere with our schoolwork. Miss Ventura, a lovely young brunette who usually dressed in well-tailored suits, opened our class just as Mrs. Sterling had by letting everyone know that she was glad to see I was back in school today.

"I am happy to see you are back with us today, Louise," she said. "I'm sure that all of you saw our Louise on TV last night. I know it made me glad that we all live in America where someone with a minority viewpoint, like Louise, can share her views. But you all should remember that our Constitution allows a woman the freedom to decide if she wants to have an abortion."

As I sat there, totally embarrassed, I began to feel very uncomfortable. Here she was paying me a compliment but at the same time letting everyone know that my opinion was just that an opinion, and a minority one at that.

"I hope that all the attention," she continued, "our little town has experienced these past few days will die down and all of us can get back to normal at our jobs and in our school."

I suppose this was Miss Ventura's subtle way of letting me and her entire science class know where she stood on the issue and that she had popular opinion and the law siding with her, as well as making sure that we all knew that our U. S. Constitution gave women the right to abort if they so desired.

I had wanted so badly to tell our class that our Constitution didn't guarantee a woman the right to an abortion, but that it was the misinterpretation of the Constitution made by our Supreme Court that gave women that right, but I felt this wasn't the time or place, so I remained silent. I knew that she had scored points with her students. I also knew that, in order for abortion to become outlawed in the future, millions of Miss Ventura's would have to have the veil of darkness lifted from their minds. And with God's help I intended to try to make that happen.

The rest of the school day proved pretty uneventful, but by the time my final class, Spanish, came to an end I was emotionally exhausted. The events of the past few days were both exciting and nerve-racking. Each day seemed to be full of new surprises as well as challenges. And I was beginning to realize that my life was about to change forever.

I was waiting outside in front of the school for my mom to pick me up when a freckle-faced girl came up to me and asked me if we could talk.

"My name is Heather Windgate," she said blushing. "I'm a junior and two weeks ago I found out that I'm pregnant. I'm so afraid Louise, and I don't know what to do."

The words all came out in a rush, as though that was the only way she had been able to say them. I felt a rush of pity for her as I remembered how difficult it had been for me to confide in Joan.

"I'm sorry," I told her. "I hope you don't plan to get an abortion like I did?"

"I don't want to but I'm terrified of my father," she told me. "He – he drinks a lot and sometimes he hits me and my mom. If he knew that I was pregnant, I don't know what he might do."

"You're in a very difficult situation," I told her, squeezing her hand in mine. "However, I just know that getting an abortion is not the answer to your problem."

"Up until last week I was planning to take the same route that you chose," she told me. "I was going to get an abortion and not tell my parents. But after I saw you on TV, I knew in my heart that abortion was the wrong way to go. I just can't take the life of the life that is growing inside of me."

For the first time I was being asked to counsel someone with a real life serious problem. I knew that abortion was wrong but at the time I had little knowledge of where a young girl in Heather's predicament could go for help. Heather feared for her life and based upon the way she described her dad I knew that she might very well be in danger if she chose to keep her baby instead of aborting it.

Since the day I had had my abortion I always carried that pamphlet with the picture that changed my life forever with me. Now I remembered that on the back page there was a number and address of a crisis pregnancy center only a few miles from Palmerville where young women could get free advice and help on alternatives to abortion. I was in no position to offer Heather the exact road she should take but I felt that the crisis pregnancy center would have the answers that she needed.

"I'm so thankful that you don't want to get an abortion, Heather," I told her reaching into my pocketbook to get a pen. "Your decision to keep your baby is a decision to choose life over death. It really is. I'm so glad you came to me. Here is the name, address and phone number of a crisis pregnancy center I think you should get in contact with. And here's my number, too. Let me just write it down for you here on the brochure. And call me anytime you need to talk." We exchanged hugs and I told her that I would be praying for her.

At that moment Heather and I seemed to have so much more in common than just attending the same high school. Even though we had just met our common dilemma had already begun to bond us emotionally.

"Heather," I said as my mom was pulling up in our blue Chevy, "I'll see you tomorrow. And how about having lunch?"

"I'd love to, Louise," she told me, smiling for the first time.

On the way home, I told my mom and Don about all of my adventures that day. But all I could think about were all the new opportunities that I hoped would be opening up for me to help other girls like my new friend Heather.

6

Evil Fights Back

By the time it was almost seven-thirty, I knew that dad would be arriving home from work at any minute. I was looking forward to sharing my day with him and couldn't wait until I heard his key in the door. My dad always greeted mom with a big "I'm home" as soon as he stepped foot in our house. This time, however, there was no greeting and I could see from the way he looked that something was very wrong.

As I began to tell him what had happened in school, he seemed to be only half listening, until, finally, I summoned the courage to ask him what was the matter.

"I received a call from Dr. Foote at the Women's Health Services Center this afternoon," he told me, lowering himself into his leather recliner. "He wanted me to know that he was planning to bring a lawsuit against our family unless you came forward and admitted that the statements you made the other day about his clinic were inaccurate."

"You've got to be kidding me!" I exclaimed. "A lawsuit! On what basis?"

"He said that his clinic always informs all of its patients about the risks of abortion and what stage of the pregnancy they are in."

"But that's a lie," I told him.

"Not according to Dr. Foote. He said that you obviously misunderstood what was told you. He even told me that you signed a consent form agreeing to the procedure."

Now I was really mad. It was bad enough that I had killed my baby but now Dr. Foote was telling my dad that I was even lying about what went on inside his clinic.

"Dad, I remember the exact words that Nurse Patterson told me when I asked her what my twelve-week-old baby looked like," I said firmly. "She said the fetus was little more than a mass of tissue or what she referred to as 'birth matter.' When I asked her what a fetus was, she said that it was just another name for the 'birth matter' before it becomes a baby. She lied to me and Joan was standing right there with me, listening to everything Nurse Patterson said. I will never retract a single word I said about that abortion clinic and the lies they told me."

"Calm down, Louise," my father said, reaching out to take my hand. "No one said that you were making up what you told the news media the other day. Are you absolutely certain about what the nurse told you?"

"I'm one hundred percent certain," I told him. "You can call up Joan. She can confirm everything."

"What about the form you signed?"

"They told me that I had to sign a consent form," I explained. I was amazed at how much this had upset me. My mouth was dry and my heart was pounding. I had never thought that these people would actually lie. "Nurse Patterson told me it was just a formality and that my parents would never know about it or anything that would take place on this day. I was so nervous that I didn't even bother to read it. I also figured that, since this was a medical clinic, I could trust them."

Now it was dad's time to hit the roof. When he heard me say that according to Nurse Patterson, neither he nor my mom would ever find out about the form I signed, his entire mood radically changed.

"That's it!" he shouted. "It's one thing that they lied to you Louise, but it's quite another matter for them to then tell you that they were also going to help you deceive your mother and me by making sure we never find out about your signing a consent form that gave them permission to kill our grandchild."

I had never seen my father so upset before. He called mom into our living room and told Don to go to his room. "If it's a fight this abortion clinic wants," he said grimly, "then we'll give them the fight of their lives. Even if we have to suffer for it."

The first thing that Dad did was to call Joan and asked her if she would come over because he wanted to ask her some questions regarding our two trips to the Women's Health Services Center. Fifteen minutes later our doorbell rang and Joan came in with her father, both of them looking very serious. My dad and Joan's father Jack had grown up together in Palmerville and must have known each other for over thirty years.

After we were all seated in the living room, Dad took a few minutes to tell them about the potential lawsuit that the abortion clinic had said they were going to bring against us if I didn't retract what I had said about them.

"Since Joan was in on this from the start," he ended by saying, "I'd like to ask her some questions."

"Ask whatever you like, Tommy," Jack said wearily. He was a short, stout man who was usually grinning from ear to ear but tonight he looked drawn and anxious and his face was pale. "Joan told me that she would do anything to help Louise."

"Joan," my dad said, "when you and Louise went to the abortion clinic the first time, can you recall what Nurse Patterson told Louise about getting an abortion?"

"She told both of us that Louise was carrying a fetus," Joan said, sitting up very straight and looking him right in the eye. "When Louise asked what a fetus was the nurse told her that it was nothing more than a mass of tissue. She called it 'birth matter.'"

"Those were the exact words she used?"

"Yes."

"Did Louise sign any forms?"

"Yes, she had to sign a consent form giving them permission to perform the abortion. They told us that it was only a formality and that her parents would never have to know anything about the entire matter."

Dad just sat there, totally speechless but clearly fuming with rage. I could see that Joan was also very upset that Dr. Foote was trying to cover up all the lies his clinic told us. She kept glancing from her father to mine and I knew she must have been wondering how much I had told my dad about the part she had played in all of this.

"Mr. and Mrs. Jordan, I am so sorry," she said, tears now flowing freely from her eyes. "If it hadn't have been for me Louise would never have gone there for an abortion in the first place. I encouraged her to get it and even lent her the money."

"Joan didn't know any more about abortion than I did," I told them. "We both thought that it was the best course of action at the time, not realizing that abortion was the extermination of a tiny innocent life."

Dad had heard enough. Going over to console Joan he put his hand on her shoulder and let her know that she was completely forgiven for her mistake. He also asked her if she would be willing to repeat what she just told everyone in our living room if Dr. Foote decided to go through with his lawsuit. Joan, without a moment of hesitation, turned to my dad and told him that she definitely would.

I was glad that both Joan and I were being honest. I had made a vow last Sunday night that I would do everything in my power to be truthful in the future. I owed that to my parents who loved me so much; and I owed it to Sally.

By now Joan had finished crying and wanted to know if she could share something with everybody.

"Mr. Jordan," she said. "I've done a lot of soul searching over the last few days. I know how deeply sorry I am for the role I played in Louise's abortion. I've asked her for her forgiveness and I have also asked God to forgive me. I believe that both Louise and God have. I only hope I can forgive myself."

Joan then went on to explain the key role that secrecy played in every aspect of my abortion. She told my parents that since I wasn't allowed to have a boyfriend at age fifteen I had to conceal the entire relationship. She then went on to describe how New York State's non-parental consent and notification laws allowed me to ensure my abortion would remain secret if I chose to keep it that way. Finally, Planned Parenthood, the organization that gave Joan the idea about the abortion option, has remained extremely effective precisely because all of their services are strictly confidential. Minors are even told they never have to tell their parents about anything relating to their sexual activities, especially abortion.

"This clinic practiced deception and told lies to Louise and me to keep us in the dark," Joan concluded, her lovely face a mask of rage. I had never seen her so upset before. "They deceived us and then they killed Louise's baby and threw her in the garbage."

She choked up then, unable to go on. Reaching into her purse she took out a folded piece of paper and handed it to my dad asking him to read what she had underlined. As he unfolded the paper, Joan told everyone that she had cut out the ad that the Women's Health Services Center had placed in the yellow pages. When Dad read the words, "Minors Welcome" and "Parental Consent NOT Required," I looked at Mom, who was now visibly shaking.

As for me, I just sat there wondering what God must think of the thousands of babies ruthlessly murdered each day by members of a profession sworn to heal and save life.

When Joan and her father had gone, Dad told me that he had made an appointment with a lawyer friend of his, Robert Finkel to get his advice on Dr. Foote's potential lawsuit. And the next morning instead of going to school he told me he wanted me to come with him to meet him. Dad was originally going to see him by himself but that all changed after he had seen the eleven o'clock news before going to bed. Apparently Dr. Foote had felt it necessary to do some damage control and had invited the news media into his clinic so that he could show everyone how clean and professionally run his clinic was and explain how his staff are trained to provide the most up to date and accurate information on all aspects of abortion to his patients.

Dad knew in his heart that everything we were doing was right and that my story had to be told. However, he also knew how evil often wins out in a world where values are often compromised for the sake of money. During his interview on the news, Dr. Foote said that he was upset by some of the remarks I had made about his clinic over the past few days and that I had deliberately misinterpreted Nurse Patterson's comments. His staff was trained to always dispense factually accurate information. He hoped that I would reconsider what I had said and welcomed the opportunity to meet with me to try to straighten out what he called some "misunderstandings."

When we reached Mr. Finkel's office a very heavyset man, who must have been in his late fifties, came out and in a loud baritone voice called out, "Hey Tommy Boy, how the hell are you? This must be your daughter, Louise. Young lady I'm honored to meet such a pretty and courageous champion for the unborn."

I smiled and took an instant liking to Mr. Finkel.

"Please come into my office," he said. "Would either of you like a soda?"

As we sipped our sodas in his comfortable office with windows overlooking the town square, he told both of us that he had seen the interview last night with Dr. Foote.

"Tom," he went on. "You mentioned to me the other day, that Dr. Foote called you up and threatened to sue you if your daughter didn't confess that she must have somehow misunderstood the information his clinic had provided her with. I have to tell you I think he's bluffing. It is very hard to sue a minor, especially over trying to interpret who said what. In reality you would have a better chance of suing him for his misleading your daughter. However, since he has a signed consent form it would be tough to win."

"Dad," I protested, "I don't want to sue anyone. I just want to let everybody know the truth about what went on in his clinic."

"I must tell you that at least in this town, Louise has a tremendous amount of support and Dr. Foote has very little," Mr. Finkel told us. "He took a calculated risk appearing on TV trying to defend his clinic. Louise, you've put Dr. Foote in a very unenviable position."

"I'm not sure what you mean," my father said, frowning.

"You see if he chooses to do nothing, the tremendous amount of sympathy you have generated around here for the pro-life cause could hurt his abortion business. But by appearing on TV and saying that you basically misinterpreted what was told you, he runs the risk, if indeed he did lie to other women, of having them come forward to support your claims. What he probably is banking on is the fact that not many women will come forward and let the entire community know they got an abortion."

"Wow, I never thought about it like that but I see your point."

"I like many Americans, didn't know much about abortion," the lawyer said, leaning forward in his leather chair. "I was always against it but I never had any strong convictions and I didn't feel it was my place to impose my morality on others. But after watching your news conference, I began to see abortion in a totally new light.

Now, I realized for the first time that none of us has the right to impose our morality on the life of the baby."

"Thanks for letting me know that you were touched by my message," I told him. "That really means a lot to me."

"What do you think we should do, Bob?" my father asked. "Do you really think Dr. Foote is bluffing?"

"Well, Tom, I think that Louise should meet with Dr. Foote. I believe we can lay a trap for him that will only help to heighten the schizophrenic nature of doctors who both deliver babies and abort others. You see if Louise's interview convinces other women to come forward, admitting that they too were lied to by people from Dr. Foote's clinic, then his reputation will be severely damaged. However, if Dr. Foote can convince the viewing audience that the medical description that Louise was given, describing what was growing inside her body, was accurate, then everyone will realize that a tiny baby was killed. Either way the nature of the abortion doctor and his profession will be viewed as either deceptive or even worse deadly."

I looked at my dad and he looked at me and we both nodded in agreement. Mr. Finkel's logic did indeed make a lot of sense. My sole desire was to help educate people on the evils of abortion and thereby hopefully cause some women to change their minds, thus saving the lives of the innocent babies. By now my opinion of Dr. Foote had changed quite a bit from the first time I met him. Back then he seemed kind and caring. But now I viewed him as one of the most evil persons on the face of the earth.

I told Mr. Finkel I thought his idea made a lot of sense and that I would like to meet with Dr. Foote. Mr. Finkel said he would like to be our legal adviser and consultant and suggested that he call the Women's Health Services Center and try to schedule a time when the two of us could meet with Dr. Foote.

"But he's going to have to agree to our little discussion in front of the TV cameras," my father said grimly. "And I want to have Robert Topaz as moderator."

Mr. Finkel nodded his approval. It was obvious that he, too, understood the power of the media. Suddenly I felt empowered knowing that a lawyer as well as my family were in my corner.

After our visit with Mr. Finkel, Dad told me he was going to go back to his store for a few hours and wanted to know if I would like to hang there with him until he closed up. I hadn't done that for years although when I was a little girl the store had been one of my favorite places. I loved watching my dad make keys and was fascinated seeing so many different tools. It would be great hanging out with him at work again.

When we got to his store, Harold and Tony came over to me and gave me a big hug. Both of them told me that they were very proud of me. Harold had worked for my dad for the past seven years and Tony has been in our store for almost ten.

As Tony and I began to reminisce, I commented how it was only a few short years ago that I used to wander the aisles and count the different kinds of nails we stocked. It was just amazing how my world had changed since then.

Our family spent a quite night together and for a change we got to discuss other issues beside abortion. We all sat together in the living room and watched a video together, one of my favorites, Disney's, *Peter Pan*.

School was great. While I did get involved with some discussions on abortion, most were low key and none of my teachers brought up the subject except Miss Ventura who casually told our class once again that, even though there were many people who held similar pro-life positions as mine, our government had long ago settled the issue by granting a woman the right to choose, explaining that in 1973, when the landmark *Roe v. Wade* decision was handed down, our highest court in the land settled the issue once and for all.

When I got home, Mom told me that dad had gone into work late after spending the entire morning on the phone, working out the details for my meeting with Dr. Foote.

"I'm not sure if your dad has finalized everything," Mom said as she came out of the kitchen holding a basket filled with my favorite fruits. "But he did say before he left for work that he thought by the time he came home tonight a meeting time and place should be decided upon."

"I'm nervous, Mom," I told her, grabbing an apple from the basket. "I don't know how I am going to feel when I see the man who killed my baby again."

"Louise Ann," she told me, now appearing totally at ease, "I'm sure that God will help you not only deal with your emotions but also give you just the right words to turn Dr. Foote's own lies against himself. And don't forget, there will be a lot of people here in Palmerville praying for you."

When Dad came home, he told us that all the details had been worked out. We would meet Dr. Foote at the WRRM studios for a taping this coming Friday at 7:00 PM with the show airing the next day at six. Roger Topaz would be the moderator and both Dr. Foote and I would each be given five minutes to give our side of what was said and done followed by a concluding statement from each of us.

For a good part of the past four months I had spent a large part of my life lying to cover up my dark secrets. It was only when I was ready to let the truth take center stage that I was delivered from the bondage of shame and guilt that I had been living with. I was not proud of my days of deception but now that the truth was finally out I felt clean inside for the first time since the day I made up my first lie in order to see Jason. I kept thinking how sorry and deeply grieved I was for innocently participating in the death of my one and only child and I kept wondering how Dr. Foote could live with himself knowing that he had personally put to death literally hundreds of innocent lives.

I had never been inside a TV studio before so when Dad and I arrived at the WRRM set I stood amazed as I looked up and saw all the lighting and wires that were suspended from the ceiling. Near one end of the set two large wooden podiums were standing about fifteen feet from each other with cameras pointing right at them. My dad had told me that each of us would be standing behind our own podium as we gave our presentations.

Mr. Finkel met us just as I was headed off to make-up and told me, in his deep baritone voice, that all of Palmerville would be rooting for me. While his words were certainly encouraging I couldn't stop feeling nervous, wondering how I would react when I saw Dr. Foote again.

Well, it didn't take long for me to get my answer. As soon as we returned to the set I saw Dr. Foote talking with Mr. Topaz. Instantly, an intense feeling of hatred began to flood my heart as I thought about what that man had done to little Sally and me. Dad saw how upset I looked and told me to try to compose myself. He, too, wanted to let Dr. Foote know how much he disliked him but understood that this wasn't the right time or place. Obviously he was right and if I didn't get rid of this anger it would come across in my remarks and I couldn't let that happen.

By now the time had almost arrived for the taping to begin and right before Roger Topaz was ready to open the broadcast I asked if I could spend a little time by myself. Mr. Topaz took me to his office and told me I could spend a few minutes in private to gather my thoughts. But instead of gathering my thoughts I found myself asking God to help me deal with my hatred for Dr. Foote. I then closed my eyes and offered up a very simple prayer: "Lord please let the truth come forward and let evil be exposed." It was now time to face Dr. Foote.

As Roger Topaz began to open the broadcast I felt as if a great burden had been lifted from me. I don't know if it was the fact that I had given my concerns over to God, or if I felt, that if I just told the truth, I couldn't lose. Either way I had a peace about what was going to take place. Dr. Foote, who was wearing an expensive looking dark blue suit, seemed calm and relaxed as he gave his opening statement.

"Thank you for giving me this opportunity to put in perspective the events surrounding Miss Jordan's recent experiences and to share with the public a little about our Women's Health Services Center facility," he said with a nod to Mr. Topaz.

"Women's Health Services Center has been in operation for over fifteen years and has been providing women with a wide range of gynecological services. Our staff of highly trained Board Certified Obstetricians and Gynecologists have been providing women with services that range from gynecological exams, mammograms and prenatal care to family planning, free pregnancy testing and abortions. Our nurses are professional and courteous and trained to keep all of our patients feeling as much at ease as possible. As the head of our center I can assure you we keep our facility clean and spotless and that all of our physicians keep constantly up with the latest advances in medical technology. We treat all of our patients with compassion and assure them that their confidentiality will never be violated. For the past fifteen years we believe we have been an important part of our community and are proud of our record of service."

It was clear to me that this was the way he intended to go, his face expressionless, and his voice, too, reciting the words as though they were memorized. And perhaps they were.

"We never talk about individual cases but since Miss Jordan has chosen to tell a national TV audience about her experiences with our center I felt it was important to let you hear our side of just what happened to her while under our care," he said, turning slightly to look at me.

"Unfortunately her statements have placed our facility in an unfavorable light and I felt it important to let our community know exactly what advice and care Miss Jordan received at our center.

"Approximately two weeks ago Miss Jordan came to our facility a very scared and confused young lady," he went on as the camera panned in on him. "She said she was pretty sure she was pregnant and came to confirm her suspicions. I personally examined her and told her that her suspicions were quite correct and that she was already twelve weeks along. We talked about her options and I let her know that one of them was abortion. I'm sure everyone would agree that I had a responsibility to do that. I also told her that she could speak with one of our nurses who would explain everything she needed to know about the procedure and let her know that she could ask any questions she might have to our specially trained nurses who have been counseling women for many years on these difficult matters."

He then went on to describe how one of his nurses had explained to me that, if I chose to have an abortion, I would find it a very safe, quick, and relatively painless procedure. When I asked about what was going on inside my body he, pausing to take a sip of water, said that his nurse told me that a tiny fetus was growing inside my womb and assured me that it wasn't yet a baby since it could never survive on its own. And then to top it off Dr. Foote turned to Mr. Topaz and added that I had been a very good patient and had left his clinic in good spirits.

I realized that Dr. Foote was a very skilled speaker, something I had not calculated on. Now he moved to one side of his podium and addressed the camera directly.

"Our center stands behind our record of quality gynecological care for all of our patients. We treat all of our patients with great respect. Our counselors explain available options to all of our clients on all of our services and I am saddened to hear that Miss Jordan feels that we led her astray on exactly what happened at our center."

As soon as Dr. Foote finished his discussion on the advice his clinic had given me, Roger Topaz told us that we were going to break for a few minutes before I would give my response. While I was waiting for the taping to resume I began to analyze Dr. Foote's comments. I could now see why so many people believe abortion is not as terrible as the pro-lifers make it out to be. My dad had told me that like any good politician, abortionists are trained to put a positive spin on even the worst of scenarios. I was fast finding out that abortionists were like magicians, magicians at making you believe things exist when in fact they are just illusions. They also use their trickery to make you see things in a totally different light than reality.

I remembered that when I was seven my dad had taken me to a magic show. It was so exciting and everything seemed so real. I will never forget the time the magician sawed a woman in half and then she got up to show everybody that somehow she was still in one piece. After the show, dad told me that all of the things we saw were tricks designed to make us believe one thing when in fact something else was actually going on behind the scenes.

I still to this day didn't know how that woman got up and walked away after I saw her in two pieces. But I did know that, when it comes to abortion the doctor transforms himself into a master of magic, using tiny innocent babies as part of his act, causing them to vanish from the face of the earth. The trick was to convince you and me that these are not viable human beings and thus what he causes to disappear are nothing more than props from his trade. To me Dr. Foote was not much of a doctor but he was a master magician.

Dad had also showed me how abortion doctors use words to paint pictures that often distort reality. Take for example the term "product of conception." Every human being alive today was, at one point, a "product of conception." But this term was used by the abortionist like Dr. Foote to dehumanize the unborn because it implies that the unborn is some kind of product like something you might pick up at the supermarket or drug store.

When a sculptor takes a lump of clay he helps to breathe life into his artwork by carefully using his tools and hands to fashion and mold the clay into something with form and substance. Often even before he completes his work we know exactly what will be the end product. When I took the life of tiny Sally at thirteen weeks, she already was a "masterpiece" that no Picasso or Rembrandt could ever duplicate or improve upon. All of her organs were already present. Her hands and feet were already "fearfully and wonderfully made." She had a heart and a mind and a soul. She was no longer "birth matter" but only six short months away from being a "matter of birth."

Mr. Topaz then announced that the taping would resume in one minute. Dad, who was standing by one of the cameras, quickly came up to me and gave me some last words of encouragement. As I looked to my right I saw the make-up woman dab a little powder on Dr. Foote's now shiny face and marveled that I was not any more nervous than I was. I think it was because I was so determined to expose him. I had a mission and it was sustaining me.

"Thank you Mr. Topaz for another opportunity to set the record straight on what happened to me when I visited Dr. Foote's clinic," I said when I had taken my podium. "First I would like to acknowledge that many of the statements that Dr. Foote has made are accurate. Everyone at his clinic was very polite to me. His facility was clean and his staff seemed professional. And yes, I was very scared and confused. But on two very important points I take strong issue with Dr. Foote's remarks."

Now it was my turn to look the camera straight in the eye.

"First of all, when I asked Nurse Patterson what my then twelve-week-old looked like she said that it was little more than 'birth matter' and a mass of tissue. According to science at twelve weeks a developing baby consists of many billions of individual cells. It has already started cell differentiation. Specialized cells in the human eye, ear and brain were being formed at the moment Dr. Foote killed my baby."

I paused to hold up the photograph and heard one of the technicians gasp.

"I challenge you to look at this picture of this thirteen-week-old fetus and tell me if this is just a mass of tissue or some amorphous 'birth matter,'" I went on. "Only a blind man or a madman can look at this picture and deny the humanity of this precious tiny life. What

Nurse Patterson described growing inside of me was not some type of 'blob' or 'thing.' My little Sally was a real person, a special child. She was not a 'thing' or an 'it.'"

I glanced at my father who was now standing at one side with Mr. Finkel. Both of them gave me thumbs up.

"As far as a discussion of what options I had available, the only option discussed was abortion. Nurse Patterson told me if I didn't have an abortion that my life would be ruined. She told me that I was not emotionally or financially prepared to raise a baby and that if I did carry my baby to term my social life would be over. What she failed to tell me was that while I might not be emotionally or financially prepared to raise my child there were over a million couples who would do anything to hold my little Sally in their arms. And these couples were emotionally and financially in a better position to raise and love my daughter than I was. Adoption is a wonderful alternative to abortion but I was never told about it. I freely admit that I was at the time more interested in getting rid of my problem quickly, but looking back I made a horrible mistake."

With the help of a professional nurse I had brought notes along with me but I found that I didn't need them. I knew exactly what I wanted to say.

"Nurse Patterson, I beg you to let other young girls that come to your clinic know that adoption, not abortion is a wonderful alternative. One gives life, the other takes life. One is selfless, the other selfish. One shows compassion, the other corruption. And one is so right, while the other so wrong."

We paused for another break. I was now feeling really confident and eager to give my final remarks. When we returned to give our concluding statements Dr. Foote closed by telling me he was sorry that I still felt misled but that he and his staff stood behind their comments. When Mr. Topaz asked me if I had a closing statement I told him it was more like an observation and an appeal.

"Dr Foote," I said, turning to look straight at him, "when my mom had an operation two years ago to remove her gall bladder she saw how scared I was not knowing what was going to happen to her when she had to go to the hospital for her surgery. She sat me down and took almost one-half hour to describe every aspect about her upcoming surgery, telling me everything her doctor had told her

71

regarding gall bladder surgery, as well as sharing all the literature her doctor had given her on her operation. But I was told next to nothing about my abortion. I now realize that the difference between a real doctor and an abortion doctor is as vast as the Grand Canyon is wide.

"Mr. Topaz I brought with me the following chart that my dad helped me construct. I think it gives a very fair presentation between two types of surgery – abortion and ethical surgery. Can I please present this chart to let people see for themselves the differences."

Mr. Topaz said he had no objections and with the help of my dad, he brought in a big flip chart that I had constructed using information from Dr. Willke's book *Why Can't We Love Them Both*. According to Dr. Willke, I began to explain, abortions are unique among all types of surgery. To a greater or less extent, in every country, abortion procedures are commonly exempt from the sanitary and professional rules required of other surgery. [15] As the camera scanned our big flip chart I began to read from top to bottom the differences between abortion and ethical surgery that exist in free standing abortion clinics in the U.S.

	ABORTION[16]	ETHICAL SURGERY
Payment	Cash at Door	Pay Later
Pathologic Exam	Seldom	Routine
Advertising	Routine	Rare
Counseling	Usually a farce	Done if needed
Second opinion	Never	If needed
Informed consent	Legally not required	Always
Kickbacks	Sometimes	Never
Record Keeping	Sketchy	In detail
Pre-op exam	Often not done until she is on the table	Mandatory and detailed
Follow-up exam	None	Mandatory and detailed
Correct Diagnosis	10-15% done on non-pregnant women	Surgeon is disciplined if he does many wrong operations
Husband's consent	Not needed	Expected
Husband informed	Not necessary	Always
Consent of parents of minor	Not needed	Legally required
Parents informed	Seldom	Legally required
Tissue disposal	In garbage	In humane and dignified manner
Burial	In garbage	Yes, if large enough
Surgical training	Not required	Absolutely required
Non-medical reasons	99%	About 1%
Cash "kick-backs"	Common	forbidden

"Finally," I said, "I would like to make an appeal to any woman out there who feels like they were given the same misleading information or no information at all before deciding to have their abortion. Please step forward and let all of these abortion mills know we will not tolerate this vast network of lies, deceptions and cover-ups any longer. Only when evil is exposed can we begin to destroy it."

And then it was over. I had met Dr. Foote face to face and I knew, as I saw him leave the studio, that I had bested him. The director and Mr. Topaz congratulated me and some of the stagehands gave me thumbs up. As for my dad and Mr. Finkel they felt confident that my presentation would serve to definitely weaken the credibility of Dr. Foote and his clinic. I could only hope that they were right.

7

Preparation for Battle

It didn't take very long to find out if my closing appeal would bring other abused and mislead women forward. At around eight the following evening, our doorbell rang and a most unexpected visitor appeared. It was Nurse Patterson!

As I introduced her to my parents, I turned to look at my mom and immediately noticed that her expression had become cold and unsympathetic. Dad, on the other hand, welcomed her into our home, almost as if he somehow was expecting her visit.

I was stunned to see her and began to feel that same intense hatred that I had when I first saw Dr. Foote at our taping. How could she be so deceived as to think her advice could have solved my problem? What did she think about my televised confrontation with her boss? And why was she now here? There were so many questions racing through my mind. I was glad Don was spending the night at one of his friends. I didn't exactly know what Nurse Patterson was going to say, but I kind of knew, whatever it was, Don didn't need to be here to hear it.

"I don't know quite where to start," she told us when she was seated on the straight-backed chair by the piano. It was clear that she was nervous because she kept pulling at her handkerchief as though she intended to tear it to shreds. Her face was now pale and her eyes were so sad looking that she seemed to be almost in mourning.

74

"I hope you will accept my sincere apology for my role in Louise's abortion," she continued. "I know that I will never be able to bring back Louise's baby but I can promise you that, thanks to her coming forward, I will never participate in helping to destroy another precious life again. Two years ago I took a position at Dr. Foote's center as an obstetrics nurse. My duties were to help care for our patients during pregnancy and childbirth. I quickly found out that Women's Health Services also did surgical abortions. And I soon discovered that over half of our patients came to us to not help them bring about a successful pregnancy but to terminate it!"

That apology meant a lot to me. I knew that it could never bring back Sally but those words were just another help to me as I continued to go through the healing process.

"I respected Dr. Foote a lot," she went on "and when he asked me to help with some of the abortion cases I agreed. At first I couldn't believe my eyes."

As she began to describe the first abortion she had participated in my parents and I just sat there totally silent. She told us that the fetus was sixteen weeks old and that Dr. Foote used a pair of big tongs with an open spoon at one end to literally tear off arms and legs and completely dismantle the baby. When she then told us that another nurse had to count the body parts to make sure they got everything, otherwise the mother might suffer an infection or some other complication, I stood up and made a beeline straight to the bathroom and fortunately made it to the toilet just in time.

All three of us had different reactions to her story. I reacted by throwing up. Mom continued to just sit there, staring at Nurse Patterson, almost unwilling to believe that all of this could have taken place in a doctor's office. Dad, on the other hand, called the whole thing disgusting and barbaric.

"How could you still participate in more abortions after that?" my mother, finally breaking her silence, exclaimed.

Nurse Patterson was now visibly shaking. She asked if she could have something to drink before she continued. I was now praying that as painful as it must have been for her to finish telling us what she had come to share that it would help in her own healing process.

After taking a few sips of water and a deep breath she went on.

"Well, let me tell you what happened after that experience. That night I went home and called my best friend Judy and told her what had happened at the clinic. Judy is a nurse, too, and she tried to reassure me that abortion was a necessary medical procedure. She shared with me that when she was seventeen she got pregnant and had an abortion. She also told me that when her father had found out she was pregnant he insisted she get an abortion. Even her boyfriend flat out refused to help her in any way if she chose to have the baby."

"Some boyfriend," my father exclaimed. "He must have been a real cad."

As for me, I thought of Jason and wondered what his reaction would have been if I told him I was pregnant? Sally was just as much his baby as mine. And when I had my abortion I killed *his* child, too! Up until now I had never really given any thought about this.

"We see so many girls who tell us the same sad story that come to our clinic," Nurse Patterson went on. "But then Judy came with the clincher. She said that given our U.S. Supreme Court decision that abortion is a woman's right how could she start telling other women they shouldn't have one. She made a lot of good points and from that day forward I chose to rely upon the medical judgment of Dr. Foote and the wisdom of our U.S. Supreme Court to override what in my heart I knew was wrong."

Nurse Patterson rose and came to stand beside me. "I knew that the sixteen-week-old fetus that Dr. Foote dismembered two years ago was not just 'birth matter' but a real human being," she told me. "When the other nurse assembled the baby parts for her inspection count I could clearly count five of the tiniest fingers I had ever seen on each hand. So that night after talking with my friend Judy I made my choice."

I turned to face her then, encouraging her to go on with my eyes. This woman had repulsed me when she had first come into the room just as Dr. Foote had at the TV studio but now I began to feel sorry for her.

"I chose to deny what my eyes had seen and what my heart was telling me. I rationalized that this was a fetus that was not yet viable, that a woman's right to choose was the law of our land and I was not in a position to impose my morality on anyone. I felt as if I was standing at a door. I could either open it and find out as much as I could about what abortion is and just who this tiny fetus I had just called non-viable was, or I could leave the door closed and allow my ignorance to act as a covering for my conscience. Needless to say I never opened that door and as a result your little baby is no longer with us. I kept that door closed for two more years until one day an incredibly brave young lady faced with a similar decision chose to open her door, and thank God, my door, too. As of today, I have tendered my resignation effective at the Women's Health Services Center. I needed to let you know that, Louise."

I think we were all stunned. This was a great victory for the pro-life cause and for me personally. I was beginning to see that Baby Sally's death was not in vain after all.

"Louise you have a powerful story to share," she went on. "And thanks to the events that have taken place over the past two weeks you have a wonderful platform from which to get the message out that abortion kills babies. Don't back down even one inch. There is so much at stake. I can tell you from personal experience that you are in for the battle of your life. There is just too much money being made by abortion doctors for them to let you stop the flow of profits they are making. And the feminist movement will do everything in their power to silence your message. In addition, I believe there is a spiritual battle going on somewhere behind the scenes."

"I think you are right on target when you say something spiritual is taking place that we can't readily see with our eyes," my father said thoughtfully. I could tell from the way he was looking at Nurse Patterson now that he was willing to accept her.

"What kind of spiritual battle are you talking about?" I asked him, leading the nurse over to the sofa so that we could sit together. I felt that she was an ally now.

"Why don't we let Ms. Patterson explain?" my father said.

"If I ever needed proof that a real live devil exists in our world then all I need to do is reflect back on the hundreds of buckets we used to catch the dismembered baby parts our clinic 'surgically' removed," she said simply. I took her hand and found it was very cold. "There is some type of supernatural battle going on for the lives of millions of babies every year. I don't fully understand it but I just feel it in my gut. Louise, if I can offer you any advice it would be to learn as much as you can about every aspect of abortion and fetal development. You must prepare for battle. You'll be facing many formidable foes in the not too distant future. Information is a powerful weapon and I believe that with your insights and presentation skills, you can open many hearts and minds."

I knew right then and there that she was right about my need for more information. And as far as the battles ahead, she only confirmed what my dad had been telling me every day for the past week. When Nurse Patterson got up to leave, I rose as well and we hugged one another. I knew I would never forget her for making me even more determined to pursue my mission. Because that was what it was, a mission.

Over the next few days five women, who also had abortions done at Women's Health Services, came forward to tell the media their stories of how they, too, were not given much counseling other than the option of abortion. Each said they had been told that their baby was little more than a wad of cells that could never survive on their own. It was interesting that three of the women used the same term, "birth matter," to describe what was growing inside of them right before they submitted to their abortion.

Needless to say the news media had a field day. By now the pro-life people in Palmerville and other parts of our nation were no longer referring to my abortion as just another taking of innocent life but as taking the life of "Baby Sally." Even the media started referring to my case that way. Right after those five other brave women came forward to condemn the Women's Health Services abortion clinic, one newspaper came out with the following headline:

"Baby Sally Abortion Nurse Resigns – Five Other Women Tell Similar Baby Sally Stories." Another headline read: "Baby Sally Death not in Vain as Abortion Nurse Resigns Position."

Within a few weeks time the bad publicity that Women's Health Services Center received was so overwhelming that, according to Nurse Patterson, their business was substantially reduced. I would like to think that, her resigning, and the other women coming forward, put a stop to many abortions that might otherwise have been performed. However, I knew that many women in our surrounding area were still probably having the procedure done just at different clinics in the area. Only God knew what was actually going on behind the scenes. There was however, one thing I was certain of and that was Nurse Patterson would no longer play a role in terminating these pregnancies before these babies decided when to come out of their wombs.

The most amazing nine-month journey any human being will ever experience all takes place even before we take our first breath. Like the movie many years ago called *Fantastic Voyage* our first nine months of life are indeed just that – a most fantastic voyage. And it is during those first three months of our maiden voyage into this world that a dazzling ninety day explosion of life so incredibly complex and moving with such awesome lightning speed serves to let every set of parents know that we are here. It was here that I wanted to be in a position to be able to describe in detail what went on during those first ninety days of little Sally's life. I had a good idea from reading Dr. Willke's book but I wanted to know so much more.

I asked Dad if I could purchase more books on abortion so I could find out the answers to the many questions I still had. I also asked him if we could invite people from the pro-life movement to our home so I could learn from their experiences what to expect as I continued to advocate on behalf of the unborn. I knew I needed to gain that vital knowledge that Nurse Patterson spoke about. After all, if I had to prepare for battle it was imperative that I understood the battlefield I would be fighting on and the enemy I would be engaged against.

I soon discovered that arranging to invite people active in the pro-life movement wouldn't be too difficult since literally dozens of phone calls had been coming into our home from their groups requesting to meet with my family and me. Dad told me he was particularly impressed by a phone call he had received from a woman from the National Alliance for Life, who told my dad that I could play a vital role in the fight for life of the unborn. Her name was Jennifer Poole and dad said he would ask her to come over and talk with me as soon as he could work out the details. Well, a few days later, Dad placed a call to her office in Washington, D.C. and ten minutes later my father returned to let me know that we would be meeting Miss Poole and one of her associates, Jack Tucker, at eight the following evening.

I must admit that by now I was finding it difficult to keep up with my schoolwork although Dad tried his best to shield me from the many phone calls we were receiving requesting interviews. He and Mom knew that my schoolwork was important but they also believed that my involvement in the pro-life cause was too important to minimize.

School flew by that day and before I knew it our doorbell was ringing. Miss Poole must have been in her early forties. She was an efficient looking woman in a tweed suit. Her hair was pulled back tight to her head, and with her amazingly high cheekbones, she was handsome rather than pretty. But she looked like someone I could trust. Jack Tucker had to be about fifty and looked a little like Principal Foster, except he was almost bald. Dad showed them into his study. I think he meant to show them that we intended to be very businesslike and I was glad of that.

"We've closely followed your activities over these past two weeks," Miss Poole said to me, taking a file of papers out of her briefcase, "and everyone in our organization is convinced that you have a unique story to tell, a story that has already begun to change hearts and save the lives of many unborn children."

My mother slipped out of the room and I knew her well enough to be sure that she would come back with some refreshments.

"Our organization is called the National Alliance for Life or NAL for short," Miss Poole went on. I liked her matter-of-fact approach. "It is a powerful Washington, D.C. based pro-life group that does extensive lobbying among politicians both at the local and national level, working to pass laws favorable to our pro-life beliefs. We were formed the year after the Supreme Court decided in favor of *Roe v. Wade* in 1974 and have been politically active ever since. Another one of our roles is to educate Americans about the evils of abortion through various media campaigns and other grassroots functions."

As she continued to talk, Mr. Tucker passed out some of their organization's literature. It looked very professional, and as I glanced at one piece of literature, I saw a picture of a tiny aborted baby that looked like it was about twelve to fourteen weeks old. In the picture a young woman in her late twenties was carrying a bucket containing the mutilated remains of a baby in her arms. The caption under this picture read: "Garbage is meant to be placed in buckets; babies are meant to be held in a mother's arms." At that instant I wanted more than anything else in the world to hold my Sally in my arms. When I told Miss Poole that, she nodded her understanding.

"Down through the years, we have spoken with hundreds of other women who feel exactly the way you do. It must be a terrible feeling. But, Louise, I must tell you, that from the moment I saw your televised news conference, and became familiar with the entire story that has propelled you to national media prominence, I felt in my heart that you might just hold the key to padlocking the clinics that serve as the slaughter houses of these precious unborn. Because, in order to win this war over abortion, we must capture the hearts of those Americans who have been seduced by the dark side of the unholy Trinity of Planned Parenthood, the radical women's rights crusaders and the abortion industry."

"I never heard of an unholy Trinity before," I said with a perplexed look on my face. "But putting it that way certainly adds a spiritual overtone."

"No doubt about it," she told me. "Much of our battle is spiritual. And prayer is an important weapon we strongly rely upon in this fight."

Dad, who was listening very attentively, looked at our guests and asked the big question:

"And how do we capture those millions of seduced hearts?"

As Miss Poole took a bite out of one of the pastries that my mom had brought us she turned to her associate and asked him to respond to my dad's question.

"Capturing hearts is such a massive undertaking," Mr. Tucker said, pausing to sip his coffee. "It can only be done by utilizing the national media as an ally instead of the foe they have been to us during these past twenty years. As you probably know, Mr. Jordan, most people in the print and TV media approve of abortion on demand for just about any reason. And since these people are the ones writing the stories and presenting their natural pro-choice bias to the average American, is it any wonder why winning the media war is crucial to saving babies?"

Miss Poole nodded her head in agreement. It was clear that both of our guests understood the battlefield I was about to join.

81

"I am thoroughly convinced that the only way the abortion holocaust in America can ever be stopped," she said, "is if a new constitutional amendment is passed guaranteeing the unborn the right to life. Back in 1865 it took the thirteenth Amendment to our U.S. Constitution to be passed in order to abolish slavery and give their humanity back to a whole race of Americans. Without this amendment, blacks would still have to stay in bondage and their only legal rights would be that they had none!"

She went on to explain that since our Supreme Court legalized abortion the unborn can no longer be considered legal persons. And as a result, with no legal rights prenatally, these tiny little ones are at the complete mercy of the abortionist.

"If we can pass a constitutional amendment," Mr. Tucker added, "establishing the unborn as a 'person' under the same definition considered in our fourteenth amendment then we could outlaw all abortions except for cases where the life of the mother is involved. This has been our driving goal for the pass twenty years."

Miss Poole then turned to me with a look of resignation in her eyes and told us that the support needed to pass such an amendment has never been on NAL's side. She then informed us that in order to pass a constitutional amendment it must receive two-thirds approval from both the House of Representatives and the Senate and then ratification from seventy-five percent of the states.

By now I was really starting to appreciate their presentation and felt that NAL was the type of organization I'd like to be associated with.

"That's a pretty high standard, Miss Poole," Dad said. "Do you really think that one day we might be able to gain that type of support among our elected officials?"

"Mr. and Mrs. Jordan, Louise has done more to place the abortion issue as a discussion topic at dining tables and office water coolers across America in these last few weeks than any other person in American history since the passage of *Roe v. Wade*. Perhaps without her being aware of it she has highlighted the fact that abortion kills babies in a way that has captured the fascination of our entire country. Her graphic 'show and tell' has been able to accomplish something that every pro-life organization in America hasn't been able to do to date; and that is to get the national media to run with the story in a highly favorable light to our cause."

"I certainly agree that Louise has been able to stir up quite a storm since she decided to break her silence about her abortion," my father agreed, smiling proudly at me. How wrong I had been to think he might ever fail to support me.

"We never dreamed that something like this would happen to us," my mom said and I thought I detected sadness in her eyes. Unlike my father, she was probably finding it more difficult to think of what had happened to me as a challenge.

"Through a unique set of circumstances something wonderfully special has been happening all across our land," Mr. Tucker told my mother handing her a stack of letters. "People everywhere are falling in love with a young teenage girl named Louise Ann Jordan. Her story has been generating incredible sympathy everywhere I have traveled to in these last few weeks. Over the last ten days alone our organization has received hundreds of letters like those you have in your hand from people who said they use to support abortion but after following the incredible story of Louise have since changed their minds. They wanted to let us know they have changed their stance as well as request literature on abortion, fetal development, adoption and other aspects on the entire abortion controversy."

"That's right, Jack," Miss Poole said. "We will never be able to bring Sally back but her death and your story and your courage - and I really believe this - has already changed the minds of thousands of women contemplating abortion. Sally's death and your life are beginning to make major inroads into the hearts and minds of millions in our nation. We must continue to use your unique story, along with your charismatic style, to seize the moment and perhaps put an end forever to this needless annihilation of our most defenseless citizens."

"Nobody has ever referred to me as having a charismatic style," I told her. "But if I do..."

"You *do* have a way with words, Louise," my father interrupted me. "Principal Foster said the same thing about you when I spoke to him on the phone the other day."

"Mr. & Mrs. Jordan, I know I'm asking a lot," Miss Poole said, leaning forward, her dark eyes intent, "but do you think Louise could take a few days off from school and come down to Washington, D.C. with us. I want her to meet other representatives from NAL and take a crash course on a host of issues concerning every aspect of abortion. I understand how important school is but also know that the lives of millions of souls are at stake."

My father rose from behind his desk. "Could you give Jill and me a few minutes to discuss this alone," he said.

"Certainly. This is a big request and a big decision on your part."

After about a five minute conference with my mother in the hall, my father returned and told Miss Poole and me that they had agreed that they would allow me to take the entire next week off from school and travel to Washington, D.C. Dad said that he was going to also take a week off from work and accompany me. Miss Poole was so excited with my father's decision that she ran over to my dad and gave him a big kiss and hug. Mom felt a little embarrassed but understood her excitement. And missing a week of school and traveling to Washington, D.C, was something nobody needed to coax me into doing.

It was now the end of October and a full seven weeks after Palmerville High became a household word across America. Miss Poole told dad that she would make all of the travel arrangements for us and that the National Alliance for Life would pay for our entire stay. Miss Poole made plane reservations for us to leave New York City on Saturday afternoon. Dad spoke to Principal Foster and got permission to take me out of school during the following week. I packed my bags Friday right after school and asked my mom if I could invite some of my friends over tonight before leaving for D.C. the next day. So that evening Sarah, Jenny, Heather, and several other friends came over to discuss my upcoming trip and provide me with some badly needed moral support.

Since the day I had my abortion I made it a point to learn as much as I could about this very charged subject. I must have read three books in addition to Dr. Willke's book and several pamphlets. That night, my friends and I discussed how absolutely amazing it was that one five-minute English class presentation could have had so much impact on an entire nation. When every one of my friends told me that they had gone out and bought *Why Can't We Love Them*

Both, the book that had impressed me so, I felt deeply touched. It was really something to see a group of high school kids spending three to four hours discussing and sharing comments and ideas about how to put a stop to abortion in America. Each of my friends kept asking me my opinion on a variety of important issues.

Heather wanted to know, "how can we not allow a woman to obtain an abortion if she becomes pregnant through rape?"

Heather's freckled face was so familiar to me now that we had become good friends. Last month she finally summoned the courage to tell her parents that she was pregnant. And to her amazement her father didn't throw her out of the house. While he strongly recommended she get an abortion, he told her that he would leave the final decision up to her. When she told her dad that she planned to give birth and then put her baby up for adoption, he said he could live with her choice.

"No one has ever asked me that question before," I told her. "But it horrifies me to even think about being raped and having to carry a criminal's child."

We were all sitting on the floor in front of the fire my dad had built for us in the rec room. Mom, of course, had provided the refreshments and every now and then would peek in on us to see how I was doing.

"I'm definitely against abortion," Sarah said, her long brown hair now glistening in the glow of the fire, "but I feel that in special cases like rape exceptions need to be made."

"I know exactly how you feel," I assured her. "But I just know that even a baby conceived through rape is still a baby."

My friend Raymond brought up a point that none of us had ever really looked at before. Raymond Barton was the best basketball player at Palmerville High and a straight "A" student. Almost every girl in school had a crush on him. But what I liked most about him was his unique way of making everyone he met feel important and special.

"You have to remember that rape is just one of those thousands of things that happen in life that just aren't fair," he said emphatically. "For example, my father drinks. And I know yours does, too, Heather. And that's not fair. But thousands of kids have the same problem. And millions go to bed hungry. And some people are blind. I read the other day that there are over forty million blind people who, if they lived in this country and had proper care and living conditions, most would be able to see. And that's not fair. But it happens."

"Raymond, wow I never looked at life that way before," I said. "You sure make a lot of sense, but what does this have to do with our discussion on abortion?"

Then Raymond really made it personal and asked me whether, if I had became pregnant with Sally as a result of having been raped, could I have aborted her. And when I shook my head, he went on to tell all of us that how Sally made her way into this world had absolutely nothing to do with her innocence, uniqueness, and humanity.

"If I understand what you're saying Raymond," Sarah excitedly said, "to abort a baby that is the product of a rape is to, in reality, impose the ultimate punishment on an innocent child for the crime of its father."

"That's exactly right Sarah," Raymond said, now standing up and walking right in front of our fireplace. "In a perfect world," he continued, "we wouldn't have all of these problems. But we don't live in a perfect world."

"But Raymond," Heather wanted to know, "what can we do to make things better?"

"Well," Raymond, now looking straight at Heather said, "I believe we should feed the hungry, work harder to find medical cures for conditions like Jerry's, and let babies conceived through rape have the same opportunities to live that all of us sitting in Louise's house have."

I determined to remember everything Raymond had just said because, as far as I was concerned it was the most profound answer I could give if anyone ever asked me that same question on rape and abortion in the future. It was an answer that would, at the very least, give many "exception clause" people something to think about.

Over the past month Jerry, the boy with Down's Syndrome, had become one of my best friends, as well as being a favorite with just about everyone else at school, a constant source of inspiration to everyone. We all loved him because of his affectionate nature and cheerful personality. And all of us were quite glad that his parents hadn't gone through with their planned abortion. Jerry thanked Raymond for sharing his comments on rape and abortion and asked if he could talk about why he felt handicapped babies also deserved a chance to live.

"It hasn't been easy for my folks, having me," he told us, pushing his dark hair back from his forehead. I was glad that he wasn't nervous about sharing with us. But then Jerry trusted everyone.

"My dad says there are a lot of bumps along the way in life," he went on, "and I tell him I'm one of those bumps." We all laughed at that and Jerry grinned.

"But you know," he said, "I'm real happy with my life. I don't play baseball like Jack Hawkins but I can watch it. And I'm a fan, you know. That's what Dad calls me. My team's the New York Yankees. And my mom told me that people who can't see beyond my limitations are the people with the real handicaps."

I turned to Jerry, smiling and nodding at the same time, to let him know he was right on target.

"And just last week," Jerry continued, "my dad came into my room and told me he was going to get me my own phone line. He said I was getting so popular that with all the time I spent on the phone nobody else was able to make or receive phone calls anymore."

At that moment the doorbell rang and my friend Eric, who worked for Lazzaro's Pizza, said that my dad had ordered pizza for everyone. There was pepperoni, my favorite and extra-cheese. Jerry took a slice of each. By now it was almost ten but nobody wanted to leave. As soon as Jerry finished his second slice he said he wanted to ask me a question.

"If a Mom killed someone like me when I was two," he said, "she'd go to jail, wouldn't she, Louise? But it's OK to kill a Down's Syndrome child before he's born. I don't understand that!"

Raymond told all of us that Jerry's logic was quite compelling and then added, "Every day thousands of people in our world will become handicapped through sickness and accidents; and many of these handicaps will be far worse than Jerry's. Should we then kill them like Jerry's mom's doctor wanted to do with him?"

"No. You don't know how important you are to us, Jerry," Sarah said, putting one arm around him. "We shouldn't let a group of nine U.S. Supreme Court Justices determine which handicaps do and which handicaps don't measure up to their standards of quality of life. You may never be a famous doctor or a scientist, Jerry but when all is said and done, I'll bet that the citizens of Palmerville will be able to say that Jerry Bedford was an important part of their community."

Jolene Tobin, perhaps the brightest girl in tenth grade, who had once told me that, during the past five years, she had read over two hundred books said she saw a fascinating piece on Helen Keller in a book she read last month and that she wanted to read a section of it to us.

"Helen Keller, although she spent almost her entire life deaf and without sight, became a symbol to the entire world of the unlimited potential the human spirit possesses to overcome personal trials and handicaps. To this incredible woman, being deaf, mute and blind, only propelled her on to greatness. She was the author of nine books, graduated from Radcliffe College with honors, contributed $2 million to a foundation to help others and once remarked, 'The Bible is one mighty representative of the whole spiritual life of humanity.'"[17]

She closed the book and put it down on the rug beside her.

"Jerry," she said, "the more I read about people with severe handicaps the more I learn that these disabilities often have been the keys to bringing out the best in people. Besides, how can anyone measure the relative value of someone with a handicap versus someone without that same handicap?"

And then she told us about a book she had just finished in which a geneticist told a story about a physician who lived in Austria. One day the doctor delivered a baby boy and a baby girl. While the baby boy was very healthy the girl was born with what we would today call Down's syndrome. The doctor followed them both for almost fifty years. The girl grew up and had to take care of her mother who suffered from a very long illness after a stroke. The boy lived to be a man who died in a bunker in Berlin. [18]

"Do you know what that man's name was?" Jolene then asked us. But before we could answer she blurted out, "his name was Adolf Hitler."

All of a sudden I could hear a collective gasp. This story didn't need any explanation. I think all of us knew the point Jolene wanted to make.

Jolene went on to tell everyone that after seeing me on TV she became deeply touched with my message and wanted to learn more about abortion. As a result, I think she had actually read more books on the subject over the past two months than I did. She asked if she could share one more quote from the current book she was reading. Of course we told her she could. And we were all ears.

"This is a statement made by a pediatric surgeon and our former Surgeon General, Dr. C. Everett Koop," she told us.

"I am frequently told by people who have never had the experience of working with children who are being rehabilitated into our society after the correction of a congenital defect that Infants with such defects should be allowed to die, or even 'encouraged' to die, because their lives could obviously be nothing but unhappy and miserable. Yet it has been my constant experience that disability and unhappiness do not necessarily go together. Some of the most unhappy children whom I have known have all of the physical and mental faculties and on the other hand some of the happiest youngsters have borne burdens which I myself would find very difficult to bear."[19]

We continued to share our opinions with one another late into the night until, when the grandfather clock in the hall struck midnight, mom came downstairs and reminded me I had a flight to catch tomorrow and needed to get some sleep. I wished all my friends good night and asked them to keep me in their prayers. I now felt much more at ease knowing I had so many of my friends supporting my views. By this time tomorrow I would be in Washington, D.C. and hopefully learning how to reach the millions of other living rooms in America with the pro-life message.

It was great taking an airplane with my dad and just spending time with him alone. When we landed, Miss Poole and two other representatives from the National Alliance for Life were waiting to greet us. We all got into a minivan and Miss Poole told us she would take us to our hotel first. After we got settled in, she would have another car pick us up and take us to the NAL headquarters where we would dine and meet other important people in the pro-life movement.

When Dad and I arrived at the National Alliance for Life headquarters, and we stepped out of the elevator onto their 7th floor main office, I was greatly moved to see a huge banner hanging over the main reception desk saying "The NAL Welcomes Louise Ann Jordan." Miss Poole came out to greet us and introduced us to National Alliance for Life president Sally Gates, a tall gray-haired lady, who told my dad and me how honored she was that we were willing to spend a week of our lives to help NAL in their battle for the lives of the unborn.

Tonight was indeed going to be a special night. The NAL had converted their boardroom into a dining room and they treated Dad and me to a wonderful catered dinner. Don't ask me how but the menu had all of my favorite foods including Hawaiian chicken. When they brought out dessert I began to wonder if dad might have participated in the menu selection for tonight. How else could they have chosen my all time favorite – a banana split with whipped cream and a cherry. If the NAL wanted to make me feel special and important they were certainly doing a great job. Mrs. Gates was old enough to be my grandmother but she knew how to relate to me as if she was just another one of my high school friends. We talked about the latest fashions, Mark Twain, movies and yes the reason for my being here – abortion.

Mrs. Gates told us that in 1978 she had had an abortion and she, like me, had knew very little what abortion was all about. She had been single, in her mid thirties and had a promising career as a Wall Street investment banker. The last thing she needed was a baby to raise. Marriage was not in her plans and she told my dad and me that she didn't even love the father of her baby. The procedure was, like mine, quick and relatively painless. Within a day or two she went back to work and felt as if her career could now proceed as normal. But for the next two years she felt as if something was now missing in her life. Yes, she was making a lot of money and even got a big promotion; but deep inside she knew that what she had done to the tiny life that use to be inside her body was wrong.

On many a night she couldn't sleep and often would stay up at night wondering if her baby would have been a boy or girl if she decided to keep it. Mrs. Gates told me that she wanted me to get a good night's sleep because the NAL had prepared a very busy day for dad and me of sightseeing and a special Sunday evening presentation on the fight for life. But first she said she had a story she wanted to share with us about something that had transformed her life.

"Back in the spring of 1987," she told us, her voice now becoming very serious, "I was having lunch with one of my co-workers and somehow the topic turned to abortion. I told John that I was pro-choice but didn't tell him that I had an abortion several years earlier. John told me that he and his wife also used to be pro-choice, but now were strongly pro-life. I asked the natural question. What changed your mind? And his answer changed my life forever. After John had told his story, I knew in my heart that I could never defend the pro-choice position again."

"That must have been some powerful story to apparently take you from the world of investment banking to become the president of NAL," my Dad observed. He had spent most of the meal talking to Miss Poole who was explaining her plans for us in detail, but now he turned all his attention on Mrs. Gates.

"It wasn't the career path I had in mind," she admitted, "but life is never very predictable is it?"

"You can say that again," I told Mrs. Gates. "I could never have planned the path I have traveled on these past few months either."

"Mrs. Gates, I'm very interested to hear this story," my father said, as he moved his chair a little closer to hers.

"Well, John told me that while he and a woman named Christina had been dating, she got pregnant. Neither one of them were ready for marriage at that time and knew that having a child out of wedlock was something they just weren't willing to do. Besides, they reasoned a child now could adversely effect Christina's investment banking career. Well, Christina was never one to make a decision without researching things quite carefully. Her doctor told her she was approximately ten weeks along and that the abortion procedure was quite simple and painless. The technical name was suction curettage in which the woman's cervix is dilated and a tube inserted in the uterus. According to the medical literature, they subsequently attach the tube to a very strong suction apparatus and the fetus is then torn to pieces and its parts sucked into a jar.

"However," as John told me, "when Christina saw her doctor again and asked him questions about this entire procedure, he told her that, at ten weeks, the fetus was little more than a cluster of cells and not a baby. Christina still felt very uncomfortable with the entire situation but she trusted him and knew how this baby would cause a major disruption to both of their lives. The abortion was scheduled later that week and true to form it was quick and almost completely painless. As they left the clinic that day they both felt very relieved that their minor complication was finally over."

"Mrs. Gates, I'm sorry to interrupt you but that's just about the same thing that happened to me when I went to the clinic that performed my abortion," I exclaimed.

"I'm sorry to say that this type of deception is the rule rather than the exception in that business," Mrs. Gates told me.

"Well, two years later, Christina and John were married and six months after that Christina became pregnant again. Right after they were married a special event happened to them both. They were invited to attend a church service by mutual friends. The pastor gave a wonderful message that night and asked if there was anyone who would like to have their sins forgiven by inviting Jesus Christ into their life. That night both of them said yes and became new Christians. After that Christina did a lot of thinking and decided that once their first child was born, she would quit her job and take the next few years to raise their child."

I was glad that they were going to keep their child but kept wondering if they would have decided to abort their second child, too, if they hadn't been married. But what Mrs. Gates was about to describe next was totally unexpected and would serve to greatly strengthen my belief in just how precious every human life is.

"When Christina went for her five month checkup," Mrs. Gates went on, "her doctor told Christina and John some very devastating news. On the basis of several tests, he had to inform them that, in all likelihood, if they decided to have their baby it would be born with a severe birth defect called hydrocephaly.

"John and Christina were both crushed," Mrs. Gates told us. "Her doctor immediately recommended that she get an abortion but they told him that they could never take the life of their child, that they believed that life and death should rest with God and not man.

Their decision rested firmly on the knowledge that Christina, who after her abortion had done a lot of research, knew she was carrying a real baby and not just some clump of cells or fetal tissue. Rather than kill their child, they chose to pray that God would heal their baby. For the next four months they had their entire church pray for them. But sadly, when the baby was delivered it was born with a condition called hydrocephaly."

Mrs. Gates paused for a moment to take a sip of coffee. It was clear that it wasn't easy for her to tell this story. My Dad gave her some time to pull herself together by explaining to me that hydrocephaly is a condition where an abnormal accumulation of fluid in the brain takes place causing an enlargement of the skull and compression of the brain.

"I can still remember John's face as he told me this," Mrs. Gates said. "They named her Gloria and during the next five years she underwent over ten surgeries but she never was able to walk and she could only make sounds with her voice. To most people she would have been a major liability but to Christina and John she was their gift from God and they loved her so much, just as everyone did who ever met her. John showed me her picture. She had the most wonderful smile. 'At six years old God called her home,' John told me, 'and even today I can tell you I miss her so very much.'"

As Mrs. Gates continued to tell John and Christina's story the heartbreaking reality of their abortion decisions became hauntingly real to me. John had told Mrs. Gates that their first baby if they didn't abort it would almost certainly have been a healthy child. Ironically, they chose to keep their second baby, Gloria, and unfortunately she was severely handicapped. But John insisted that Gloria was a wonderful child in her own way, and when she died a special part of their family was taken from them. Despite the fact that Gloria brought with her many challenges John and Christina never once felt that they should have gone through with the abortion. While she was never able to experience many of the things most little girls love to do she did enjoy finger painting, eating ice cream and playing with her Barbie dolls.

When Mrs. Gates mentioned Barbie dolls my mind immediately started reviewing my entire collection wondering which one might have been Gloria's favorite. She must have been a very special child whom God had given the gift of life for six precious years.

When Mrs. Gates finished this powerful story, she leaned back in her chair as though she were exhausted and Dad poured her more coffee. It was clear that the impact this story had had on her was profound. As she went on to tell us, for the next few weeks she hadn't been able to stop thinking about the abortion she had years earlier. She, too, had decided on death to an almost certain healthy child. But she too now knew it wasn't man's place to make the decisions on which babies can live and which babies should die. Shortly after this time Mrs. Gates told us how she became active in the pro-life movement and for the past three years had served as the President of NAL.

Dad and I thanked Mrs. Gates and Miss Poole for a wonderful evening and headed back to our hotel. Our nation's capital was a far cry from Palmerville but I felt comfortable being here. I was really looking forward to meeting new people active in the movement and learning more about life in the womb. While I was anxiously waiting to see how this week would unfold something inside of me kept telling me that this wouldn't be my last trip to D.C.

8

Eddie Moss

Jennifer and Mrs. Gates acted as our tour guides that Sunday. It was awesome! We had so much fun visiting the many Washington D.C. memorials, monuments and government buildings. I must have taken three rolls of pictures that day. By the time we finished an early dinner and traveled back to NAL headquarters, I was pretty tired. NAL had prepared a special presentation just for me highlighting a brief history of the pro-life movement from the late sixties to the present.

For the next three hours dad and I listened intently to a variety of speakers who spoke on a wide spectrum of pro-life/pro-choice issues. What really made an impact on me was the passion with which each pro-life advocate delivered their presentation. And the diversity of occupations each pro-lifer was engaged in was equally amazing. Mr. Samuels and Mrs. Terry were doctors. Mr. Gilbert was an U.S. Congressman from Tennessee. Jane Gonzalez was a housewife and mother of three small children. Eddie Moss was the owner of a big chain of restaurants in the Midwest. Mrs. Billings was a registered nurse. Aida Jones ran a Crisis Pregnancy Center right here in D.C. And Mr. Todd, Mr. Seaver and Mrs. Chen were on the board of NAL.

Each person gave a ten-minute presentation on some aspect of the abortion issue, every presentation more powerful than the one before it. From seven to almost nine these ten speakers were able to masterfully dismantle the pro-choice position plank by plank. Three of the presentations still stand out in my mind to this day.

Dr. Barbara Terry spoke about the different abortion techniques and how cruelly and inhumanely they were administered. As she described each technique she was careful to replace the pro-choice terminology with what really was going on inside the mother's womb. For example in a Dilation & Curettage, D & C, abortion the pro-choice description would be "the use of a curette to help remove fetal tissue from the mother's uterus." In reality, according to Dr. Terry, in a D & C abortion the abortionist uses a loop-shaped steel knife to cut into pieces the developing child and then proceeds to scrape the dismembered baby into a basin. Bleeding is usually profuse as the tiny baby is killed.

I'll never forget how Dr. Terry described a saline abortion.

"During this technique a pregnancy is terminated by injecting a salt solution into the amniotic sac," she said. Dr. Terry was a very petite young woman, perhaps in her mid thirties, who was fond of gestures. "Normally this procedure, induces labor within twenty-four hours, causing the fetus to be expelled," she said, pointing to one of the many slides she had brought with her. "But, in reality a saline abortion should more accurately be called a salt poisoning abortion. In this type of an abortion a long needle is inserted through the mother's abdomen into the baby's sac. The abortionist then removes some fluid and a strong salt solution is injected. The unsuspecting baby swallows this poison and begins to suffer terribly. It takes over an hour for the baby to die as he kicks and jerks violently. The helpless baby is literally being burned alive as his outer layer of skin is completely burned off. Within twenty-four hours, labor will usually set in and the mother will give birth to a dead baby."

When she turned to the D & X type of abortion I began to wonder how another human being, in the name of medicine, could perform such a monstrous act. Even dad was in shock as Dr. Terry let us know just how low an abortionist could actually go.

"Louise," she continued, "I'm sorry to be so graphic in my descriptions but reality often can be quite brutal in life. Even the pro-choice movement has a hard time showing a D & X, Dilation and Extraction, abortion in a non-ghastly manner. The proper name for this procedure is partial birth abortion. Abortion advocates contend that this procedure is necessary to preserve the life or health of the mother and in many instances the babies already have severe handicaps. These claims are highly questionable. In fact a very high percentage of these babies are normal, and since the procedure is done often after four or five months, most of these babies are viable if delivered and given intense neo-natal medical care. What is not open to debate is the barbarism of this procedure.

"In a partial birth abortion the doctor uses forceps to grab hold of the baby's leg. He then pulls the baby's leg out into the birth canal. He then delivers the baby's entire body, except for the head. Then he jams a pair of scissors into the baby's skull and proceeds to open them to enlarge the hole to make room for inserting a suction tip before sucking the baby's brains out. When the brains are removed, the baby's skull collapses and the baby is delivered quite dead."

Mrs. Terry closed her presentation by telling me that if the American Society for the Prevention of Cruelty to Animals ever found out that anyone ever treated animals the way abortionists treat babies there would be a great outcry of inhumanity. And rest assured their lawyers would step in to stop this type of treatment.

The second talk, one that really touched my heart came from a young registered nurse named Emily Billings. Emily worked in a hospital that delivered babies but also performed abortions. She told my dad and me that, the first time she assisted in an abortion, she couldn't believe that a doctor used his medical instruments to pull arms and legs off a tiny baby still in its mother's womb. The abortionist assured her that everything he was doing was perfectly legal and ethical.

As she told her story my heart broke once again as I reflected on that horrible day back in September when baby Sally was dismembered and then discarded. Mrs. Billings then continued to relate the incredible dilemma she found herself in.

"When that doctor saw how distraught I was at having witnessed a real abortion for the first time," she said, "he sat me down and told me why abortion was a very necessary medical procedure. He told me how many teenagers would have their lives ruined if they had to keep their babies to term. Finally, he told me emphatically that we had no right to impose our brand of morality on a woman who chose to abort her fetus. At the time those arguments seemed to make sense, so I closed my eyes and my heart from that day forward whenever I assisted in an abortion.

"Fortunately I assisted in more live births than abortions and I was somehow able to keep my perspective in focus that in both cases the mother had the right to make the final choice on either having her baby or aborting it. One day, however, we had to perform an abortion on a woman who was approximately twenty-two weeks pregnant. She was huge but we were successfully able to abort her baby. Within fifteen minutes after I had cleaned myself up we got an emergency call that a woman down the hall had just given birth to a tiny one pound four ounce, twenty-two-week-old premature baby. I had to rush to the intensive neo-natal care unit and watch as three doctors frantically worked to save the life of that helpless infant.

"Louise, as I tried my best to help those doctors save that baby's life, I began to see that I was acting as if I was a schizophrenic. Here I was, just a half-hour ago, helping to take the life of a twenty-two-week-old preborn. And now, exactly one half hour later, I was doing everything in my power to help save the life of another preborn exactly the same age – twenty-two weeks old - as the baby I just helped kill!"

Well that night Nurse Billings had gone home and took a good long look at herself in the mirror and decided she didn't like the person she saw. She loved being a nurse and loved babies. As an obstetrics' nurse she had always viewed her role as someone sworn to help bring healing and comfort to sick infants and mothers and to assist in delivering life from the womb. That day she realized she had broken her oath to help deliver life many times over, whenever she participated in an abortion.

"Louise," she said, "I can tell you that ever since that day, seven years ago, I have never participated in another abortion; and I never will again."

But perhaps the most compelling testimony came from a sixty-six-year-old balding man from Kansas – Eddie Moss. What touched me the most about Eddie was that he was willing to put his convictions into action. Eddie was a millionaire many times over. He owned a chain of three hundred restaurants that did business in fifteen states. He told me he was very active in his home state of Kansas in the pro-life movement. In fact he was the head of all NAL Midwest activities. When Sally Gates had informed him that I would be spending a week at NAL national headquarters, he had insisted on flying down to meet me. I had never met a millionaire before Eddie, and I couldn't wait to tell all my friends back in Palmerville that a multi-millionaire flew all the way from Kansas just to meet me. As Mr. Moss began to tell us just how involved he was in the pro-life movement, I began to wonder how he had any time left to run his restaurants.

"Louise, when Sally called me to let me know you were coming to Washington this week, I told her that I wanted to meet you and personally thank you for all you are doing for the pro-life cause," he began.

"I'm flattered that you would come all the way to D.C. to meet me," I said, smiling. This was the kind of person no one could help but like.

"Mr. Moss," Dad added, "I think you've definitely made my daughter's day."

"Well, it's not often someone so young can make such a powerful statement for life."

"Louise, Jennifer and I invited Eddie down not only to meet you but to share a little about the work he is doing in the Midwest," Mrs. Gates told us. "Eddie please let our guests know what you've been up to the last few years."

"Well, for the past ten years I have spent a large portion of my time and wealth fighting to help prevent young women from taking the lives of their very own flesh and blood through abortion. But I wasn't always active in the fight for life. In fact I use to think that we had no business telling a woman what she should do with her own body. To me, abortion was a totally private decision that each woman should decide for herself."

"What happened to make you see things differently, Mr. Moss," I asked.

"Everything changed for me when my granddaughter came home from school one day and showed me a photograph from a high school paper she had just written," he began.

"Her English teacher had asked each student to write a paper on a controversial issue aimed at trying to influence people who had an opposing viewpoint to change their minds. Now my granddaughter

99

Katie chose the issue of abortion in America. The paper was only four pages long, but right at the end, she pasted on a photograph of a fourteen-week-old fetus she had cut out from a magazine. Right under her photograph, she wrote: "Question: Did you know that this tiny baby has a perfectly functioning human heart? How could anyone have the heart to kill it through abortion? Answer: They don't!!!"

"That makes a persuasive case, all right," my father said. "Your granddaughter makes me think of Louise."

"Right then Katie accomplished what she had set out to do," Mr. Moss told us. "She changed my mind. I have a copy of her paper with me that I hope both of you will take a look at later on. It's been ten years since my young granddaughter changed my stance on abortion and during that time I've been trying my best to change minds too."

"You must be awfully proud of Katie."

"Yes, Mrs. Moss and I love her to death."

"You mean love her to life, Eddie."

"I think I like your expression better than mine Louise," he said with a broad smile.

"You know Louise, during these past ten years I have spent a lot of my own money to open and fund Crisis Pregnancy Centers in over ten states. My wife and I have supplied literally tons of clothing to young, expectant mothers. For the past five years our company policy has been to give any employee $10,000 if they choose to adopt a child. My wife and I have helped fund and produce ten anti-abortion videos. In addition we have opened our home to several young women who, because they had decided to keep their babies instead of aborting them, were thrown out of their homes. We provided the love and support that these young girls so desperately needed and I am happy to say all of them decided to deliver and keep their babies."

"Funny how a simple picture can motivate the heart," I said.

It seemed a little eerie, but in both of our lives a simple picture had changed forever the way we would view life and live life.

"That's quite profound Louise," Mr. Moss said. "But I have learned down through the years that telling the truth is indeed always the best policy."

"I only wished I practiced that policy a lot sooner than I am now doing," I told him.

"Don't we all," Miss Poole agreed. She then put her arm around my shoulder just like my mom always did when she sensed I needed to be comforted, and at that moment I did.

"I run my restaurant business to make money and provide a decent honest living for my over two thousand employees," Mr. Moss went on. "But one thing I never do is to compromise on my principles of honesty and integrity. We stand behind everything we sell and my convictions dictate all of my business dealings. As a result of these core values I have always endeavored to present our pro-life arguments in an honest and non-deceptive manner. My goal has always been to save babies and educate women on the evils of abortion and the alternatives available to them and not to shame them into changing their minds."

This was the sort of person I wanted to be associated with, someone willing to put all their resources and energies on the line for a just cause. And I just knew that this would not be the last time our paths would cross again.

At the conclusion of the presentations, NAL showed us a special thirty-minute video that documented the history of the fight for life since *Roe v. Wade*. After the video, Mrs. Gates told us that we would be closing the evening by enjoying Washington's best pizza – DeVito's. It was delicious and I felt like royalty being treated to so many of my favorite foods. NAL made me feel like part of a wonderful big family. But as I ate my pizza and drank my soda, I felt a deep sense of sadness knowing that every day thousands of our most innocent and precious new citizens would be stripped of their dignity, humanity and their very lives.

I asked Eddie if I could read his granddaughter's paper on abortion. He gave me his copy and told me that it had a special note attached to it.

Her paper was full of excellent pro-life arguments but it was her personal note that really moved my heart:

Dear Louise,

Over the past two months, I have been following your story with great interest. Almost ten years ago, I wrote this paper as an English class project. When I wrote it I could never have imagined the impact that my paper would have on my grandfather. His dedication to the entire right to life movement has been a constant source of inspiration to me. When he told me he was flying to D.C. to meet you, I asked him if I could attach this personal note to my paper which he told me he was going to share with you. Louise, your courage and convictions have served to renew my spirit into believing that we still can put an end to this monstrous American genocide called abortion.

My grandfather has given the last ten years of his life trying to rescue as many of these babies as possible, but he has only been able to do so much. Now, because of a unique set of circumstances, you have been able to do something quite remarkable. No matter how the pro-abortion forces have tried to use their negative spin, they have been unable to quench the powerful central theme of your message: abortion kills babies. Right before my grandfather left to meet you, I told him that there was no doubt in my mind that you, Louise have a special calling on your life.

Newspapers all across America are depicting your story in a positive light. Students in English classes all across our nation are writing thousands of papers just like the one you have in your hand. In Kansas alone at least five nurses at local abortion clinics have tendered their resignations. Churches in all fifty states have the name of Louise Ann Jordan on their prayer lists. And yes, a sixty-six-year-old balding man named Eddie Moss was so moved by your story that he dropped everything from his busy schedule to fly to Washington to meet you. And in my own humble way, I, a twenty-six-year-old mother of three small children, just wanted to let you know I love you.

God bless – Katie.

I also believed that God had given me a special calling. The big question in my mind, however, was did I have the courage and emotional temperament needed to stand up to all the negative attacks I was sure to face in the near future. I certainly was going to need a lot of encouragement along the way and thankfully Katie's note gave me a heavy dose of it.

9

A Strategy for Life

That night as we traveled back to our hotel room I remarked to my dad that with so many powerful pro-life stories out there why was mine in particular receiving so much incredible attention.

"I asked Miss Poole that same question earlier in the day," he told me. "As we were leaving tonight, she asked us to join her for breakfast tomorrow and she would try to answer my question."

"Dad I can't believe how exciting all this is."

Being in a new city, and meeting new people made me realize just how lucky I was. I had always wanted adventure in my life but I never expected this much so soon.

"Well, hold on to your seat," he said with a grin, "because she also told me that she wanted to lay out how NAL felt they could use you in helping them launch their most dynamic nationwide anti-abortion campaign ever."

"No way, Dad!" I exclaimed. Could all of this really be happening to me? Was NAL really going to risk so much of their resources on Louise Ann Jordan? I was almost afraid to ask how they planned to use me but my curiosity couldn't wait to find out.

"That's what she told me," he replied. "You can ask her about it tomorrow over breakfast."

"I can't wait."

"Me too."

We gave one another a hug as we got out of the cab. My father had always been a happy man and affectionate but I had never seen him like this.

We met Miss Poole at eight and dined in the hotel at a quaint restaurant called *Oliver's*. As I stared at the pancakes, eggs, bacon and fruit I had ordered, I began to realize that the way they were feeding me if I wasn't careful by the end of the week I might just gain ten pounds. "Louise," Miss Poole said, "I know that you and your dad have lot's of questions on why we feel that you are so unique to the pro-life cause. Before I try to answer them however, I would like to tell you how I came to work at NAL."

Miss Poole was wearing a neatly pressed dark blue suit. She always looked so professional. Whenever I was around her I felt secure and comfortable. She was so upbeat and sharp as a tack.

"Last night I told my dad that I bet you were either a teacher or a stewardess," I said.

"Those are good guesses," she replied, pausing to sip her coffee, "but before I joined the staff here at NAL I was a vice president at a major New York City advertising agency. One day I got a call from Sally Gates. She wanted to know if our firm could help them with a new pro-life ad campaign they were working on. I told Mrs. Gates that our firm had never worked with a right to life group before but asked her if we could meet for lunch later in the week to discuss the concept. We both agreed and scheduled our lunch meeting."

I leaned toward her, prepared to listen carefully. These personal stories I had been hearing were simply fascinating and obviously life changing.

"Before I met Sally, I knew very little about abortion," Miss Poole went on. "But after spending nearly two hours discussing the work and mission of NAL with her I began to understand why right-to-lifers believe so strongly that abortion kills babies. As we continued to eat and talk Mrs. Gates made such a powerful case against abortion that she convinced me that the issue of choice really boiled down to the right to choose to keep a baby or kill a baby.

"I'm sure that both of you know that the job of an ad agency is to design ads that put our client's products in a favorable light," she went on briskly. "It is our job to convince prospective buyers why they need to purchase a certain product."

One of the things that intrigued me about her was her ability to put her emotions behind her when she needed to. I was beginning to realize how necessary this might be for me, as well.

"Designing an ad campaign to convince a mother not to terminate her pregnancy must have been a real challenge for you," I said.

"It certainly was, Louise. After our lunch I told Mrs. Gates that I wanted to work with NAL but felt before our firm could design a marketing campaign, I would need to know as much as possible about abortion."

"That's exactly the same approach I took before I made my speech on national TV back in early September," I told her.

"Ladies, great minds think alike," my father said, trying his best not to laugh too hard.

"I appreciate the compliment," she told him, smiling.

It was clear to me that these two liked and admired one another. And that was important to me. If I was going to work with NAL, I wanted my family's approval all the way.

"Well," she continued, "I spent the next week learning everything I could about abortion. My main objective was to understand how the pro-choice forces used their 'spin' to justify abortion. That knowledge would prove invaluable in helping me to mount a pro-life counterattack."

It seemed that Miss Poole had received an MBA from Arizona State University with a major in marketing. She told us that she had been a rising star at her ad agency and had worked on many major corporate accounts. When she met Sally Gates she told her that designing a campaign to save the lives of tiny innocent babies would be a challenge and a welcome relief from the pet food, beer, breakfast cereals and various other consumer products she normally worked on.

As she read both right to life and pro-choice literature she was amazed at how two different sets of eyes could view a tiny developing baby so differently. Her agency was paid to design ad campaigns that sold their client's products. They weren't paid to judge how valuable these products were to society nor if these products in the long run benefited or harmed their users. As an advertising executive it was her job to find a way to induce people to buy what her commercials were promoting.

She told us that it was her habit to use a large yellow legal pad of paper to help her lay out the positive and negative aspects of the products she tried to promote. In this way she would be able to know which good qualities to boost and enhance and which bad qualities to mask and hide. She had learned from years of experience that her yellow legal pad often proved invaluable in laying the groundwork for many a successful advertising campaign. After her week of extensive research on a variety of issues viewed from both the pro-life and pro-choice camps, she decided one evening to take out her yellow pad and begin to write down her observations. However, in this case, her product was not a pack of cigarettes or a box of breakfast cereal but a tiny package of human life.

As was her custom, she took a ruler and drew a line with her pen right down the center of the first sheet of paper. But before she decided to analyze this incredibly charged issue, she went back to her desk and pulled out another yellow pad that had her early notes on one of her most successful campaigns ever – Bold Gold Cigarettes. She felt that there was a very powerful parallel between cigarettes and abortion based on her study of both. On the top of her legal pad she wrote down "Bold Gold Cigarettes." On the left side she wrote the word positives, and on the right side the word negatives. She then showed us her original cigarette analysis. As I began to read her list I was amazed at what I found:

Positives	**Negatives**
Makes one look mature	Causes lung cancer
Tastes good	Causes yellow teeth
Makes one look sexy	Causes yellow hands and clothes
It's a man's thing	Causes severe coughing
Makes one look cool	Causes Heart disease
Creates a sense of security	Causes Emphysema
Makes you look sophisticated	Contains Carbon Monoxide
Macho	May Complicate pregnancy and cause fetal injury and premature birth

I was impressed. Miss Poole certainly knew how to state her case. Even if I hadn't believed that cigarettes were a threat to everyone, I definitely would have been certain of it now. And, of course, no one should forget what a danger they are to the unborn.

Dad nodded his head vigorously and I remembered that he had told me that he had once smoked but that, when I was born, he had stopped.

It was clear that she thrived on being able to make her points clear which was, I supposed, what made her such a successful advertising consultant. I hoped that in the future I would find my own talents as well suited to what I knew I had to do.

"If you take a close look at the list," she said, "you'll notice that the positives appeal mostly to external perceptions of how people might view you if you smoke. Clearly smoking is very harmful to ones health but the benefits focus only on positive perceptions, which by and large have been created by clever marketing campaigns down through the years. A woman wearing nice perfume and having soft feminine hands is sexy. It took Madison Avenue, however, to somehow convince us that the smell of cigarette breath and having yellow fingers is OK as long as we keep smoking."

"Cigarette smoking has always been bad for ones health," my father noted, as he reached down to pick up a fork he had accidentally knocked off our table. "But I guess it wasn't until the sixties that we began to learn just how unhealthy smoking is. By the nineties everyone knew that cigarettes were harmful, but yet why do so many people still smoke?"

"As the team leader who handled the Bold Gold Cigarette account," Miss Poole said, pausing to take a quick glance at her watch, "it was my job to create positive illusions surrounding the smoking experience. These positive illusions had to create a strong enough motivation for the smoker to outweigh the clear negative impact that cigarettes inherently have. I certainly knew that smoking was an unhealthy habit, and I thanked God I didn't smoke. However, back then I also realized I was getting paid very good money by my firm to make sure that Bold Gold became a winner. I knew, just from looking at my yellow legal pad that, in order to make Bold Gold a winner, I would have to make those who smoked them appear to be losers. I think I can say without boasting that I was very good at what

I did, and within three years of their introduction into the marketplace, Bold Gold became a big seller to the eighteen to thirty-five-year-old crowd. Today, whenever I see a young person smoking Bold Gold it saddens me to know I played a part in slowly poisoning their life."

"I guess we all have done things we're not proud of," I told her.

Even now, almost two months since I had aborted baby Sally, I was still struggling with self-blame. Although I knew that lives were being saved because of my pro-life activities, I still couldn't completely erase the memory of what I had done to my baby.

"When I was in the Marines, I had my own list of things I wished I had never done," my father assured her.

"But the past can be a wonderful teacher, if we are willing to learn from it," Miss Poole continued, clearly reassured by our response. "When I began to work on the NAL account, I once again took out my yellow legal pad and began to pattern my pro-life campaign based on the approach I took with the Bold Gold Cigarette account. As I started to write down the positives and negatives of abortion, I began to see a very disturbing pattern arise. The parallels between Bold Gold Cigarettes and abortion were proving to be strikingly similar."

Jennifer gave each of us a copy of her analysis. As I looked at the list I could see she had done her homework well:

Children of the Womb

Positives	**Negatives**
A woman should have a right to her own body.	An innocent child will be put to death.
Unwanted children will not be born.	Mothers wanting to adopt babies will be denied the chance.
Handicaps can often be discovered in the womb and these babies can be aborted; saving them a lifetime of suffering.	Mothers having abortions suffer many emotions scars for years after their abortion.
Abortion is a constitutional right.	Unborn granted no constitutional rights.
Teens spared the emotional, financial and psychological challenges an unwanted child will bring.	Abortions can complicate future pregnancies.
An unwanted child can be a big inconvenience to a mother's career.	Minors can often get an abortion without parental notification or consent.
Rape victims shouldn't be forced to bear the rapist's child.	Abortion destroys an entire class of humans.
Abortion is another family planning tool.	Abortion is irreversible.
Abortions are necessary when a woman's life is in danger.	Almost all abortions are done purely for the sake of convenience.
Legalization makes back alley abortions unnecessary.	Legalization encourages abortion as just another method of birth control.
Women should control all aspects in the decision to keep or abort her child.	Husbands and their unborn child have no say in the decision to keep or abort.

"If you look at my list," Miss Poole said, after I had finished reading it out loud, "most of the positives revolve around lifestyle issues. Pro-choice forces have been very successful in using their positive arguments to keep the laws of our land, and a great majority of our TV and print media, both news journalists and Hollywood celebrities, solidly in support of a policy of abortion on demand."

"I agree with you completely," I told her. "I know how it affected me."

"Did you know that the great middle ground alternative of adoption is rarely discussed as a viable option by the pro-choice side," Miss Poole said, turning to my father, "and in fact is often discouraged. And as far as the negative consequences to the unborn, which in one hundred percent of the cases is their complete destruction, whenever an abortion is successful, they have been able to claim that since the unborn are not considered persons, what's the big deal!"

Miss Poole told us that after spending a week analyzing the entire abortion issue with an open mind, and dissecting all the arguments, both pro and con, it became clear to her that abortion kills a living member of the human race.

Furthermore, as she had continued to ponder the parallel between abortion and cigarettes, she had picked up a pack of Bold Gold's and read: "SURGEON GENERAL'S WARNING: Smoking Causes Lung Cancer, Heart Disease, Emphysema, And May Complicate Pregnancy."

"The dangers of smoking are known to everyone, yet millions of Americans still smoke," she said. "That abortion is harmful to the unborn is perhaps the greatest understatement ever made. Yet, when we strip away all of the facades, well over a million of these defenseless little ones are basically put to death for the sake of convenience."

Miss Poole then told me something that I will never forget.

"Louise, when I designed the marketing campaign for Bold Gold Cigarettes I had to find a way to get people to use a product that clearly states right on the package that it's very hazardous to your health," she said. Her voice was soft now but very firm. "By law I couldn't remove the Surgeon General's warning disclaimer so I had to ask smokers to deny reality and believe the illusion that smoking Bold Gold was clearly a status symbol." She then turned to my father. "The reason why so many still accept abortion as an important legal right and necessary medical procedure is that the media and pro-choice supporters have joined forces to suppress the truth and distort reality."

"I think you hit the nail right on its head," my father said as he waved the waiter over and ordered more coffee.

"Could you say something about the use of language employed by the pro-choice camp?" Dad asked. "You must know a lot about that sort of thing."

"Using language to help convey concepts and influence people is of paramount importance," she agreed. "As a former advertising executive, I can tell you that proper word choice is critical in the design of any marketing strategy. Carefully chosen words can help paint pictures in our minds that can influence the way we see things and eventually influence our behavior. As I studied the way pro-choice individuals used their words, I noticed that they carefully chose terms and phrases that either distorted reality or hid the truth."

She once again pulled out another yellow page from her legal pad that outlined the words and phrases pro-choice supporters used to describe abortion. She then contrasted these terms with the pro-life viewpoint. As I examined her sheet I began to see how these skillfully chosen word substitutions could definitely influence how one views abortion:

Pro-life Terms and Phrases	Pro-choice Terms and Phrases
Unborn baby, preborn baby	Embryo, fetus, birth matter, pregnancy tissue, product of conception (POC), feto-placental unit
Abortionist	Doctor, surgeon
Womb	Uterus
Abortion Chamber	Health Clinic
Death to innocent life	Termination of pregnancy
Right to Life	Reproductive freedom
Pro Life	Impose our morality
Unborn baby is a person	Fetus is not a person

Armed with her marketing savvy and her knowledge on abortion, Miss Poole had been able to design a highly effective strategy for NAL. She told us how NAL believed that the Right to Life posters and slogans that her agency had come up with had been instrumental in causing many young women to change their minds and not go through with contemplated abortions. But Miss Poole's involvement in the right to life movement didn't stop when she finished designing the NAL marketing campaign. She told us that she became a passionate pro-lifer, and after about a year, was asked if she would like to join the staff of NAL and use her talents on a full time basis in the fight for life. She had agreed and for the past several years has served as Chief Strategist for Marketing and Communications at NAL.

By the time we were done with our breakfast discussion it must have been almost ten-thirty. Miss Poole told us that we had a two o'clock meeting in the NAL boardroom to discuss the future direction NAL felt it wanted to go in as well as the role they wanted to use me in. By now my curiosity was getting the better of me.

"Why does NAL feel that I'm so special to them?" I asked her as the waiter brought the check.

"You'll just have to wait to our meeting to find out," she said teasingly. I was glad that we felt so comfortable together, particularly since that meant that my work for NAL might compliment hers.

"I'm just as excited as you are Lou," Dad told me, "but we need to follow the NAL timetable."

It seemed like an eternity until two o'clock but finally the time for our big conference had arrived. Attending the meeting, beside dad and myself, were Miss Poole, Mrs. Gates, Mr. Moss, and several other NAL executives including their Chief Counsel and head of Governmental Legislation and Affairs, a Mr. Seaver. During the next six hours we participated in what I believe was clearly the most important "Strategy for Life" summit conference ever held. It was at this meeting that we laid the groundwork for the most powerful and innovative fight for life campaign ever launched.

Mrs. Gates began by anticipating my question as we sat around a long mahogany table in a room with tall windows that looked out over the Capitol. It was a brisk, blue, windy day and the flags across the way were rippling through the air.

"Louise," she began, "Jennifer asked me to explain why we feel so strongly that we can use your unique presentation and passion for the unborn in so many new and exciting ways in the fight for life." Mrs. Gates had a presence about her that was hard to put into words but when she spoke everyone made sure to give her their undivided attention.

"Over the years, there have been many interesting stories demonstrating that the unborn clearly are human life," she told us, "but the media has never devoted too much attention to these stories. A million unborn babies are killed in the most monstrous ways imaginable each year and the media stands by almost in complete silence. But if one overly zealous pro-lifer bombs an abortion clinic and kills an abortionist, the media lets the entire country know all about it through hundreds of newspaper articles, TV newscasts, and cable talk shows."

I knew that this was true because when an abortion doctor was killed last year in Atlanta it was all over the news for days.

"The media has done everything in its power to cause untold millions of Americans to still deny the reality that abortion kills babies," Mrs. Gates said, her voice now choking up a bit. "It is not open to debate that the pro-abortion forces have been able to control almost all the news about abortion that we see in our newspapers and on our TV's month after month and year after year. The pro-choice lobby has been able to use their muscle and influence skillfully to dictate to the media just how they should describe what abortion is all about. Through years of gross misrepresentation of what is really going on inside the womb, millions have bought the lie that the unborn is not a person. The truth has been hidden for far too long and as a result millions of intelligent people have been trained to deny it."

"I have a perfect example of just what you're talking about, Mrs. Gates," I said disregarding my father's frown. I knew that he didn't want me to interrupt but what Mrs. Gates had been saying had made me think of something important, an analogy that NAL might be able to use.

"Hundreds of years ago," I began, "there were millions who denied the truth that our planet earth revolved around the sun. Today every schoolboy knows that the earth revolves around the sun. But back in the 1400's, scientists believed that the earth was the center of the universe and that the sun revolved around it. And those who disagreed with this scientific 'fact' ran the risk of being branded a heretic. But almost five hundred years ago, a Polish astronomer named Nicolaus Copernicus believed that the sun, rather than the earth, was the center of the universe. He stated that the earth and all the other planets moved through space and revolved around the sun.

Copernicus was scared to publish his theory for fear he might be labeled a heretic. Isn't it strange how, back then, his theory could have cost him his life, while the prevailing theory of his time would, if you held it today, brand you as a candidate for the 'loony bin?'"[20]

"That's a great example, Louise," Mrs. Gates told me, smiling gratefully and I saw Miss Poole making notes. "I'll have to remember that. Another example concerns fetal development. One hundred years ago we knew almost nothing about what was going on inside a woman's body during her nine months of pregnancy. Today, however, thanks to tools such as real time ultrasound, we can see the truth with our own eyes. Young and old can now view the wonderful secrets of the womb. A rapidly developing human being, a unique person, is alive and well. The truth is there. It can either be accepted or denied. Sadly, the media has cast its vote in favor of denial."

She leaned toward me then, her blue eyes shining. "Over the past two months something totally unprecedented has happened," she said. "Our entire country has fallen in love with you, Louise. I believe that they view your story as a breath of fresh air amidst the massive sea of cynicism that America finds itself engulfed in. From political and sex scandals to lies and cover-ups, it is rare when someone admits to a horrible mistake and then exposes themselves to face whatever consequences may come their way. Your refreshing honesty and delightfully charming personality has fascinated even the media. Couple your unique qualities with the most impact-driven show and tell presentation that most of us have ever seen and you have the stuff that even the pro-abortion media cannot resist to cover. For the first time since *Roe v. Wade*, the right to life movement is being given unprecedented positive publicity solely because of one sixteen-year-old girl – you!"

I was stunned. Could they be talking about Louise Ann Jordan from Palmerville, New York? Did these impressive people really feel that I could contribute something important on a national scale?

"Louise, when you talk all America is listening," Mrs. Gates assured me. "I can tell you that you are having a major impact on the way abortion is being treated in the news. We've received three times the volume of phone calls and letters requesting information on abortion and alternatives, and in requests for literature. We have seen a ten-fold increase in requests for our posters and pictures of the unborn. Even requests for media interviews with pro-life representatives have reached an all time high. After talking to many of my colleagues at other pro-life ministries throughout the country, I found that they all are experiencing the same inundation of requests for information. And perhaps the most telling sign that something wonderful is happening in our fight for life is the fact that the abortion lobby is launching a massive attack aimed at discrediting the right to life stance we hold to so dearly."

She was clearly excited now. Her eyes were aflame with passion and her enthusiasm for what she believed in was quite evident in her voice.

"We are being called intolerant, anti-choice, bigoted, anti-freedom, judgmental, seditious, and a host of other negative adjectives," she went on, looking as animated as I had ever seen her. "In addition we are told that we are imposing our morality and putting people on guilt-trips. Hate mail has also gone up by over three hundred percent during the last month alone. It may sound strange but we are just delighted that we are being attacked with such ruthless vigor because all of this means that our message is beginning to reach more and more people each and every day. It's clearly becoming more difficult for pro-choicers to keep the truth hidden. The dark and evil world of abortion is being exposed to the light. And I'm excited to share that the slogan, 'Why Can't We Love Them Both,' is picking up steam. We must now seize the moment and do everything we can to use you and the media to turn the tide once and for all back to life from death for the millions of precious little souls caught in the middle."

She paused for breath and turned to face me. "Louise," she said, "if you don't think you have already made a huge impact just listen to this letter we received last week from a girl in Florida.

Dear National Alliance for Life:

I am a seventeen-year-old from Miami named Nicole Simon. I, like so many young girls, thought I knew what love was all about. As a result I made the mistake of equating sex with love. Well, about three months ago my world came crashing down right before my very eyes when I found out, that despite taking birth control pills, I was pregnant. My mom, dad and boyfriend told me that my only option was to get an abortion. My parents accompanied me to the clinic on a Wednesday and helped make all the arrangements. We scheduled my abortion for the following Tuesday morning.

But on the night before my surgery, my dad and mom decided to watch the Louise Ann Jordan news conference. After they finished watching, they both looked at one another and realized that they had to cancel my clinic appointment. Dad knew very little about abortion, but after watching and listening to Louise Ann Jordan, he determined that no one was going to kill his first grandchild. My father told me that he and my mom had made a horrible mistake in forcing me to get an abortion. And they now promised to do everything in their power to help me raise my baby. Somehow, I knew in my heart that I was carrying a real baby and I was so happy that I was no longer being forced to take the life of my child.

I am now five months along. And with the full support of my family, I'm happy to report that while I am scared, I'm excited that I soon will be a new young mother. I just wanted all of you at NAL to know that the literature I received from you several weeks ago has helped me understand so much more about the evils of abortion and the joys of motherhood. If you ever get the chance to talk with Louise Ann, please let her know I pray for her every night. Thanks to her, our family has truly bonded together over the past two months. Please let her also know that my doctor told me I am going to have a little girl, and that I have already picked out her name – Louise.

Sincerely,
Nicole Simon

As Mrs. Gates finished reading this tribute, Eddie Moss apparently noticed that my eyes were full of tears because he gave me a tissue and a big hug. "Mr. Moss," I said gratefully, "I can't believe that my story is having such a big impact." Eddie paused for a minute, as his eyes seemed to pan the entire room, and then told all of us that he believed my impact was just starting to be felt.

For the next five hours, Washington, D.C.'s newest think tank went into action. Here we were, a millionaire businessman, a former investment banker, a hardware store owner, a lawyer, a former advertising agency executive, a tenth grade high school student, and several other key NAL personnel all joining forces in an attempt to participate in the biggest rescue mission in the history of humanity. By the time we were finished sharing our ideas, we all felt that we had come up with a winning strategy in our fight for life. The stakes were very high. We all realized that. If we didn't succeed in our mission countless millions of children would never be able to step foot in a playground, never be able to play hide and seek, and never be able to have their mother's read them bedtime stories.

While doing a lot of talking Mrs. Gates also did a lot of writing. She jotted down all of our ideas and helped to carefully construct our master battle plan. Throughout our discussions we all were in unanimous agreement that in order for America to put a stop to abortion we would have to launch our campaign on several strategic fronts, and she recorded this. By the end of our meeting, she had put the finishing touches on what we sincerely believed was the right strategy to capitalize on this most providential series of events. The following manifesto was to serve as our guiding principles over the next two years as we armed ourselves, for what NAL called, in honor of my aborted baby, *Operation Sally*. Its eight keys to success were as follows:

1. We must constantly let America know that "Abortion Kills Babies." Until this concept becomes a certainty in the minds of our citizens, we will never be able to win the war. If Americans still believe that abortion only removes "birth matter," then the inconvenience that an unwanted child brings will still triumph and the killing will continue.

2. We must not only try to save the life of the unborn but let the mothers of these precious babies know that we love them too. "Why Can't We Love Them Both," must become a powerful new rallying cry from every Right to Life group across our land. We must do everything in our power to let these new mothers to be know that we understand their very difficult situation and are here to provide whatever help, support and love we can.

3. We must use every form of media, including TV, radio, newspapers, Internet, and outdoor advertisements to educate and persuade America that "Abortion Kills Babies" and that this silent holocaust represents everything that America doesn't stand for. We must make our citizens understand that our very humanity is on trial. And we also must use the media to let our slogan, "Why Can't We Love Them Both," ring true all across our country. We must let everyone know we genuinely stand behind this principle by our actions.

4. We must mobilize a massive group of pro-life supporters who can share their knowledge with family, friends, neighbors, and coworkers.

5. We must launch a massive personal letter writing campaign targeted to our Congressmen, Senators and other legislative leaders informing them about the true nature of abortion. People from all over our land must let their legislative leaders know that the time to pass a constitutional amendment establishing the "personhood" of the unborn, and thereby putting an end to legalized abortion is right now.

6. We must design and implement other powerful presentations like that of Louise Ann Jordan's to highlight in a high impact way what abortion is all about.

7. We must launch a major educational campaign aimed at our young people to teach them the three "A s" – Abstinence, Adoption and Abortion.
    Abstinence prevents a major problem from ever coming about and thus saves a woman from having to choose between life and death.
    Adoption allows a woman to choose life and not death for her baby when she can't handle raising her child.
    Abortion enables a woman to make the horrible choice of choosing death over life.

8. We must ask people of faith everywhere to pray for the conscience of our nation and the right to life for every unborn baby.

Eric Seaver, the tall, preppy looking young man who had offered several excellent suggestions during our meeting explained to us that all of these initiatives would prove crucial to building up the positive public sentiment against abortion needed to help Washington look to the possibility of creating a new amendment protecting the life of the unborn. For the past six years Mr. Seaver had been NAL's head of Governmental Legislation and Affairs, and was an expert in D.C. politics. During that time he had worked tirelessly to pass legislation favorable to the unborn, often a very difficult task since defeats were often massive and victories small. But his spirit and courage to fight the battle were as solid as a rock.

Miss. Poole told us she had begun to sense a shift in the way the media was covering the abortion debate. She had been working on several different ideas over the past few weeks and felt very excited that the atmosphere was now right to implement them and that I would be a key player in the entire overall campaign. But she had one concern and she went about explaining it by telling all of us about the table a story concerning a black man called Jackie Robinson.

According to Miss Poole, Jackie Robinson was the first black person ever to play "Major League Baseball." Before 1947, blacks could only play baseball in their own special Negro Leagues. By being the first to cross the color barrier, he became subject to intense cheers and boos that had nothing to do with how well or poorly he performed on the baseball diamond. Many believed he had no right to play ball with whites. People would spit and curse at him and some even threatened to kill him. Everyone was looking to Jackie and wondering could he handle the pressure and succeed at the plate and in the field. Jackie Robinson proved that he could and won the battle that shattered the color barrier for all those who would follow after him.

Just as I had made an analogy with Copernicus to demonstrate a point about the truth, I could see that Miss Poole was using Jackie

Robinson to show me that I might have to face some very difficult times ahead. She certainly was giving me a lot to think about.

"Louise, you are a very pretty young girl," Miss Poole told me. "Those big baby blue eyes, cute little nose and bubbly personality are so easy to fall in love with. However, there is a large group of people out there who will look at you as the devil. You'll be hated, mocked, cursed at and yes, don't be surprised if death threats even come your way. I felt that I must warn you and your dad well in advance that this battle for life will be intense and at times bloody. I believe you will become the central figure in this fight and will prove to be the main voice and chief advocate for the over one million unborn facing annihilation each year but it may be dangerous."

I knew that I might have to endure some negative reactions but the way Miss Poole was describing everything was really scary. Was I getting in over my head? I certainly cared for the lives of the unborn but the last thing I wanted to be was a martyr. My heart was pounding now, but I was glad she was letting me know what I might have to face in the future.

"To millions of women this privilege to abort their unborn young, if they deem it necessary is taken to be a sacred constitutional right," Mrs. Gates said in her motherly way. "And you by continuing to defend the unborn will be working to strip this 'right' from them. Louise, we need you so much right now but we also need a Louise who is willing and able to handle the antagonism that will come at her from all directions. I ask you to take tonight to sit with your dad and talk and pray with him to see if you want to join with NAL as we fight to stop this, our national holocaust – abortion."

For the past two months dad and I had frequent discussions about the dangers I would be going up against the more I continued to speak out against abortion. My parents loved me so much but they always told me that the decision on this matter was up to me. They seemed prepared to accept whatever level of involvement and commitment I wanted to make.

"I don't need tonight to think any more than my father and I have done about it," I said resolutely. "Abortion is the personification of evil and I want to do everything in my power to help put an end to its practice."

As I looked at all of them in turn I knew that, even though I might have to endure intense persecution, I wouldn't have to go it alone. I was proud to know them and I knew that they would be a powerful support group. I only hoped that the decisions we made this day would help us cross a much more important barrier – that between the life and death of many future doctors, lawyers, carpenters, housewives and yes even a few other Jackie Robinson's.

It was now Eddie's turn to share but before he started to speak he reached into his briefcase and pulled out an envelope which he placed on the table. Mr. Moss was now beaming with excitement and he stood up as if he had something important to share.

"In order to implement our eight point strategy we will need a great deal of additional funding. I think you know that all of us at this table are involved in the business of saving lives. When a young teenage girl, contemplating an abortion, reads some of our literature, and as a result changes her mind and decides to have her baby, our funds actually help save the life of a tiny human being. Can you imagine that one small booklet, that perhaps cost fifty cents to print and mail, has the power to save the life of a human soul!"

Mr. Moss certainly knew how to capture the attention of his audience. By now it was dark outside but I sat there riveted by every word that came from this most impressive man from Kansas.

"As you all know I am a businessman and I say with all humility a pretty successful one. I run my business with a keen eye focusing on the bottom line. We care for our customers and employees but we also look to make a fair return on our investment. But I challenge anyone to find an investment that can yield a greater return than saving the life of a fellow human being. Just think that with an investment of less than a dollar we can help another human heart continue to beat. And who knows if this new addition to the human race may one day grow up and be the person who finds the cure for cancer? While financial returns are important they cannot compete with the rich dividends that accrue by allowing another human being to continue on their journey through life. The way I look at it, investing money in the pro-life cause is an investment opportunity of a lifetime. We need to stress this aspect to our current contributors and future investment partners.

"Our most important resource in America today are our children. Since it is well known that today in our country one out of every three conceived babies will be killed by abortion[21] we are literally destroying one third of our most precious and perishable resources – our future children. Every child that we can save from being dismembered at an abortion mill is one more resource that can contribute to the betterment of society." Mr. Moss then handed Mrs. Gates the envelope that he had placed on the table a few minutes earlier. "Sally, please accept this check for one million dollars as my investment in *Operation Sally*."

I think we were all in a state of shock. Mrs. Gates just stood there speechless, and when I turned to look at my dad, he was just sitting there with a look of amazement on his face. This was indeed some way to end a meeting.

That evening dad and I visited the Lincoln Memorial. President Lincoln was a special president. It was his resolve along with a mighty and bloody civil war that helped to bring about an end to slavery well over one hundred years ago. As I looked into the eyes of the imposing marble figure rising high above me I kept wondering if the time was now right to fight a different but yet very similar type of war. Our weapons, however, wouldn't be guns but words, but our goals would be the same – to ensure that all persons, including the unborn, are allowed to experience certain unalienable rights, and that among these are Life, Liberty, and the Pursuit of Happiness.

10

Sharon Brolly

During the rest of the week I spent most of my time meeting more people from NAL as well as other leaders in the pro-life movement. They shared so much information with me about abortion, adoption, the law, fetal development, history and other areas that I had never even heard about that I felt as if I was packing an entire school year of study on one of my subjects into just one week. I must have seen ten videos on the subject and I even talked with former abortionists, actually handling the tools used to perform an abortion. I spoke with women who had been maimed for life from botched abortions, and even spoke with a young man who was aborted but lived when his mother's saline abortion didn't go as planned.

I spent an entire afternoon listening to five experts in the field of fetology describing, almost on a day by day basis, how the tiny life within a mother's womb develops. I studied case histories on how abortions had severe psychological effects on women. We spent another morning discussing the difficult issues of rape, incest, fetal handicaps and a host of other difficult issues. Throughout most of my learning time, Jennifer Poole and my dad were with me. During this intense educational training I really started to bond with Jennifer. I truly admired her unrelenting passion to end abortion. She was a woman with a mission and I felt as if I, too, was a young woman with a similar mission.

Time traveled very slowly during our stay in D.C. I felt like a giant sponge, soaking up everything that came my way. At the end of each day, dad and I would spend time alone reviewing what we had learned and discussing how I might be able to use this new knowledge in the weeks ahead. These proved very special times for me, just being with and talking to the man I loved more than any other man in the world. It had been just two short months ago when my world came crashing down all around me. I had shamed my family and my God and killed my baby. I had deserved to be punished and grounded for life. Instead I had been told how courageous and special I was. I had been treated with love and compassion by both my mom and dad. Somehow God had taken the worst thing that had ever happened to me and turned it into the blessing of life for many babies whom might otherwise have been aborted.

Our return flight was early Saturday evening, and while I was a little homesick, I knew I was going to miss the many new friends I had made this very special week. And, as it happened, Friday night was going to prove to be a very special one. Jennifer had asked my dad for permission to take me to a special restaurant, just the two of us because she wanted to share some thoughts, just one girl to another before I returned to Palmerville.

With dad's blessing, the two of us drove off to a quiet part of this wonderful city to a very elegant Italian restaurant where we were escorted to a table for two in a charming room full of oil paintings of scenes from Italy. Just before we started to eat a waiter came over and serenaded us on his accordion. From entree to dessert, the entire experience was something I would not soon forget. We must have spent three hours just enjoying one another's company, our conversation and the food. We laughed as we exchanged stories from our childhood and she even told me about her private life and her boyfriend, an electrician named Barry. She was sophisticated but at the same time down to earth. In fact, she was everything I wanted to become – beautiful, intelligent and dedicated to a cause.

As our evening was coming to a close I began to confide in her about how nervous I had become just thinking about the incredibly high expectations everyone seemed to be placing on me. I needed someone to help me understand just what these amazing past two months were really all about. I guess Jennifer sensed this nervousness and this was one of the main reasons she wanted to talk with me alone.

"I just marvel at how mature you are for your age," she told me, as we were served the most delicious cheesecake I had ever eaten. "Louise, for you to hold a nationally televised news conference less than one week after having your abortion and to speak with such clarity, wisdom, conviction and force is beyond my comprehension. The poise you demonstrated when you answered question after question so convincingly made me realize that God was going to use you in ways that I still can't fully fathom. I still cannot believe how someone with such a minimal knowledge of abortion could give answers with such deep insight as you gave that night."

"I can't fully understand it either," I confessed.

"It must be a special gift from God. There's really no other way to explain it."

"My mom said exactly the same thing, that God has a special plan for me. And if He has a special plan He will supply the grace and skills I need to carry it out."

"Louise, if Barry ever asks me to marry him and we have a daughter I pray that she'll turn out just like you. Stay strong and never let future discouragement get you down. Everyone at NAL has fallen in love with you. You're part of our family and we are here for you. Because of you, hundreds and perhaps thousands of babies have already been spared their date with death. And I believe with your help one day the number may climb into the millions."

By now my eyes once again began to fill with tears but this time they were tears of joy knowing that I was helping to give life to many precious little ones. As we left the restaurant and drove back to the hotel, Jennifer said she wanted to share one more story with me about another life that I had impacted.

"Louise, I am sure you remember a lady named Miss Brolly."

"I'm afraid that name doesn't ring a bell."

"She was the young lady from your news conference who had one hand."

"OK, sure I remember her."

"Well," Jennifer said, as she stopped for a red light, "when you told her that 'morally speaking' it would be wrong to take the life of a fetus with two perfect hands and then allow her to live, having only one hand, Sally and I just looked at each other in total amazement. I personally know Sharon Brolly. She is a top-notch newspaper reporter from Chicago who has always been very pro-abortion. I'm sure your remarks must have made her quite upset at the time."

"I never meant to be cruel, Jennifer," I explained. "But, somehow when I saw that Miss Brolly had only one hand and could still make light of a fetus that had two, I felt it necessary to make my point in a bold way."

"Well, I received a phone call from Sharon three weeks after you made those comments and to my complete surprise she shared with me that after your conference she went home and began to stare at the two perfectly formed tiny hands of a thirteen-week-old fetus. As she looked at those hands she began to count fingers. When she finished counting to ten she then looked at her hand and began to count. When she got to five she stopped and for the first time in her life understood why an abortion is not about a woman's right to choose but about a baby's right to live. The following day she wrote an editorial for a major Chicago newspaper entitled, *Why I Can No Longer Support Abortion*."

When we reached the hotel, Jennifer told me that during the next week the entire staff of NAL would be taking our eight point battle plan and designing specific implementation projects. As Jennifer delivered me safely to my dad, in our hotel room, she asked him if she could drive us to the airport tomorrow so that she could fill both of us in on some of the future plans NAL had for my involvement in the fight for life. She also wanted to see just how much time my dad would permit me to spend on the many upcoming conferences, rallies, TV appearances and the host of other projects that NAL would be spearheading. Miss Poole let both of us know that the role I would be playing would be limited only by the amount of time I would be willing to commit to.

The next morning, as Jennifer skillfully wove in and out of traffic on the way to the Ronald Reagan Airport, she described what the next two years of my life could be like working with NAL.

Just before we went to our gate, Jennifer told us that she had saved a surprise for last.

"Since you have decided that you are going to work with us, Louise, even though I know you still need to discuss your level of commitment with your family," she said, giving me a hug, "I'm going to arrange for you to be on *The Bob Jacobs Show!*"

And without even giving either of us a chance to respond, she was gone.

Jennifer had given both of us quite a lot to think about on our flight back home. Bob Jacobs was perhaps the most famous talk show interviewer in the country. My mom loved to watch his show because of all the famous people he interviewed. I was afraid that when Mom heard that I might be a guest on his show she would probably pass out. By the time our plane had landed, both Dad and I were overwhelmed that so many people were ready to place their confidence in me. Dad was just delighted to see how his little girl had matured during these last two months. And to be honest with you I, too, was amazed at how I had grown.

When we got home, both Mom and Don ran to the car to meet us. There also must have been at least fifty of my friends on hand to greet my return. Dad made a little speech, standing there on the porch, holding Mom's hand. He said that we had been treated like royalty from the time we had stepped off the airplane till the time we boarded our flight to return home and took a few minutes to share one or two highlights from our trip before we both thanked everyone and went inside the house, accompanied by a few of my closest friends who wanted to hear everything.

After about an hour of talking, my friend Jenny asked if she could get more involved in the fight for life. As soon as she asked me that question just about every one of the others began to echo the same sentiments. Clearly they understood the serious nature of my celebrity status and wanted to help in any way they could.

I told everybody that if they wanted to help there would be plenty of things they could do and when I told them that one of the executives from NAL felt she could arrange for me to be interviewed on *The Bob Jacobs Show*, everyone screamed and, just as I had feared, my mom almost passed out. These indeed were exciting times at the Jordan home.

By ten Dad told everyone that it was getting late and that our family needed a little time to relax. As soon as the last of my friends had departed, he told me that he really needed to discuss my level of involvement with NAL with my mom and so I went upstairs with Don to watch TV and unwind a little. I hoped that Mom would be as understanding as Dad was. But there was the fact that I was still in school to discuss. I knew that. But I also knew that their decision would rest on what was best for me in the long run. And I thought I knew what that would be.

The next morning we all went to church, as usual. It certainly was no coincidence that our pastor's sermon was on the sanctity of human life. After service, Dad took us out to lunch at Mom's favorite restaurant, *The Blue Whale*. Don and I really enjoyed eating there too because of the two giant fish tanks that were always well stocked with the most exotic fish we had ever seen. Don ordered crab cakes while the rest of us had the lobster dinner. And as we ate we began to discuss my future. To my surprise, Mom began to tell me that both she and my father, after discussing all sides of just what was at stake, had decided that they were going to leave my level of involvement with NAL entirely up to me. After hearing about everything that had gone on in Washington, Mom had became convinced in her heart that my message and story had to be shared with as many people as possible. She felt that God clearly had singled out her daughter for a special assignment that was of the utmost importance.

"Louise, I love you so much," she told me, taking both my hands in hers, "but my little girl is no longer a little girl but a powerful advocate for the most innocent and helpless of all of our citizens, the unborn. There are over a million silent voices each year desperately crying out for your help. How can I stand in the way of this massive plea for help? Whatever level of commitment you decide on, your father and I will back you one hundred percent."

"Thanks, Mom," I told her. "I love all of you so much. And thanks for giving me so much freedom to make my own decisions. Putting your trust in my judgment means so much to me."

The last time I had to make a major decision I made it all by myself and unfortunately I now must live with its tragic consequences for the rest of my life. Thankfully, I planned to make all of my future decisions only after careful consultation with my family and NAL.

"Your mom and I have seen you mature so much these past two months that we feel quite confident that the decisions you make will be well thought out and solid," Dad said. "But don't forget we're here to offer you our advice. And please never hesitate to ask us if you feel you need help in sorting out any issues that come up."

"Don't worry about that," I assured them. "I value your advice a great deal. You know that. I plan to bounce most of my ideas off both of you before I make any major decisions."

During my entire week in D.C. my heart had been moved by each person I had met and with each presentation they had given. As I learned more and more about what was taking place inside the womb I knew that I wanted to do everything in my power to help put an end to abortion on demand in our country. I decided that when my training was over I wanted to devote my life to defending the unborn, if my parents would only let me. With their stamp of approval I knew that everything was about to change with my life forever.

That night at the dinner table I let my parents know that I wanted to get totally involved in *Operation Sally*. Jennifer Poole had given me her home and cell phone numbers and told me to call her anytime and for any reason. After we had finished eating, Dad said I could call her and let her know of my decision. When I told her I was making myself totally available to NAL, Jennifer let out a loud thank you that almost hurt my ear.

"Louise," she said excitedly, "I plan to call Sally Gates as soon as we finish speaking to let her know the wonderful news. I also plan to contact the producer of *The Bob Jacobs Show* tomorrow morning to see how soon we can get you on. As soon as we can set up a date I'll let you know. Meanwhile, if there is anything you need from us, let us know immediately. And if you have any ideas about things you would like to do, please share them with either Sally or myself. We're a team, and with the help of God, we can win this war. God bless you! I'll be in touch."

As soon as I got off the phone with Jennifer, I called Jerry, Sarah and Jenny and told them that my life was about to change quite dramatically. I asked all three of them if they could come over the next day after school so that I could fill them in on more of the details of what NAL was planning to do with me as well as share some of my ideas on how Palmerville could get more involved in launching *Operation Sally*.

Going back to school that Monday was an amazing experience. As soon as I entered the building, I saw a giant banner that read, "Welcome Back Louise." All of my friends were so happy to see me. But I got the biggest welcome back greeting of them all from Principal Foster. He grabbed my hand and escorted me to his office. When I told him what had happened during my week in Washington and about my plans for getting more involved in the right to life movement, he assured me that Palmerville High would do everything it could to help me in my schooling.

"Louise," he said, now sounding more like a friend than a principal, "my office is always opened to you. Please let me know if you need anything or if you would just like to talk."

As I headed off to class with a smile on my face and a great joy in my heart, everyone seemed to have a smile and a wave. My teachers were especially happy to see me and Mr. Henderson, my U. S. History teacher, said he wanted me to share what took place during my week in Washington with our class. "Even though we aren't suppose to talk about abortion," he said, "I feel that your talk would fall under the heading of current events."

By now I was getting use to speaking in front of all kinds of groups of people and so, even though I hadn't had a chance to make notes, my presentation went very well. And so did the entire day until I entered Miss Ventura's science class.

Miss Ventura's pro-abortion stance may have had many supporters around the country, but in Palmerville, her viewpoint was fast becoming a minority one. While my friends in science class were happy to see me back, Miss Ventura clearly didn't share the same sentiment. In fact, her subtle ways of putting my pro-life viewpoints down gave way to outright open hostility to both my views and to me. I will never forget the reception I got from her on that first day. Right in front of the entire tenth grade science class she proceeded to give me a lecture on women's rights.

"Miss Jordan," she said, with a sinister look in her eyes, "I hope you realize that it took women in our country over one hundred years of tireless fighting to gain the right to vote. And it took women almost two hundred years of tireless fighting to gain the right to privacy over their own bodies. There are literally millions of American women who will not stand idly by while a sixteen-year-old publicity-seeking girl tries to undo two hundred years of our fight for equality and struggle for freedom. You will discover that your foolish position will in the end not stand the test of time. I would suggest that we all now turn to our study of science and not social rebellion. After all what Miss Jordan is proposing is to overturn the U.S. Supreme Court's decision on a woman's right to choose."

All the joy I had felt that morning disappeared and in its place was taken fear and humiliation. I felt so embarrassed and deeply hurt. It was one thing to disagree with my beliefs but quite another to question my motives and integrity by accusing me of being a cheap publicity seeker. I kept a curb on my emotions until school was over but then I couldn't stop crying and I was in no mood to share with my friends the plans I had for Palmerville and *Operation Sally*. I told Jerry, Sarah and Jenny that I needed to go home and be by myself for a while and that I would call them later on.

Mom greeted me with a cheerful hello, but she quickly realized that I had been crying.

"Louise," she said, as she took off her apron, "why have you been crying? Please come sit in the kitchen and tell me what's the matter."

"Mom, everything in school was going just great until I got to my science class," I told her as I wiped my eyes with a napkin from the kitchen table. "As soon as we sat down Miss Ventura started to attack my pro-life stance and then me personally. She called me a publicity seeker and totally humiliated me in front of the entire class."

By now Mom's big hello had been replaced with an even bigger sigh.

"I feel so sad for Miss Ventura," my mother told me. "She is clearly more concerned with a woman's right to choose than with a tiny innocent child's right to live. Louise those stinging remarks that were hurled your way today will not be the last ones you will hear in the days to come. In fact, in a way I'm actually glad that Miss Ventura attacked you."

"Mom," I protested. "How can you be happy that your daughter was ridiculed and mocked in front of all my friends!"

Before my mom answered my question, she stood up and walked over to the oven where she had been baking cookies. As she opened the oven door, the smell of freshly made chocolate chip cookies momentarily took my mind off Miss Ventura. As she set the tray on the table she began to explain the reasons behind her strange pronouncement.

"I'm sure it must have felt great being in the presence of so many pro-life supporters and leaders of the movement during this past week," my mother told me, as she took a bite out of one of the cookies herself. "It's important for you to know that so many people are with you in the fight for life. But it's also important to know very early on that in a war the enemy will try everything in his power to discredit and destroy his opponent."

"I think I'm beginning to see your point."

"As you defend such a noble cause as the right to life, your feelings often are going to get hurt by people who hate what you stand for. I know that right now you must really be hurting, Louise, but use this experience to grow. And fight these personal attacks with love. There are millions of other Miss Ventura's out there. Always let these blind supporters of death know that we love every mother facing the difficult decision of what to do when faced with an unwanted pregnancy. But also stand firm and let those mothers know that we equally love the precious life that they are carrying."

What Mom said brought so much comfort to me during what was, perhaps, one of my deepest moments of despair. I took her words to heart and thanked her for her wisdom. And with that, I went up to my room and knelt by my bed. Closing my eyes, I offered up a prayer for Miss Ventura. It was a simple one but I knew that it would prove to be a powerful weapon behind the scenes as *Operation Sally* got underway.

"Lord," I said, "please open Miss Ventura's eyes and let her see that each baby in the womb is a gift of Your handiwork and is indeed 'fearfully and wonderfully made.'"[22]

After that simple prayer, I felt renewed in my spirit and decided to invite Jerry, Jenny and Sarah over so that for the rest of the day we could begin to plan just how Palmerville could get involved in *Operation Sally*. I was now fully armed for battle.

11

Children of the Womb

It was great spending time with my friends and exciting to see that all of them shared the same desires that I had toward putting an end to legalized abortion in America. Mom said that they could all stay for supper. By the time my father got home from work the dinner table was just about set up. Mom had brought out her best set of china and prepared a turkey dinner with all the fixings. Dad asked Jerry if he would like to say grace. Even though Jerry had some big learning disabilities he never ceased to amaze me. His simple prayer underscored his simple life and reminded us that Jerry's inner beauty rested in his wonderful way of letting everyone around him know that life was a great gift from God, and the simpler we lived it, the more enjoyment we would find.

Jerry asked us to hold hands and close our eyes as he began to pray: "Dear God, thank you for letting me be here with Louise and her parents and with my friends Sarah, Jenny and Don. They are all good people. The food sure smells good and the table is set up so pretty. Dear God, bless this food to our bodies and bless those tiny bodies that may never be able to taste food because their moms are contemplating aborting them. Amen."

After a prayer like that, we all had an even greater resolve to wage war against this mass killer named abortion, knowing that with each passing day thousands of these tiny bodies would never have the prayer that Jerry prayed answered. We exchanged a multitude of ideas, but by the end of the evening, we all voted that we wanted to do something unique right here in the city of Palmerville. We called Dad and Mom up to my room and told them that we hoped that they would support our plan to establish a new museum dedicated solely to *Children of the Womb*. This new museum would be located right in the heart of Palmerville, and that through exhibits, videos, and lectures, we would depict the wonderful humanity and plight of *Children of the Womb*. We already had a lot of ideas for different exhibits. The only thing we didn't know was where we could obtain a building to house them.

Both of my parents thought that a museum dedicated to the unborn was a fabulous idea and gave us two thumbs up. But I knew that I would still need the support of NAL to help us set up the exhibits and provide us with literature and videos as well as guidance and financial assistance. Dad suggested that I give Jennifer Poole a call to bounce our idea off her. If she gave her approval, then we could get the ball rolling.

I quickly found Jennifer's phone number in my pocketbook and gave her a call. When I explained our proposal to her, she immediately pledged NAL's complete support to our project.

"Louise, your *Children of the Womb* museum is a brilliant idea," she said. "I'd like to fly up this Wednesday to discuss your project further with you and your friends and see how NAL can help you."

"That's perfect," I told her, delighted. "All my friends are dying to meet you."

"Great! Then I'll see you Wednesday."

I just couldn't contain my excitement.

"It's a go, everyone!" I told them. "NAL is going to support us fully and help us set up our museum."

"Wait until I tell my Mom and Dad!" Jerry exclaimed. His face was now beaming with pride.

"But where can we put our museum?" Sarah asked.

"Maybe, we should just build a new building to house everything," Jenny added.

By now it was getting late and Mom reminded us we all had school tomorrow. Dad, always the gentleman, offered to give all three of my friends a lift home. That night, as I lay in bed, my mind kept churning out different ideas for our museum. I was so excited about our new museum that I couldn't wait to tell my friends at school all about it.

The one big question that was still outstanding was where could we house our *Children of the Womb* museum. Most of my friends really liked the idea and we had a great discussion at lunch over possible exhibits. Principal Foster stopped by at lunch and asked if he could join Sarah, Jenny and Jerry at our lunch table.

"I really think that a museum dedicated to the unborn is a great idea," he said, "but I feel that Palmerville might not be the best place for it, simply because the crowds that it might draw wouldn't be anywhere as large as the crowds a major city like New York could command. But I would suggest that, in order to test the idea, we set up a temporary exhibit here to see how people would respond. If the museum proved popular we could then seriously consider constructing a brand new building in a major city to house a permanent collection."

"That makes a lot of sense to me, guys," I commented, looking down the table at the others. "If we took this approach we probably could set up something on a small scale very quickly while the mood of the country is on our side."

Principal Foster even had an idea on the perfect place to set up our temporary exhibits. The city, for its small size, had a fairly large hotel called the Meeting Place Inn right in our downtown area. It was the tallest building around, standing twelve stories high. It often would serve as a conference center for businesses as well as a convention center for several small trade shows.

I was very familiar with the place. My friends and I would often stop by to view all of the hustle and bustle that went on. We felt like being in a big city whenever we visited the Meeting Place Inn. The hotel had two big ballroom/conference rooms and Principal Foster felt that, if we could rent one of them for say two weeks, we could set up our *Children of the Womb* displays and see how the public would react to them.

Principal Foster then added that he was good friends with the owners of the hotel and felt confident that, if one of the rooms were not already booked, they would be willing to allow us to set up our temporary museum. The plan seemed perfect and I asked him if he could stop by tomorrow evening to meet with us when Miss Poole came by to discuss everything. During the rest of the day, my mind was far from schoolwork. Wednesday also came and went by quickly as I eagerly waited to meet my friend Jennifer again, this time on my home territory.

Our meeting was set for eight that evening and coincidentally Jennifer booked a room at the Meeting Place Inn for her overnight stay. She listened as we described many of our exhibit ideas and Principal Foster's desire to set up a temporary museum there. She liked everything she heard and told us that NAL would supply everything we needed to open our bold new presentation, including all the funds. The only major question that remained was could we book the Meeting Place Inn and if so how soon?

Principal Foster took out his cell phone and asked my father if he could place a call from a quiet place. Dad walked him to his study and about fifteen minutes later he returned with a great big smile on his face.

"I just finished speaking with Tom Jenkins, one of the hotel owners," Principal Foster told us, "and he wants to help Louise in her crusade. He told me that we could have the first two weeks in December; and that we could use his bigger ballroom, the Palace Room. When I asked him how much our two-week stay would cost, he said to tell Louise, 'It's on the house.'"

Miss Poole looked amazed. To rent a big ballroom for two weeks would normally cost thousands of dollars and the Meeting Place Inn was giving it to us for free. We were now confirmed to host *The Children of the Womb* exhibit from December third to the sixteenth at the Meeting Place Inn in Palmerville, New York. Since it was already November eleventh, we had only three weeks to get everything ready. It would be a very tight time frame to work with but we had to succeed and succeed we would.

During those next three weeks, my life was a whirlwind of activity. Balancing going to school with two trips to Washington, D.C. to help design and construct our exhibits was both exhausting and exhilarating. The entire staff of NAL had a lot of great ideas too for making the exhibits both attractive and powerful and worked twelve to fourteen hour days, right up to the time of our opening, gathering materials, and getting everything ready to ship and then assemble in Palmerville. The final test would come on the Saturday and Sunday before the exhibit was scheduled to open on the following Monday. Could we assemble our eighteen exhibits in the two days left to us after a previous convention ended in time for our Monday opening?

Tom Jenkins gave us permission to begin our set up starting that Friday evening. As it turned out that extra time proved invaluable since we needed every extra hour to get things ready. During those three amazing weeks, Jennifer was busy behind the scenes making sure that the media would provide us maximum exposure. While perhaps only a few thousand people might be able to view the *Children of the Womb* presentation in person, we hoped to provide millions more the privilege of taking a guided tour of our unique pro-life exhibits through the magic of television.

Jennifer was also busy making arrangements for my appearance on *The Bob Jacobs Show*. She hoped that over the next week or two she could finalize a date, hopefully sometime in January.

By eleven Monday morning everything was ready to go. Our grand opening was scheduled to begin with a special sneak preview opened only to invited guests, along with TV reporters and journalists, of course. There must have been over one hundred prominent leaders from the pro-life movement on hand. Eddie Moss flew in and an old adversary, turned ally, Sharon Brolly, the newspaper reporter from Chicago even greeted me warmly. Cameras were everywhere and as 7:00 PM approached my heart was beating a mile a minute.

Sally Gates, NAL President, was on hand to give her opening remarks, looking absolutely radiant in her red silk evening dress.

"Ladies and gentlemen," she began, "distinguished colleagues and members of the media on behalf of the National Alliance for Life we welcome you to view with us a most remarkable series of exhibits that we have entitled *Children of the Womb*. Each day in America over four thousand children of the womb become children of the grave. Each day in America over four thousand precious little lives, just beginning their journey through life, are snatched from the warmth, safety and sanctity of their mother's wombs and in ninety-nine percent of the cases executed because of the crime of being inconvenient. We have put together what we believe these totally innocent victims would want you to see and consider before you choose to end their lives through abortion. It is our hope that after you finish the tour you may understand why abortion always destroyed a unique human life and is always the wrong choice. While I will be talking with you about each exhibit I ask you for one favor, please let your heart be your true tour guide. Let's begin."

For the next two hours, Sally Gates described what each exhibit represented as well as some of the thinking behind why it had been chosen. While each of the eighteen separate displays clearly had a powerful impact on those viewing them, there were several in particular that touched the hearts of even the staunchest pro-choice advocates in attendance that night.

Our first exhibit was entitled *The Wall of Life*. We had assembled twenty-five beautiful full color portraits of children, ranging in age from two through seven, who almost never made it to the photographer's studio to pose for these charming pictures since each one of them had once been scheduled to be aborted. In all twenty-five cases the mother was getting ready to enter an abortion chamber to end their lives when, because of being presented with information explaining why getting an abortion would be a horrible mistake, they changed their minds. Because these women faced the reality of what an abortion is truly designed to accomplish – the death of a child – each changed their minds, and as a result, these beautiful children were here to say thank you to groups like the NAL for letting them live.

Underneath each picture on *The Wall of Life* was the name of the child, their age, where they lived, and a brief testimony of how thankful each mother was for choosing life over death. During each day of the exhibit, NAL brought in the mother from one of these children to share her actual testimony of what changed her mind. These children looked so precious that to think that they had almost been mutilated and horribly destroyed at some abortion mill was almost too painful to contemplate.

Right next to *The Wall of Life* another exhibit entitled, *The Pit of Death* stood in sharp contrast since it was as gruesome as *The Wall of Life* was delightful. It consisted of a small circular two-foot high plastic swimming pool that must have been approximately five feet in circumference. Inside this so-called "Pit" were literally hundreds of small baby body parts.

Members of the NAL team had taken hundreds of their small, actual size, true to life models of babies from ten to twenty-two weeks gestation, torn them apart, and threw them into this makeshift grave. There were detached arms, legs, fingers, toes, eyes and even entire severed heads. Other life-size models were only partially torn apart and still others were perfectly whole with hardly a blemish on them. Crushed skulls, ripped opened rib cages and a host of other partially severed bodies made *The Pit of Death* the most realistic portrait of what happens to *Children of the Womb* after they finish their date with the abortionist.

After Sally Gates briefly explained what *The Pit of Death* represented, she pushed a button and we heard a three minute audio presentation from a former abortionist describing in graphic detail how some of these tiny ten to twenty-week-old babies had made their way into the "Pit." As this former doctor of death described some of the abortion techniques he used to tear these babies apart literally limb from limb, I could see several of the reporters looking into *The Pit of Death* and then back toward *The Wall of Life,* and could just imagine what must have been going through their minds as they tried to reconcile these totally irreconcilable images.

One of my favorite presentations was the *See How I Grow* exhibit. A beautiful set of nine unbelievably lifelike baby models were lined up in a row, showing the progression of life in the womb from one month right up until birth. Each successive model added one more month of life to the developing baby until the last one represented a live birth at the end of a normal nine-month pregnancy.

Under each model there was a description of the type of development a baby is undergoing during that month of its growth written by an internationally known scientist. Each model was specifically handcrafted for the *Children of the Womb* exhibit and was completely lifelike. After reading the descriptions of what was taking place with the first three models it became crystal clear that by the time we finished with the third one, that all human body parts and the baby's complex internal systems were already present at that stage. The remaining six models almost seemed anticlimactic since by the end of the twelfth week of a pregnancy all body systems are functioning.

After the third model a plaque was inserted which Mrs. Gates read aloud to the group.

"By the end of the twelfth week of a pregnancy, generally called the first trimester, the U. S. Supreme Court has ruled, 'For the stage prior to approximately the end of the first trimester, the abortion decision and its effectuation must be left to the medical judgment of the pregnant woman's attending physician.'[23] Basically our U.S. Supreme Court has given the abortionist the supreme authority to decide on whether over one million babies a year will be able to live or die.

"Leaving a medical judgment decision completely in the hands of an individual who has a huge financial stake in choosing death puts the lives of these first trimester babies at a distinct disadvantage.

"However, there are certain medical facts about what has taken place in a developing baby by its twelfth week of growth that are not open to judgment, according to our most up to date scientific knowledge. No one can debate the following scientific facts regarding fetal development by the end of the twelfth week of a normal pregnancy. Each normal twelve-week-old preborn baby can boldly claim the following statements about its own humanity:

1. The baby has a perfectly formed and beating heart that is pumping its own blood.[24]
2. The baby has a brain and active brain waves.[25]
3. The baby can swallow.[26]
4. The baby can squint with its eyes.[27]
5. The baby's stomach is already producing digestive juices.[28]
6. The baby has ten fingers, ten toes and even fingernails.[29]
7. The baby can suck its thumb.[30]
8. The baby's liver is already making blood cells.[31]
9. The baby's taste buds are forming.[32]
10. The baby can smile and frown.[33]
11. The baby can kick, turn its feet, and curl and fan its toes.[34]

12. The baby can make a fist, move its thumbs, and bend its wrists.[35]
13. The baby can turn its head and open and close its mouth.[36]

"There can be little debate that at twelve weeks' gestation the miracle of birth in reality has just about been completed. All of a baby's incredibly complex body systems are up and running.[37] During the next six months refinements and additional growth are the only things added to each one of these precious 'children of the womb.'"

As I looked around the crowd surrounding this exhibit, I noticed that only two middle-aged women were expressing their disbelief that a three-month-old fetus could do so many things. As reporters continued to snap pictures and take notes I could see that some were visibly shaking their heads as if to acknowledge that they, too, were learning some new secrets from the womb.

Right behind this progression of life stood a five-foot tall model of a dinosaur that also appeared very lifelike consisting, as it did, of an intricate network of bones. Right in front of the dinosaur was another plaque which read:

"Tyrannosaurus – A carnivorous dinosaur with small forelimbs and a large head that roamed the earth fifty million years ago.

"Archeologists in some cases have come across one or two dinosaur bones and have been able to construct complete dinosaurs such as the Tyrannosaurus seen here. How much of this reconstruction is science and how much sheer imagination is certainly a valid question to ask. But if scientists can, with a fair level of certainty, claim that the Tyrannosaurus you are viewing is a solid representation of what roamed our earth fifty million years ago, how then can anyone question the unique humanity of a twelve-week-old fetus, which today is alive and well and can be seen by all?"

Another exhibit was the brainchild of Jerry Bedford who had suggested that if we eventually wanted to have a constitutional amendment passed that would outlaw abortion we would need the support of quite a few members of Congress. He said one way the city of Palmerville could show their support for this amendment was to let our U.S. Congressman, Todd Oliver, know just how we felt about the evils of abortion.

"People who make our laws ought to know about this," Jerry kept saying over and over again. I thought it was wonderful how he always managed to remember the important things. And his parents were so proud of what he was doing to help.

Two weeks ago Jerry and about twenty of our friends from school had begun to go door to door urging everyone to write or type a short personal letter to Congressman Oliver, conveying disapproval of abortion and seeking to enlist his support to help end this American tragedy. The response was simply incredible. Within a matter of one week, over five hundred personal letters were sent to Congressman Todd Oliver's office in Washington, D.C. We also asked everyone who wrote Congressman Oliver a letter if they could give us a copy since we planned to use them in a special two week exhibit on abortion, right here in the city of Palmerville.

We collected over four hundred of these individual personal correspondences and assembled them in an exhibit which Jerry entitled *Letters for Life*. This exhibit consisted of a large bulletin board that must have had over fifty of these letters attached by pushpins and thumbtacks. Most of them were short and came straight from the heart. One in particular said it best. It was written by an eleven-year-old named Betty Fox and was only four lines long:

Dear Congressman Oliver:

Abortion is wrong it kills babies. Adoption is good it lets babies live. If a mother doesn't want her baby why can't she just give it away instead of killing it. Please let's encourage adoption and not abortion.

Jennifer Poole had made a special point to invite Congressman Oliver to our sneak preview. He had told her that he was pro-choice but went on to add that, in his ten years as a U.S. Congressman, he had never received so many letters on a single issue as he had received during these past two weeks. His office had logged in over five hundred letters on abortion and that every one of them was against it.

Well, you can imagine his surprise when he began to read the letters we posted on our *Letters for Life* bulletin board. When Mrs.

Gates began to talk about this exhibit she asked Congressman Oliver, whom she had been told was in the room, if he would like to make a comment on our unique display since every letter on the board was addressed to him.

"I never knew that I was so popular," he told us, making his way to the front of the group and straightening his tie. "In all seriousness, as many of you know I have long supported a woman's right to choose. But after seeing such a tremendous outpouring of support against abortion I thought it was important that I find out why so many people would take the time to write me a personal letter. If I receive three or four letters on a subject, that's usually a lot. But to get over five hundred letters on the same issue is unheard of. So one day last week I went home and took about one hundred of them and read every one. By the time I was halfway through I began to understand things about abortion that I never knew or even considered. I can't promise you that I will change my stance but what I can promise you is that I will seriously consider everything I have read and what I have seen in these exhibits."

There were marked signs of approval from a good many of our guests and I saw that that had not gone unnoticed by Congressman Oliver. I expected that, whatever his personal opinion about this issue was, he would listen to the electorate and, if they were anything like the people in this room, it would be clear to him that he had better not underestimate how this one single issue could play a key role in determining whether he would be re-elected. Jerry's simple idea made me realize just how powerful the written word could be. And I was beginning to get excited as I pondered the implications of going national with a "Letters for Life" campaign.

Next we moved on to a very simple but powerful exhibit we named *Sounds from the Womb*.

"Many pro-abortion advocates know that with the advent of modern medical equipment we can hear the sound of a baby's heartbeat while still inside a mother's womb," Mrs. Gates said as she walked over and opened the door to the exhibit's booth. "Obviously they don't like to talk about this fact since they know that if a mother knew and then actually heard her tiny baby's heartbeat she might change her mind about going through with an abortion. However, what many people don't know is that, early on, we can listen to a baby's heartbeat. With the aid of an ultrasonic stethoscope, we are able to actually listen to the sound of a six-week-old baby's heartbeat.[38] In fact, we recorded this for all of you to hear when you step into our *Sounds from the Womb* booth. At six weeks many women don't even know they are pregnant, yet they can hear two distinct and separate heartbeats within their own body if they choose to listen."

There was a fluttering of interest and I knew that, after this presentation, many of these people would come back to listen. When I had heard it earlier, when the exhibition was being prepared, my stomach began to turn when I realized for the first time that when I had aborted Baby Sally not only was her heart beating but it could even be heard if I only had known how to listen.

"Also inside our *Sounds from the Womb* booth is another recording of a baby crying," Mrs. Gates went on. "While most people wonder what's so special about a baby crying, since after all that's what all babies do, they become amazed as we tell them that the cry they hear is coming from a six-month-old baby still comfortably resting inside his temporary nine month shelter – the womb. While almost everyone believes that a baby can't cry until it is actually born, the truth is quite a different thing."

Mrs. Gates went on to explain that, although the watery environment in which the unborn baby lives presents small opportunity for crying, which does require air, the unborn knows how to cry, and given a chance to do so, he will.

Jennifer had already told me the story Mrs. Gates was beginning to tell and I couldn't wait to see how everyone would react when they heard the surprise ending.

With a playful look in her eyes, Mrs. Gates told our visitors that, in one particular instance, a doctor took x-rays after injecting an air bubble into a baby's amniotic sac and noticed that the air bubble had covered the baby's face. She then concluded by telling everyone this amusing but true eyewitness account of what happened next.

"'The whole procedure had no doubt given the little fellow quite a bit of jostling about, and the moment that he had air to inhale and exhale they heard the clear sound of a protesting wail emitting from the uterus. Late that same night, the mother awakened her doctor with a telephone call, to report that when she lay down to sleep the air bubble got over the baby's head again, and he was crying so loudly he was keeping both her and her husband awake.'"[39]

Everybody started to laugh but I just couldn't as I thought back to the first time I listened to the sound of this preborn crying and understood that sometimes even these millions of silent voices, destined to be aborted, could literally be heard crying out. These cries from inside the womb are just another sign that a tiny person is letting all of us know – I'm here.

A very touching set of full color photographs, fifteen in all, formed our *Adoption – The Magnificent Compromise* exhibit. Similar to *The Wall of Life* these fifteen young children and young adults, ages eight to twenty, all had one thing in common - they were put up for adoption immediately after birth instead of being aborted, thanks to the fact that the mother's had been told about this option and guided through the adoption process.

As our invited guests began to read the stories behind the faces in these photographs Mrs. Gates shared some very moving comments.

"If you look at these different photographs," she proudly began to explain, "you will notice that adoption is no respecter of race, color or physical condition. John Hood is black. Jessica Finney is Korean. Gail Gonzalez is Malaysian. Steve Painter was born with spina bifida. Jill Kennedy was born blind and Randy Musso is from Romania. And you will note as you read each one of their stories that all of them are enjoying life and looking forward to a bright future.

"When it comes to pregnancy, one woman is faced with a major problem – a baby that she feels will ruin her life. Another woman is faced with an equally major problem – she can't have children and she feels that without a child her life is so incomplete. And that's where the wonderful alternative of adoption comes in. Adoption allows both women to solve their own very different problems by sharing with one another the most precious gift known – a new born baby.

"Basically all pregnant women are faced with three major choices once an unwanted pregnancy diagnosis is confirmed. She can decide to give birth to her baby and keep it thus adding one more precious picture to *The Wall of Life*. Her second choice is to abort her child and have its remains join the other gruesome victims now residing in *The Pit of Death*. Or she can choose "The Magnificent

Compromise" of adoption and make another woman, unable to bear children, a very happy and grateful parent. I pray that every woman in America will choose to either keep her baby or place it up for adoption."

By now Mrs. Gates was almost finished with her guided tour. We had two more exhibits to view and I was very pleased the way each presentation was put together. The entire NAL team had done a fabulous job in assembling this truly unique way of looking at life in the womb. But what was really exciting was the fact that I was now part of that team.

Why Can't We Love Them Both was our next to last exhibit and consisted of a twelve-minute video specifically put together by NAL for our *Children of the Womb* presentation. It was continuously shown on a giant screen TV and was a warm and compellingly sensitive view of the plight of each woman facing an unwanted pregnancy.

In one segment a sixteen-year-old teen shared how she was told by her father to either get an abortion or pack her bags. She felt she had little choice but to abort her child or face being thrown out of her home. The counselor at the crisis pregnancy center she went to explained that, if her dad decided to go ahead with his threat, she could choose to stay with one of the two wonderful families that would be willing to let her live with them during her pregnancy. Life was very precious to these two special families, both the life of the unborn as well as the life of the brave young mother carrying her child.

Another portion of the video showed an eighteen-year-old high school senior crying because she felt she had to choose between either having an abortion or not being able to go to college. Another pro-life counselor told her how she could give her the names and phone numbers of several young women who, when they were in the same situation as she, had decided not only to have their babies but attend college as well. All of them could tell her that while it had not been easy, it had been worth it. This video made it clear that having the support of other women who have traveled on the same road was a key way of letting young mothers-to-be know that they are not alone.

The final clip took us to San Francisco where the follow-up care between a crisis pregnancy center and an abortion clinic were contrasted. Some of the follow-up services provided by the crisis pregnancy center included:

Helping expectant mothers obtain badly needed maternity and baby clothes.

Providing free prenatal monthly checkups for women that couldn't afford these services.

Holding weekly meetings where young women could meet to share their feelings and experiences in a warm and loving support group.

Placing women into temporary homes when abusive relationships made staying at home impossible.

Sharing information on adoption and helping them through the entire process if they chose this wonderful option.

When it came time to showing some of the follow-up services provided by the abortion clinic only one was listed:

Going to the bank to deposit the cash that the abortionist received in exchange for putting another baby to sleep forever.

It was our hope that this video would begin to let women know that pro-lifers are concerned not just with saving the life of another baby but in respecting and loving the mother too.

Our final display was intended to be a chilling indictment on the entire abortion industry and was titled simply, *Do you Know Where your Baby is Sleeping Tonight?* Right behind the display plaque explaining the exhibit were the following objects: a baby bassinet, a crib, a large glass jar, a bucket like the one that movie theaters use to hold popcorn, a big black plastic bag, a garbage can and a big green dumpster.

The plaque went on to read:

"Two out of every three babies born in America today will enjoy the comforts of sleeping in a bassinet or crib on their first day home from the hospital. Unfortunately one out of three babies born in America today will spend their first night away from the clinic in either a jar, a bucket, a black plastic bag, an old garbage can or thrown out with the other trash in a big green dumpster."

As I stared at that dumpster, my mind flashed back to the night I climbed into another big green dumpster that looked exactly like the one in our museum. Sadly I knew all too well where my baby spent her first night home from the clinic.

Over the next two weeks crowds of people streamed through the doors of the Meeting Place Inn to visit our experimental museum and the positive press coverage we received was awesome. We taped a tour of the exhibits, hoping that one of the major TV networks would air our *Children of the Womb* presentation. Unfortunately they all declined to do so and we had to settle for having it shown on a host of local and cable stations. However, the response to our TV tour was so overwhelmingly positive and the support and encouragement we received so uplifting we just knew that we had to find a permanent home for our temporary museum.

The success of our museum exceeded our wildest expectations. When our two weeks were up we all vowed to try to find and fund a permanent place to display our exhibits and add even more pro-life displays. NAL suggested that Washington, D.C. would be an ideal place to build a museum and set up an exploratory committee to look into all the complex aspects such a major project would involve.

Jennifer Poole knew that if *Children of the Womb* became a success that we should expect a major counterattack from the pro-choice camp. And sure enough, the day our exhibit closed, a full page stinging condemnation ad appeared in twenty of our nation's largest circulating daily newspapers.

Jennifer and I were sitting in one of the hotel rooms that had served as a temporary office during our exhibition run when she began to enlighten me on what to expect from our adversary. We had become very close during the past two weeks and I was beginning to view her as part of my family.

"Those ads must have cost over $300,000," she said, frowning as we stared at the ad she had spread out on one of the beds. "And yes, it is very well prepared and skillfully designed to paint our cause in a very negative light."

"They're certainly trying to make our museum look bad," I said.

"Not just our museum, but our entire movement and even our very character."

"That sickens me, Jennifer," I told her. I was trying to stay calm but it wasn't easy knowing that they were attempting to destroy everything we had worked so hard to accomplish.

"That's just the way they run their operation. Louise, you had better get use to it."

"Believe me I'm learning what to expect from them in the future awfully fast."

Their ad labeled our museum displays as deceptive, inaccurate and a crude attempt at sensationalism. We were accused of using scare tactics to discourage a woman from exercising her constitutional right to seek and procure a safe and legal abortion. We were again tagged with the labels of being morally intolerant, anti-choice, bigoted, judgmental, and seditious. The ad further went on to sound a rallying cry asking all women of America to unite and defend their constitutional right to obtain an abortion.

While we designed each of our displays to portray a different aspect of the abortion debate in a powerful - and yes sensational way - everything about the exhibits were totally accurate. Sadly, this clearly could not be said of their pro-choice ad attacking our movement. If anyone was guilty of using scare tactics to defend their position, it clearly was not us as can be seen from the following portion of their ad:

"Women in America," it read. "Down through the years, we have fought long and hard to obtain equal rights. We fought hard to win the right to vote and won. We fought hard to be able to hold public offices and won. We are still fighting to earn the same pay as men do for equal work and are closing the gap. And we waged a critical campaign to control our right to privacy over our own bodies and won a major victory when our U.S. Supreme Court confirmed our constitutional right to terminate a pregnancy if we choose to.

"But now we must unite as never before because several groups are trying to turn back the clock and take away one of our most precious and cherished rights. If we ever lose our right to obtain safe and legal abortions as it exists today thanks to *Roe v. Wade*, we would have to go back to the dark ages again where clothes hangers and unsafe abortions would be our only course of action when we felt that abortion was the right choice to make. The back alley abortion must forever remain a thing of the past. We must not allow this giant step backwards to ever take place. Please write and call your elected officials at every level of government and let them know that abortion must always stay safe and legal. If you cherish this right, you'll get involved in the fight."

While our museum was now officially closed the battle for the "Children of the Womb" was just getting ready to be fought on several other major new fronts.

12

Christmas: A time to Ponder

Christmastime at the Jordan home was always a very special time of year. Friends, family, food, gifts and Jesus provided all the elements that made up this special season. Ever since we were little, my brother and I couldn't wait until Christmas morning. Every Christmas morning, for as long back as I can remember, Don and I would run downstairs to just stare at all the beautifully wrapped presents that Mom and Dad would place under our tree.

Opening our gifts would always have to wait, however, because it was tradition in our home for Dad to read us the Christmas story first. As in the past, he would walk over to a special small wooden table in our living room, that had placed on it, what he said was one of his most precious possessions – our one-hundred-year-old family Bible. Dad would often tell us that this giant large print edition of the Holy Scriptures had been in the Jordan family for four generations. I can still remember how on many a night dad would gather the entire family together, and right after dinner, read from this wonderful book. But since it was Christmas, Don and I knew that he was going to read from the book of Matthew. We all sat back and listened as dad began:

"'Now the birth of Jesus Christ was on this wise: When as his mother Mary was espoused to Joseph, before they came together, she was found with child of the Holy Ghost.'"[40]

As my father continued reading the wonderful story of the birth of Jesus to us I couldn't help but marvel at how this two-thousand-year-old story, perhaps more than any one single event so influenced the history of mankind.

As I listened to the familiar story my mind began to ponder the difficult predicament that Mary and Joseph found themselves in.

"Dad," I said when he had finished, "I wonder what must have been going through Joseph's mind when he discovered that Mary was pregnant?"

"I think he must have felt betrayed at first wondering why Mary had been unfaithful to him, until the angel of the Lord appeared to him in a dream, telling him what had really happened."

"Louise," my mom added, "Joseph loved Mary. He must have been devastated knowing that the one he loved and trusted so much could have done such a thing."

Dad then began to explain to us some of the customs of biblical times.

"Kids, even before Joseph and Mary came together, under Jewish law they were betrothed to one another, which was as binding as modern marriage."

"You mean since they were a betrothed couple they were regarded legally as husband and wife?" Don, wanted to know.

"Yes, and only a divorce could break the contract. And that's what Joseph was planning to do."

"But why a divorce?" Don and I both asked at the same time.

"Well, Joseph knew that, if Mary was discovered to have become pregnant through adultery, she could be stoned to death. I still believe that he loved Mary and didn't want her to have to face that possibility. I guess he felt that if he put her away from him quickly that might just solve this concern. Again, all of these thoughts clearly changed when the angel of the Lord spoke to him."

"Mom, I dare say that, if this couple had lived today, Mary would have been strongly advised by many not even to let Joseph know she were pregnant but to get an abortion and thus save herself from possibly having to face the death penalty. Dad, the mere thought that Mary could have aborted the Son of God is something I had never considered until just now."

"I wonder if Joseph ever suggested that option to Mary?" Dad mused.

"I don't think we'll ever be able to know that," I remarked, still feeling stunned that my mind had even thought of that possibility.

"Maybe when we get to heaven, we can ask Mary," he told me, "but for now we can only speculate on what the two of them may have discussed."

With that dad began to re-read the following portion of scripture:

"'But while he thought on these things, behold, the angel of the LORD appeared unto him in a dream, saying, Joseph, thou son of David, fear not to take unto thee Mary thy wife: for that which is conceived in her is of the Holy Ghost. And she shall bring forth a son, and thou shalt call his name JESUS: for he shall save his people from their sins.'"[41]

"The rest is history," Dad said, shutting the heavy leather covers. "Joseph and Mary made all the right choices and 2,000 years later hundreds of millions of people each Sunday attend Church to worship, without a doubt, the most influential person who ever walked the face of the Earth – Jesus Christ."

Just then the telephone rang. I ran for the phone and as soon as I picked it up Jennifer Poole began:

"Louise, I'm just calling to wish you and your family a very merry Christmas."

"Merry Christmas to you too Jennifer," I said. It was always good to hear Jennifer's voice. She and I were becoming closer and closer with each passing week. She was now much more than just my mentor. She was now my close friend.

"Louise I have great news," she added in an excited voice. "Bob Jacobs has agreed to interview you on his Thursday night, January 18th show."

"I can't believe you did it, Jennifer. You're just unbelievable. I'm so excited and nervous all at the same time."

"I know you must be, that's only natural. Louise, I know you're on your Christmas break but we want you to come down to D.C. for two days so we can discuss strategy for the show."

I was so excited that I told her yes right on the spot.

"I'll call you back later today to work out the details," I went on. "But I gotta go and tell the family. My mom is just going to freak when I tell her the news."

"Jennifer Poole just called to let me know that on January 18th I'm going to be on *The Bob Jacobs Show*," I called out as I raced back to the living room.

Mom clearly couldn't believe what she was hearing. "My little Louise on *The Bob Jacobs Show*," she said, now looking even more excited than I was. And Don, too, seemed thrilled that his big sister was going to be on TV again. "I just have to call and let Aunt Jane know right away. She just won't believe it."

"Jennifer asked me if I could spend two days with her in D.C. to help prepare for the show," I went on looking from one of them to the other, hoping they would say yes. "Please can I go?"

"Yes you can go," Dad said, grinning. "And this time I'm comfortable enough to let you travel on your own. Your mom and I have discussed this and we both feel that you're mature enough now to travel by yourself for short stays. I'm very comfortable with the staff at NAL and know that you'll be in very good hands."

During this past summer, when I had found out that I didn't need my parent's permission to get an abortion, I had felt like an adult. Yet I knew in my heart back then that I was still just a scared young girl. Today, just four months later, my dad was in effect telling me that he could now treat me as if I was a mature young adult. And this time I felt like one.

Two days after Christmas, I found myself sitting in Jennifer Poole's living room, a guest at her house, discussing my upcoming appearance on *The Bob Jacobs Show*. For the next three hours, we discussed a wide variety of subjects from making sure I got my facts correct to how to keep good eye contact with Mr. Jacobs and the TV audience. We reviewed our recent museum exhibits, devised ways to counter the negative attacks on our position that were sure to be raised, examined the latest scientific facts on all aspects of fetal development and even discussed what I should wear to the interview. We also spent a lot of time talking about the adoption alternative.

During my second day in D.C., I spent eight hours at NAL headquarters working on our twin strategy. We wanted to let the public know that abortion kills babies, but we also wanted to let women who were facing the decision to abort, to know that we loved them as much as their baby and stood willing to help them in any way possible. Right after lunch both Jennifer and Mrs. Gates staged a mock interview with me where, for the next two hours, they hit me with every pro-choice argument imaginable in order to see how I responded when difficult questions came my way.

Because it was common knowledge that Bob Jacobs was solidly pro-choice and a very tough interviewer, Mrs. Gates called me names and attacked my character. She questioned my motives and asked why anyone should take a tenth grader seriously in any discussion of such a complex and sensitive topic. Jennifer explained to me that our mock interview was designed to test how I would hold up under the pressure of being questioned by a master interviewer.

By the end of two solid hours of intense grilling, I was exhausted. It felt strange to have my two new friends try to assassinate my character and attempt to put a black mark on the integrity of our entire pro-life movement. But after my interview, I was happy to hear that they were more than satisfied with my performance.

"Both of us think you did a great job," Mrs. Gates assured me. "Your counterattacking skills are simply tremendous, Louise. You clearly show a great depth of knowledge and exude passion."

"Thanks for the compliments," I replied, as I sank into Jennifer's big, beige recliner. "I felt kind of nervous but not afraid. How do you think the TV audience would react to the things I was saying?"

"You still can use a little polishing up," Jennifer told me with just the hint of a frown. "Both of us noted your nervous habit of playing with your hair. That's a definite no-no. We also need to work on your eye contact. Sometimes it seems that you are just staring into space. Another area we can improve upon is the selection of words you use to highlight some of your points. Better word choice can help us paint a more accurate picture of the true evils of abortion and the deception that pro-choice advocates use to state their case."

I can honestly say that those two days were very well spent. Both Jennifer and Mrs. Gates gave me lots to think about and work on during the next few weeks as I prepared for my interview. As they were putting me on the plane back to New York, Mrs. Gates said that for the next three weeks the entire staff at NAL would be keeping me in their prayers. And she promised to come out to Palmerville with Jennifer sometime during the next few weeks to help me with any last minute preparations. She also told me to please call her or Jennifer if I needed anything or had any questions. With those warm words of advice, off I flew back home.

It wasn't easy but over the next two weeks I was able somehow to juggle doing all my schoolwork as well as to prepare for my big TV appearance. On the final weekend leading up to my Thursday interview I asked several of my close friends to come over and pepper me with their toughest questions.

On Tuesday, January 16th, just two days before I was scheduled to appear on *The Bob Jacobs Show*, Mrs. Gates and Jennifer came out to Palmerville to see how I was doing. They also wanted to fill me in on the massive negative publicity that the pro-choice lobby had orchestrated against our cause during the past few weeks. While I had been busy getting ready for my big interview, the pro-abortion lobby was also quite busy. They were moving full speed ahead with perhaps their most extensive and expensive campaign ever to undermine all of the progress we had made during the past four months.

"According to some research that Jennifer has put together," Mrs. Gates told my entire family as we all were relaxing around the fireplace in our living room, "we estimate that our pro-choice friends have spent over five million dollars in the past two weeks alone on newspaper ads, TV spots, billboards and Internet messaging. They've also done a great job in organizing their faithful. Just last week as you know they were able to bring over three hundred and fifty thousand pro-choice demonstrators together in our nation's capital to participate in a massive rally in support of a woman's right to choose."

"I hope that one day when we have our rally we can double that number," I remarked, not realizing at the time the prophetic nature of my words.

"That's a pretty ambitious goal," Jennifer said as both she and Mrs. Gates nodded their heads.

"And you know," Mrs. Gates continued, now looking a little sad, "the major theme of their campaign has focused on three main areas. Their first thrust was to state that no one had any right to impose their own personal brand of morality on a woman when it came to what she should do with her own body when facing an unwanted pregnancy. The second phase was to attack our very integrity, character and motives. And finally, we are being accused of actively working to undermine a woman's constitutional right to privacy over her own body."

It was obvious to me that everything they did was designed to distract people's attention from what really is at stake. They clearly had little concern with the plight of the central person involved in the entire controversy – the unborn baby!

"And I hate to say it," Jennifer now added, "but because of this major pro-choice push we are definitely seeing some of the tremendous support and positive publicity we've received since the beginning of September begin to wane."

"But let's not talk about this now," Jennifer said. I knew that she wanted to keep everything upbeat for me. My Mom and Dad felt the same, which was why they invited all my friends to a party at our house the night before I was going to leave. It turned out to be a wonderful party. Mom had bought the most colorful paper goods I had ever seen and even made sure that all of my friends signed a giant card wishing me good luck on the show.

When we had finished the cake and people were beginning to wish me luck, Jennifer took the floor. She was wearing a red turtleneck sweater that almost matched the color of her cheeks, which were now flushed with excitement. "I have a surprise announcement," she said.

"We believe that Louise's interview is going to set the stage for our most important and extensive pro-life ad campaign in history. And because of this we have been working very hard during these past few weeks designing new ads, buying extensive newspaper space and TV time, designing an incredible pro-life website, getting our own billboard space and yes planning the biggest rally for any single cause in the history of the United States. And this takes money, lots of money."

For a moment, my breath caught in my throat. Was she going to tell us that all this was more than NAL could afford?

"Well during Louise's first visit to us in D.C.," Jennifer went on, "she met another very special person named Eddie Moss. Eddie is a multi-millionaire who owns a large chain of family style restaurants in the Midwest. He also is one of the most active and passionate advocates for the unborn in the entire country."

"Guys, you would love Mr. Moss," I interrupted. "He's a real millionaire but also real sweet."

"I can't argue with that, Louise," Jennifer said. "As we were discussing various ideas on a host of pro-life issues Eddie came up with a brilliant idea. According to Eddie every dollar given in support of the fight for life could give the donor the opportunity to get in on what he called 'the investment opportunity of a lifetime.' Right away he began to call on many of his well-to-do friends and business associates asking them to make an investment in 'life.'"

Dad and I glanced at one another. Both of us had seen that Mr. Moss was a consummate businessman but neither of us could ever have guessed what Jennifer was about to share.

"Since that time Eddie has traveled almost 10,000 miles," Jennifer went on. "He's visited ten states, sharing this message with literally hundreds of influential and wealthy members of his circle. And today I'm happy to let you all know that thanks to the tireless efforts of Eddie Moss we have raised over ten million dollars for the official launching of *Operation Sally,* which we have timed to coincide with Louise's appearance on *The Bob Jacobs Show.*"

I took a deep breath while the others cheered. Ten million dollars was an enormous sum of money. We finally had the war chest we needed to educate America on what was really at stake in the abortion controversy. However, at the same time I was extremely nervous. NAL had timed their *Operation Sally* launch and their ten million-dollar investment to coincide with my interview on *The Bob Jacobs Show*. In my heart I knew that, if the interview didn't go well, our launch would suffer a major setback. This added pressure was not something I wanted to have to deal with right before my show date.

After everyone departed for the evening I asked my dad if I could speak with him about something that was really making me very nervous. Dad was always willing to talk and he asked me to join him in his study.

"Dad," I said, feeling like a little girl again, "I'm starting to panic. I can't believe that NAL is investing so much money in their new marketing strategy and relying on my interview to jumpstart the entire campaign. While Jennifer and Mrs. Gates meant well sharing the great news about their new funding with us, this news has had just the opposite effect on me. Instead of giving me added encouragement I feel as if a great deal of added pressure has been placed on my shoulders."

My Dad nodded his agreement. "Being interviewed on a major coast to coast television show in prime time would make almost anyone nervous no matter how you cut it," he said, pulling the drapes across the long window behind his desk. The room closed in on itself and immediately I felt safer. But tomorrow I would have to leave all this and I had no way of knowing what was waiting for me out there. "Come sit here close to me," my dad said, patting the footstool beside his leather chair. "Over the past four months wherever you have gone and spoken, perhaps without even knowing it, you have been under far greater pressure than having to worry about getting a ten million-dollar marketing campaign off to a good start. Life and death have always been what's at stake whenever you've shared your views on abortion. And thanks to your powerful message thousands of women have already changed their minds and chosen to give life to the precious child they are carrying."

He put his hand on my shoulder and looked me straight in the eyes.

"Thursday night when Bob Jacobs tries to make you nervous or trip you up with his questions, know that millions of people all across our country have you in their prayers. You also need to realize that you have the truth on your side and the truth is always stronger than a lie. Finally, you need to know that God will give you the words to speak as He has wonderfully done ever since you made your commitment to be a defender of the defenseless. Thursday night is your night to shine and for *Operation Sally* to get off with a bang. Louise – Go for it!!!"

Dad, as he had done so often in the past, gave me the best advice anyone could ever give. While I was still feeling pretty nervous right up to the start of the interview I had a quiet confidence that was sky-high by show time. I was definitely ready to go!

13

Show Stopper

The Jordan family was up early Thursday morning because a limousine was scheduled to pick all of us up at ten to drive us to *The Bob Jacobs Show* studios in Manhattan. The trip from Palmerville to midtown Manhattan took approximately two hours, time enough for me to rehearse in my mind at least a dozen times some of the things I wanted to share. Our family checked into one of the most expensive hotels in the city. We did a little sight seeing during the afternoon visiting Rockefeller Center and the United Nations. Early in the evening, we dined at a very fancy French restaurant but I really couldn't enjoy the food because of all the butterflies in my stomach. We arrived at the studio at six-thirty and by seven, I headed off to make-up, after which Dad and I were taken to the actual television set to meet Bob Jacobs. The show was a live telecast that aired from 9:00 to 10:00PM.

Mr. Jacobs, a handsome, well-built man must have been in his early fifties. His well-trimmed black beard made him quite distinguished looking. For the next forty-five minutes we talked quite a bit about what had been going on with my life during the past few months and I must admit that he was very charming and made me feel quite comfortable. He shared a little about his background and that he had two teenage daughters. I hoped in my heart that his easygoing nature would remain that way during the interview, although I knew that probably wasn't likely given how pro-choice his views were. His strong stance in favor of abortion, however, could clearly provide me with an opportunity to expose the flaws in each of his arguments. And that was my objective. When it was ten minutes to show time, Dad gave me a big kiss and wished me luck as he left the set. Show time or showdown, either way I was ready to give it my best.

At nine sharp the show's theme music began to play and a deep baritone voice which appeared to come out of nowhere announced: "It's now time for the number one interview show in the country, hosted by America's king of talk. Ladies and gentlemen, live from studio 3B in Midtown Manhattan, it's *The Bob Jacobs Show*."

As the show's theme music played, the camera zoomed into the set where I was seated at the same round table as Mr. Jacobs. Just where the next hour would lead us I had no idea. I only knew that it was time for the show to begin.

"Good evening," my host said in that familiar voice, beloved by so many. "Tonight we have a very special guest, a young woman who made history back in early September by aborting her own baby and then telling her tenth grade English class that she was a murderer. Though she is only sixteen, it is fair to say she has caused quite a stir in the very complex national debate on whether abortion should remain legal. I am delighted to have as my guest tonight, Palmerville, New York's most famous citizen, Louise Ann Jordan."

As he began his opening introduction, I tried to remember everything that Jennifer and Mrs. Gates had taught me. I kept thinking about the need not to slump in my seat, playing with my hair, and, God forbid, not panicking. When it was my turn to respond I took a deep breath and said my opening statement, which I had fortunately memorized word for word.

"Mr. Jacobs," I said, relieved to find that my voice was firm and steady, "I'm very thankful for giving me this opportunity to share with your viewing audience a message from over thirty million of your potential viewers who couldn't be here tonight because of their very untimely deaths. On their behalf, I thank you for opening up your studio home to hear their story."

"Louise," he said, looking a little surprised, as if my opening remarks had caught him off guard, "I just realized that in my six years as host of this show that you are the youngest person we have ever had as a guest. I guess that makes you special in yet another way. Normally sixteen-year-old girls' first priorities are boys, talking on the phone and going to movies. It's pretty rare that someone as young as you has taken such a passionate stand on a social issue, let alone one so controversial as abortion. Tell me, do you miss not doing the things most of your girlfriends enjoy doing?"

It wasn't clear to me where he was going with this line of questioning but I reminded myself to be watchful in case he meant to lay any traps for me.

"I still like to do all the things you just mentioned," I told him, smiling, "and I consider myself a very average and normal teenager. In fact I must have been to the movies at least six or seven times since I aborted my baby this past September. I must confess, however, that I haven't had too many opportunities to date."

I think that my mentioning my abortion jolted him a bit and I found myself hoping it had because I had no intention of letting him present me as a typical teenager. I had an important message to convey and I needed to make sure he didn't capitalize on my youth and inexperience.

"Over the last few weeks the news hasn't been very favorable for people like you who are fighting to make abortion illegal again," he went on. "Newspaper advertisements and TV spots have painted everything you are trying to accomplish in a very negative light. How do you feel when your cause is labeled a danger to a woman's constitutional rights and your rhetoric is called judgmental and moralizing?"

I paused for a moment as I gathered my thoughts on how to respond to this first attack on our movement. I looked into the studio audience and noticed that women were in the majority.

The lights were very bright and for a moment I lost my train of thought. I started to panic and noticed that my heart was now beating extremely fast. The show had just started and I was already at a lost for words.

Then, all of a sudden, my mind flashed back to the sights and smells of death that I experienced the night I climbed in that big green dumpster at 247 Bolton Road. As I relived that horrible event, I knew that too much was at stake for me to fail now, and with that, I offered a silent prayer to God, asking Him for His divine help to give me the words He wanted me to share. As soon as I offered up my prayer I felt as though I had been given just the right reply to his question.

"To be honest Mr. Jacobs," I said, "I feel very sad for the people who have spent so much money buying newspaper space and television time trying to convince you and me that it's OK to abort innocent babies, whom they present as nothing more than trash or, at best, excess tissue. What really bothers me, however, is that every day over four thousand perfectly healthy hearts are silenced forever through legal abortion in America. And, Mr. Jacobs, although you may not realize it, each time one of these tiny hearts is silenced another heart is broken since another woman, who would desperately love to adopt a baby, is deprived the opportunity."

Mr. Jacobs chuckled in a patronizing sort of way. I could see that one of his interviewing techniques was to make you feel that he was agreeing with you when in reality he was just setting the stage for a rebuttal.

"I must admit that if I were on a debating team I would definitely want you as one of my teammates," he told me. "You seem to have an answer to just about every pro-choice argument. And the fact that they have spent several million dollars over the past few weeks alone, is proof to me that you are definitely gaining support for the pro-life cause. In fact several very influential pro-choice leaders have told me privately that they view you as the single biggest threat in America to undoing everything they have fought so hard to establish. Tell me, how do you think you've been able to put so many of your adversaries on the run?"

"I really don't consider myself a very eloquent speaker," I told him, keeping in mind that he might be trying to trip me up with compliments. "However, what I do know is that when I look at all of the scientific facts in an objective way the only conclusion that I come away with is that abortion kills babies. And killing babies is a monstrous crime, not only against the innocent baby but against all of humanity."

As I began to look out into the audience, I became fascinated by the variety of expression, ranging from women who looked heartbroken to those who looked consumed with hate. I knew that our discussion was bound to elicit strong emotional reactions but I could only hope that by the end of the evening most of them would be of the heartbroken type.

"I'm going to be honest with you, Louise," Mr. Jacobs said. "Over the past ten years, I have been a strong supporter of a woman's right to choose. In 1973 our U.S. Supreme Court ruled that a woman's right to her own body in decisions concerning a pregnancy is, within certain boundaries, absolute, something that our Constitution guarantees. As you probably know from studying history most scholars regard our Constitution as a magnificent document that serves as the bedrock on which the great freedoms we have today in America are built upon. Reproductive freedom is a foundational right for all women in our society. If the pro-life movement were to succeed with its agenda, this most cherished right would be stripped away from every woman contemplating an abortion. Are you actually suggesting that we overturn our very Constitution?"

I was on firm ground again. This constitutional argument was one that I was well prepared to meet head on.

"I freely admit that America is the greatest country in the world and I wouldn't want to live anywhere else," I said. "But if you carefully study the history of our Constitution, I think you will find that it has often been in need of serious repair, especially when it comes to the question of rights and freedoms."

"All right then," he told me, leaning back in his chair, "Can you give me an example of what you think needs to be repaired now?"

"Ever since its ratification back in 1787, our Constitution has been seriously flawed," I told him, not forgetting to look at the red eye of the camera so that I could be looking straight at our viewing audience, as well. "In fact, as you look at the amendments that subsequently had to be passed, our Constitution, you realize that if it had been left unamended, it would today be the underlying governing document in a society that allows slavery to exist, denies blacks and women the right to vote and even allows our young men at age eighteen to die fighting in wars but remain ineligible to vote until they turned twenty-one. It took the passage of our XIII, XV, XIX, and XXVI Amendments to ensure that these great injustices and freedom robbers would no longer remain the law of our land."

"You certainly know a lot about our Constitution, young lady," he said and I could see that by the way he phrased each compliment there seemed to be a string attached. He clearly had his own agenda and I needed to guard against becoming too overconfident.

"Thanks, I try to keep current with my history homework. But the point is that I'm sure you would agree that we should all be grateful that these amendments were passed correcting our nation's past discrimination based upon skin color, sex and age."

Mr. Jacobs looked into the camera and smiled as though I had said something amusing. It was clear to me now that he was patronizing me, trying to point out by inference that I was just a girl, not a Constitutional scholar. "Are there any other areas of discrimination you feel our Constitution still needs to address?"

"Yes," I told him. "There still remains one great frontier of discrimination we need to abolish and that is discrimination based on place of residence. Today when a baby is conceived, he or she faces a one in three possibility that its warm and safe initial home, the womb, will become his or her tomb. Even very conservatively speaking, one out of every four women who become pregnant will opt to abort their child. To me that's discrimination of the worse kind. Destroying innocent life purely because they happen to be conceived in the 'wrong womb' is an unspeakable tragedy. And that's why we need the passage of one more constitutional amendment guaranteeing the unborn the right to life."

"Where do you get all of your statistics from and are you comfortable that they are reliable and not just being greatly exaggerated?" he asked me.

"I have always enjoyed working with numbers," I said. "In fact math is my favorite subject in school. Statistics can often tell a very interesting story. However, I agree with you. If used improperly, they can be very deceptive and misleading. For example, if we consider that there are conservatively speaking 1.4 million abortions each year in America and 4 million live births then simple math will tell you that approximately one in four babies will be aborted this year. These are cold hard facts that cannot be disputed.

"However, people who support the right to have abortion on demand say that each abortion ends an unwanted pregnancy and thus only an unwanted child is put to death. People who are pro-abortion, therefore claim that only unwanted children are killed. However, statistics show that these babies, while not immediately wanted by their biological mothers, are very much in demand by couples looking to adopt them. It all depends on what the question is and who you ask."

"That's all well and good, Louise, but I think you're really asking those women to sacrifice quite a lot by expecting them to carry their baby to term just to make two complete strangers happy. Unfortunately we have to pause for a break, but don't touch that dial we'll be right back to continue this fascinating discussion."

As soon as we broke for a commercial, I heard two women in the audience cursing me. One of them even expressed the wish that my whole family would drop dead. I really became frightened as the other one tried to make her way onto the set. Fortunately, security immediately escorted both women out of the studio while the rest of the audience buzzed with excitement. When Mr. Jacobs saw how scared I was, he got up from his chair and came over to put his arms around me, reassuring me that everything would be OK and apologized that anyone in his audience would pull such a stunt. He then got up and walked right into the audience area and said angrily:

"This is an absolute disgrace. Louise is my guest, and I promise you that, if anyone pulls something like that again, I'll have them arrested. I know that not everyone agrees with her position, but I certainly don't need any help from this audience to ensure that the other side of the abortion controversy is represented."

I thanked him for speaking up for me and realized once again that not everyone wanted to hear my message. Even though I might be uncomfortable with the questions Mr. Jacobs threw at me I was now no longer uncomfortable with him. I was actually now happy to get back to our discussion.

"When you aborted your baby back in early September of last year," he began when we were back on air again, "you made a lot of women very uncomfortable by saying that you killed your baby. If I recall correctly, you told us then that you were about thirteen weeks pregnant. Since no fetus can ever survive on its own at thirteen weeks, to say you killed your baby is quite a stretch. Don't you think it's quite unfair to accuse by implication those women of murder, who elect to abort their fetus at the end of their first trimester of pregnancy?"

"Perhaps if I had became pregnant one hundred years ago, my statement about my having murdered my thirteen-week-old baby might be considered sensationalism since we knew next to nothing about fetal development back then. But I have learned that, when we discover a fact that clearly disproves a previous belief we once held, we can either change our belief to fit the new facts or continue to believe in something that is clearly not true."

"And just what are those facts we are choosing to deny, Miss Jordan," he asked me, looking me straight in the eyes.

"Science," I responded, "has conclusively proven that, during the first trimester of a baby's habitation in the womb, an explosion of life is taking place. At twelve weeks the technical term for what's growing inside the womb is a fetus. But the reality is that at twelve weeks a masterpiece of ultra-complex unique life is present, which we call a baby. All of its systems are functioning and if you choose to open your eyes the only conclusion any rational person can come to is that to terminate this precious life, is to kill a real baby. Mr. Jacobs, whatever reason a mother may give to justify aborting her baby, she cannot escape the fact that this procedure will kill the child she is carrying. We now have the knowledge of what is going on inside a pregnant woman's body. We know a baby is present. The only question that remains is whether we are going to continue to deny reality and continue aborting babies."

As we went to another commercial break, I took a few moments to gather my thoughts. I felt as if I had made a lot of good points but I still couldn't figure out if Mr. Jacobs was willing to concede any ground.

"You have presented some thought provoking ideas tonight, Louise," he began. "However, the fact remains that many well respected members of Congress, the entertainment industry, the medical profession and even many members of the clergy still feel that a woman should have the final right over her reproductive decisions and the option to seek an abortion if she so desires. I think Justice Blackmun said it best when he commented in his opinion in *Roe v. Wade*, and I quote, 'We need not resolve the difficult question of when life begins. When those trained in the respective disciplines of medicine, philosophy, and theology are unable to arrive at any consensus, the judiciary, at this point in the development of man's knowledge, is not in a position to speculate as to the answer.'[42] Just last week I attended a dinner of religious leaders who support a woman's right to an abortion. In all honesty, Louise, with so many well respected leaders in our society disagreeing with your viewpoint, how can you categorically say they are all wrong."

Once again his compliment was immediately followed by a hard hitting question but this time I was prepared to put forward one of my most powerful arguments.

"Politicians base a lot of their decisions on what they think their constituents support," I said. "If they feel that supporting a pro-abortion agenda might just cost them an election, they may very well begin to view the pro-life position in a much more favorable light. The abortion doctor obviously has a vested interest in wanting to keep abortion legal since he stands to gain a great deal of money from each abortion he performs. And the liberal entertainment industry is not only a staunch supporter of abortion on demand but it is even trying to redefine the definition as to what constitutes a legal marriage. If they could have their way, homosexuals would be allowed to marry and birth control and condoms would be available to everyone."

"But what about people in the clergy who disagree with you, Louise? Are you going to tell me that they are also wrong?"

"You know Mr. Jacobs, that's what truly grieves me the most," I told him. "Today there are Christians and Jews who say they have a deep love for God but yet see no problem in destroying innocent life. I'd ask those in the church today who support a woman's right to choose some simple questions."

I knew my next comments might offend a lot of Mr. Jacobs viewers but I felt that this was the right time to take people out of their comfort zones and challenge them to view abortion in a new and most disturbing way.

"Can you picture a woman seeking counsel from Jesus Christ on what to do with an unwanted pregnancy?" I asked. "Can you picture Jesus Christ, the personification of gentleness, compassion and love, telling that woman that abortion would be the best course of action under her circumstances. And now just imagine Jesus Christ accompanying this frightened and confused woman, now twenty weeks along, to the abortion chamber? And finally can you picture Jesus Christ standing by her side, gently holding her hand, and telling her everything will be OK, while the abortionist begins to tear away the baby's tiny arms and legs from its body and then proceeds to crush the baby's skull before he removes it from the womb and tosses it into a garbage pail?

"Jesus Christ is without a doubt the most influential and compassionate person who ever walked the face of our planet. Even those people who deny his deity acknowledge that he was a great man and a wonderful moral teacher. The mere thought of Jesus consenting to and participating in an abortion is impossible to imagine. I therefore ask anyone who identifies with the name of Christ to also identify with what he stands for. If Jesus came to help heal the sick, love the poor and help widows and orphans, don't you think that he also would try to save the lives of our most precious and innocent members of society – the baby in the womb?"

For a moment Mr. Jacobs said nothing and I was aware that a total silence had settled over the studio. For that moment no one even moved.

"You make a good case, Louise," Mr. Jacobs said finally, clearing his throat. "I would find it a little difficult to picture Jesus Christ helping a woman get an abortion. But let me ask you this. What happens when a woman becomes pregnant as a result of rape or incest? And do you actually believe a woman should be forbidden an abortion even when her doctor tells her that the child she is carrying will definitely be born with a major physical handicap? Can you be so cold as to demand that a woman complete her pregnancy even under these devastating conditions?"

"I think that you make a good point," I replied, reminding myself to avoid any sort of direct confrontation. "What should our response be when these tragic circumstances beset a woman? One of the things I try to do whenever I have the opportunity to share my ideas about why I believe abortion is wrong, even in the cases you just described, is to make people carry out their arguments supporting abortion to their logical conclusions. Sometimes this has proven very effective in causing people to change their position."

"I'm a pretty open minded guy Louise," he said. "Why don't you hit me with your best example."

"OK. Say your seventeen-year-old daughter all of a sudden became severely brain damaged and paralyzed from the waist down as a result of a car crash. What would you do now that she has become totally dependent on you, your wife and her friends for everything, clearly a great burden, both emotionally and financially to you?"

"God forbid, Louise. I don't even want to go there."

"Neither do I, Mr. Jacobs. But unfortunately this scenario happens every day to some family in our society. Most people I'm sure would view your daughter as a drain on our valuable resources. What should we do with your daughter? Should we kill her since her value to society has now been greatly diminished? No, never! She is still a human being who is special in the eyes of God and I am sure still equally special to you."

He was nodding his head now and I felt a thrust of energy as I realized his self-confident and patronizing attitude had been greatly muted, at least temporarily.

"For the past seventeen years you have grown to love and cherish your daughter," I pressed on. "But what if this same accident and resulting severe handicap happened to her when she was just one-year-old? Should your response be any different since you only know her for one year instead of seventeen? Again, I pray not."

"I think I'm beginning to see where you're taking us, Louise," Mr. Jacobs said slowly. "Say a mother discovers that at twenty weeks gestation this same type of a handicap was very likely to occur in their child. Rather than have to deal with a handicapped child, many would choose to abort. But your comparison still seems a little extreme and unfair."

"It might seem extreme to you," I told him, "but the arguments for killing a handicapped unborn child are valid only if we are willing to kill living children possessing these same handicaps. But I'll go even a step further. You wouldn't dare entertain the thought of putting your seventeen-year-old severely handicapped daughter to death if, God forbid she ever did become disabled? But yet you wholeheartedly support a woman's right to put to death her perfectly healthy developing child within her womb which is the case in over ninety-nine percent of legal abortions."

My remarks were not meant to be cruel or to hurt Mr. Jacobs' feelings, but only to help him to see how inconsistent his position was. And then I remembered that the last time I had used this argument in public was with Sharon Brolly, the news reporter with one hand. I could only pray that one day Mr. Jacobs would see the light as Miss Brolly had.

"I love both of my daughters very much," he told me. "If a tragedy like the one you described ever happened, I guess I would have to deal with it as best I could. But you're right, death would never be an option. But what about rape and incest? How could you expect a woman to carry the child of her rapist, or let's say the child of her own father?"

"I'm glad you asked that question," I replied. "To be honest with you, if a fifteen-year-old girl were raped and became pregnant as a result I would counsel her, in most cases, not to keep her baby. However, I would never counsel her to abort. The emotional trauma of being raped, coupled with the many other problems a girl so young would face in having to raise a child, makes the adoption alternative the optimal choice in these cases.

"Adoption, to put it very bluntly turns one person's garbage into another person's gold. Adoption is a win - win - win decision. When a woman decides to put her baby up for adoption instead of aborting it, she often is spared the tremendous feelings of guilt, grief and regret. While, on the other hand, women choosing the adoption alternative are often filled with joy, knowing that their child is being raised by a special family that couldn't have their own. And finally, the baby wins because he gets to live instead of die."

Mr. Jacobs looked thoughtful. "This is one area where I tend to agree with you, Louise," he said. "I've noticed that many people in the pro-choice camp are not very supportive of the adoption alternative, and that's disturbing. But I think every potential mother knows in her heart that if she ever did give birth she would find it incredibly difficult to give away her child. I have personally spoken to several women who have told me that they would rather abort their child than deliver it, and then put it up for adoption."

"That's very true. And the sad reality is that many people who are pro-abortion are anti-adoption. Many abortion clinics while mentioning adoption as an alternative to abortion have, nonetheless, in practice strongly discouraged it. In fact they have painted the decision to put up a baby for adoption in many cases as a fate worse than death. In the days and months ahead, we plan to do everything in our power to help make adoption the special middle ground that can bridge the gap between both sides." I leaned toward him smiling. "Mr. Jacobs," I said, "I hope you will join us in promoting this wonderful alternative to abortion?"

"I agree that adoption seems to offer some compromise for both sides and is something that should be explored further."

At that moment the show's theme music began, signaling that we were going to another break. So far I felt that I was more than holding my own against Mr. Jacobs. I was comfortable with what I was saying now but I wondered how much discomfort I was creating in those who did not agree with my stand. The cameraman was counting down with his fingers and I knew it was time to face the firing line once again.

"Louise," Mr. Jacobs said, taking a sip of coffee, "the one common thread I see running through your arguments is that you honestly believe that the unborn is a person, no matter what the stage of gestation."

"That's my contention exactly," I told him firmly. "The unborn is indeed a person and thus deserves to have the right to life."

"But for every person who feels that a fetus is a person, I can find you someone who disagrees. I'm sure you know that on legal grounds there has never been a case in U.S. law in which a fetus has been considered to be a person as the term is used and found in the Fourteenth Amendment of our U.S. Constitution. In fact the State of Texas failed to find even a single case. In the *Roe v. Wade* decision I quote again: 'On the other hand, the appellee conceded on reargument that no case could be cited that holds that a fetus is a person within the meaning of the Fourteenth Amendment.'"[43]

I was impressed that Mr. Jacobs was so familiar with *Roe v. Wade*. But I was willing to bet he wouldn't be as knowledgeable with another landmark Supreme Court decision.

"While I understand that you personally are against abortion under just about all circumstances, Louise," he said politely, but with a touch of sarcasm in his voice, "you cannot impose your own view of morality on an entire nation. I'm sure you wouldn't advocate imposing your own personal religious beliefs on people of differing faiths? Tolerance has always been a key to the American way of life and our system of beliefs and that's one reason we must never impose our views of abortion on a woman contemplating one."

"I hate to disagree with you," I told him, realizing that his persistence was the key to his attack on my ideas. While being perfectly pleasant and commending me on my presentation and my arguments, he continued to press his case. "Unfortunately," I continued, "our courts have been in the business of imposing their views of morality for a long time. I wonder if you are familiar with another equally famous U.S. Supreme Court decision handed down in 1857 by then Chief Justice Taney that dealt with the issue of keeping slavery legal in America. The exact case was called *Dred Scott, Plaintiff in Error, v. John F. A. Sandford.*"

"I am not very familiar with that case although I have heard of it, but knowing you, Louise I think I am about to learn something about it now."

He turned to smile at the audience, and as they began to laugh, I reached into my briefcase and pulled out a blue folder.

"I just happen to have the entire opinion of the Court with me," I told him. "I hope, after the show, you will take a copy home with you. It really makes fascinating reading. I wonder if I could please take a minute to read a portion of this 1857 landmark case?"

"I think all of us are curious to hear what our Supreme Court had to say on this case. Go right ahead, Louise."

"The following is a direct quote from Chief Justice Taney," I said, opening the folder.

"'It is difficult at this day to realize the state of public opinion in relation to that unfortunate race, which prevailed in the civilized and enlightened portions of the world at the time of the Declaration of Independence, and when the Constitution of the United States was framed and adopted. But the public history of every European nation displays it in a manner to plain to be mistaken.

"'They had for more than a century before been regarded as beings of an inferior order, and altogether unfit to associate with the white race, either in social or political relations; and so far inferior, that they had no rights which the white man was bound to respect; and that the negro might justly and lawfully be reduced to slavery for his benefit. He was bought and sold, and treated as an ordinary article of merchandise and traffic, whenever a profit could be made by it. This opinion was at that time fixed and universal in the civilized portion of the white race. It was regarded as an axiom in morals as well as in politics, which no one thought of disputing, or supposed to be open to dispute; and men in every grade and position in society daily and habitually acted upon it in their private pursuits, as well as in matters of public concern, without doubting for a moment the correctness of this opinion."'[44]

Mr. Jacobs scowled. It was clear that he had never expected to hear something that made my argument for me so compellingly. "I can only conclude that back in 1857 our Supreme Court decided to go with what they viewed as the prevailing opinion of their time," he admitted. "It appears as if they tried to justify their opinion based on surveys of what people believed and not on what was in the best interests of an entire race of people. I guess back then our U.S. Supreme Court was very colorblind."

"That's exactly right." I told him then that surveys and popular opinion were the guiding lights that helped illuminate our country's most brilliant legal minds back in 1857. Slavery was legal back then. That was the law. However, when a law is so fundamentally unsound, and the impact of following it is so devastating to millions of people, we must do more than just change the law. I then went on to point out to Mr. Jacobs that eight years after the infamous Dred Scott decision, our U.S. Constitution was amended. It took a great and bloody Civil War to ensure that this long overdue amendment, the XIII, was passed in 1865 finally putting an end to slavery. The addition of our XIII Amendment was a drastic step but it was necessary to correct a major flaw in the way our society functions. If slavery were allowed to continue, as sure as night follows day, our humanity would still have to be called into question.

"I think I know the next direction you plan to go now," he said, looking dead serious, "but I can tell you I'm not comfortable with it. I concede that our U.S. Supreme Court erred badly by classifying blacks as property, but I hope that you're not going to tell us that we should view the unborn in exactly the same way as blacks? A fetus clearly is not a person in the sense that a Negro slave was. That comparison would definitely be an unfair one."

"Mr. Jacobs," I said, "you're right about my direction but unfortunately we're travelling on different roads."

I went on to explain that blacks in America during the first half of the 1800's were stripped of their personhood and made to be nothing more than property. Today our U.S. Supreme Court has chosen not to learn from the past. I told Mr. Jacobs that, while reading the entire *Roe v. Wade* decision, I had noticed that Justice Blackmun had traveled the same route as Chief Justice Taney. He had conducted a survey of people's views in the past on abortion, and when he discovered that many found abortion acceptable, he then felt more comfortable in classifying the unborn into the same category as Justice Taney did with blacks. Just as Chief Justice Taney stripped away personhood from the black man, Justice Blackmun stripped personhood away from the unborn. And just as Justice Taney classified blacks as property, Justice Blackmun classified the unborn as the property of its owner – the mother.

It was time to make a personal appeal before the next and last break in the program.

"Starting today," I said, "I pray that all of you watching this show, who believe in the sanctity of life for all ages, will help me fight a new civil war against those members of our society that have chosen to close their eyes to our great American Holocaust – abortion. Our weapons will be our words and our educational advertisements. Our battle cry will be the silent screams of the millions of unborn victims who lie dead in the trash heaps of America. And our goal will be the establishment of a new constitutional amendment guaranteeing the unborn the right to life. Our abortion laws are fatally flawed and only a constitutional amendment can once and for all rescue an entire class of people from mass genocide."

"I really admire your compassion and concern for the unborn," Mr. Jacobs said stiffly and it was obvious that he was annoyed at my persistence. "But I'm just not comfortable with your comparison of a black slave to a fetus. Do you have any tangible evidence to support your claim that a fetus is a person? But, before you answer, we have to take another commercial break."

During our final break, Mr. Jacobs told me that I would make a first rate defense attorney. I wanted to believe that he was saying what he really thought but I couldn't understand why he was being so complimentary when I had been demonstrating the weaknesses in each of his arguments.

"I have to say you've really been a delight to have on the show," he said, assuming his usual gracious persona. It was impossible to measure his sincerity and I could only hope that I had made a dent in his prejudices. Even more important, had I managed to persuade some of the millions of people watching to change their minds? "You certainly are an excellent spokesperson for the right to life movement," he went on. "And I'm deeply encouraged to know that there are young people like yourself who are concerned about the important issues of our time. I only wish that there were more of our youths willing to take a stand and fight for a cause. But before I let you go, I'm very curious about this issue of personhood. As I asked before the break, can you really justify calling a fetus a person?"

"Well why don't we start with the concept of viability?" I asked him. "Viability basically is the ability a baby has to live outside its mother's womb before the normal nine months' gestation is complete. And to a large extent this ability is a function of the state of our medical technology."

"But what does that have to do with a fetus being a person?" he pressed me.

"Well, did you know that if a woman became pregnant during the nineteenth century and had to deliver her baby prematurely, say at seven months, its chances of survival were almost zero?"

"We aren't talking about the nineteenth century tonight, Louise," Mr. Jacobs snapped back.

"Hear me out," I told him. "But today, thanks to our sophisticated neonatal…"

"I suppose you're going to argue that a premature infant can be kept alive now," he interrupted me. "I think we all know that, Louise. No one's trying to set medicine back a century, you know."

I was angry, but I knew I couldn't show it. A lot depended on my remaining calm.

"I'm talking about viability, Bob," I said. Up to now I had been careful to use his last name, to be respectful. But he had taken the cuffs off and if he wanted to fight dirty, I was ready for him. But with only a few minutes left in the show, I hoped I wouldn't need to resort to saying something I might be sorry for later on.

"Bob, I would like to finish answering your question if that's OK with you," I said in my most sheepish voice.

He nodded his head for me to continue.

"As I was starting to say before, thanks to our advanced neonatal intensive care units, babies delivered prematurely, at as early as six months, stand a very good chance at survival. As a result if, at six months a fetus becomes viable, and if we induce labor at that point and allow modern medicine to take over, what do you suppose will happen?"

"Obviously, a premature baby will be delivered," Mr. Jacobs, curtly replied.

"Well, it's pretty clear to me that another tiny person will be born. Thus when we perform an abortion on a twenty-four-week-old 'viable' fetus we put to death a 'viable' person."

"But even in this case Louise, you're still talking about a premature infant and not a fetus. I hope you can come up with a better example than this one."

"Mr. Jacobs," I began, "today our society likes to define life in terms of which body systems or organs are functioning and which are not. I'm willing to accept that but only if we are willing to apply these same standards to all classes of people. For example, what do we call a person who no longer has measurable brain waves? Most of us would call that person dead. And if you're dead then you certainly can't be considered a person, now can you?"

He had another big smile on his face.

"I think we all can agree on that point, Louise," he said, laughing. But this time there was only a ripple of amusement and, looking out at the sea of faces, I realized that most of the audience was concentrating absolutely on what I was saying. There was nothing funny about any of this and they knew it.

"It's interesting to note that today, thanks to the tremendous advances in science, we have a clear consensus by just about every doctor and scientist that a tiny developing baby has measurable brainwaves at forty days,"[45] I said. "It's strange how eager we are to pull the plug on a person who is on artificial life support the moment his brain stops functioning. Yet women seeking an abortion insist on killing their baby whose brain is clearly functioning at forty days!"

The TV host continued to grin but I knew from the expression in his eyes that he knew he was on the losing end of this argument.

"Based on that logic I bet you're going to tell us that since a fetus has brain activity at forty days we should consider six weeks as the timeframe for establishing personhood?" he said.

"No, I think we can still go back even earlier. And by the way, at forty days we really can't call what's inside a mother's womb a fetus since that classification isn't even appropriate until around seven to eight weeks gestation. Now let's consider the human heart. If a person no longer has a heartbeat death usually results. And if you're dead, you're no longer a person. When someone suffers a massive heart attack, the undertaker is usually summoned. When the death certificate is typed up, it essentially states that this individual can no longer qualify as a person under the meaning and language of our XIV Amendment of the U.S. Constitution. Yet, we have a clear consensus by just about every doctor and scientist that at twenty-one days a mother has within her body two separate beating hearts.[46] Tell me how can you call a man whose heart has stopped beating dead but not call alive a baby at three weeks gestation whose heart is already beating?"

"From brainwaves to heartbeats. That's indeed a fascinating way to view the unborn, Louise. I can't deny that those are functions we all associate with life and death. But unfortunately we have run out of time."

He paused and suddenly I was aware that whatever he said next would be absolutely sincere.

"Louise," he said, "I really want to thank you for coming on the show. Your passion and commitment to the pro-life cause is most remarkable, especially for someone of your tender age. Your depth of knowledge and keen insights have certainly given all of us who disagree with your position plenty of food for thought. Ladies and gentlemen, this truly has been a unique night of television. God bless you, Louise Ann Jordan and good night."

With that Mr. Jacobs extended his hand to shake mine. He told me to not be a stranger and come back and visit again. Don't ask me how, but from that moment on I felt that one day, in the not too distant future, the two of us would be joining forces to defend life instead of taking it.

That night before I went to bed, I took the time to write the following letter.

Dear Mr. Jacobs:

When I let my mom know that I was going to appear on your show, she got so excited I thought she might have a heart attack. When I asked her what she liked most about you, she said, "Bob Jacobs is a man of great integrity. I really appreciate his honesty and intellect. He's also not afraid to ask those tough questions that most interviewers shy away from. In my book he's one classy gentleman."

Well as I began to prepare for some of those tough questions that I knew would be headed my way, I started to wonder just how did the original Bob Jacobs Show come into being. I hope that the following behind the scenes look at just how The Bob Jacobs Show came into creation will give you a better appreciation for the sanctity of human life, even at its earliest stages of development.

When a sperm and an egg cell unite, a most unique and wonderful miracle occurs: life begins. And that's how you began, as a single cell. That original Bob Jacobs cell, no bigger than the period at the end of a sentence, contained all the genetic materials needed to allow your precious life to begin its journey through time. And during your first eight weeks of existence an awesome explosion of life was occurring at breathtaking speed.

And I just marvel at the genius within you even at conception. Your one original cell knew how to exchange matter and energy in such intricate ways as to form entire body systems within that initial eight weeks of life. And the knowledge that must have been contained deep within its chambers is truly staggering.

From the moment of your conception, you became the master of your destiny and environment. That original Bob Jacobs cell was supplied with all the knowledge and plans needed to create the most dazzling array of differentiated cells, organs and body systems that, when viewed as a unit, we call life. You did it all! Yes your mother played a role by allowing you to use her womb as your temporary dwelling for nine months. And yes she supplied you with the raw materials needed to grow – nutrition and oxygen. With room and board secure you began to design and create a masterpiece that no

Picasso could ever paint or no Rodin could ever sculpt. While the canvass you used was hidden from everyone's view I would have given anything to watch those first eight weeks of the real Bob Jacobs Show.

Bob, with you acting as designer, director, producer and lead actor, I could have told you well in advance that you would become an instant hit. And if everything went according to plan your show would probably have a run of seventy to eighty wonderful years. But for any show to have a long run, it must have a great plot and a wonderful cast of characters. At conception The Bob Jacobs Show was really born. It just took nine more months to get everything in place for its gala opening. After the first eight weeks, most everything was set for the show. The remaining seven months were needed to add the finishing touches.

The plot was terrific: "Unique life explodes onto scene. Bob Jacobs is destined to change the way TV interviews are done." By the end of eight weeks the following casting was complete:

Heart was cast very early on at three weeks. By the end of week eight he became quite a leading man. He was beating up quite a storm and couldn't wait for opening night to arrive.

Arms and Legs got a call at four weeks[47] and became an instant hit with Heart. In fact Heart promised to support their movements for as long as the show ran.

At thirty days Blood was hired to make sure that the entire cast was well fed.[48] Everyone was amazed how Blood never seemed to take a break but was going about its task 24-7. Between the fourth and fifth week of production Mouth, Ear, Nose and Eye applied for a part.[49] They admitted that they were just starting out but promised that, by the end of the eighth week of production, they would all be major contributors to the show. They were signed to a lifetime contract and immediately Heart and Blood took them under their wing.

Brain had been on the set since about the time Heart was cast but it wasn't until week six that she felt she was ready to contribute to the show. By this time, she was really making waves with the entire cast and from that point on it became evident to all that Brain would make a great leading lady for Heart.

180

By the last week of casting, week eight, Heart and Brain began to take a very active role and were happy to welcome Stomach, Liver, Kidney and Taste Bud[50] to the set. By the fifty-sixth day Bob Jacobs was already destined for great stardom. By now the show was in full-scale production and the only thing that could prevent it from becoming a smash hit was a negative review by your mother and an early termination notice.

I know that a lot went into the making of The Bob Jacobs Show and I just wanted to say thanks for allowing me to appear on the adult version.

Sincerely,
Louise Ann Jordan

14

Changing Hearts

With *The Bob Jacobs Show* now behind me, I could only pray that my appearance would help with our launch of *Operation Sally*.

When we were together in the limo, being chauffeured back to our hotel room overlooking the park, Mom and Dad congratulated me. I knew that they were biased but I had to agree that I thought that even Bob Jacobs had been given something to think about. I really missed my little brother right then. I wished he could have come along but Dad felt it best for Don to stay at home this time given the seriousness of our short trip to New York City. But I knew that he had been watching me on TV and I hoped he was as proud of me as Mom and Dad were.

"I'm very interested to see just how the media will treat your interview," Dad said as the hotel doorman approached our car.

By the time we got to our hotel room that Thursday night, there was a message waiting for us to call Jennifer Poole at her home in Washington, D.C. I excitedly pushed the numbers on the hotel phone and nervously waited to hear how she felt the interview went. Her comments truly floored me.

"Louise," she said, "in all my years working to educate America on the evils of abortion and the sanctity of human life, I have never seen a more powerful, honest and convincing presentation. You countered every one of Bob Jacobs' clever retorts and turned all of his arguments around on him. And the best thing was that, by the end of the interview, he was visibly moved."

I thanked her for all the help she and Mrs. Gates had given me and when I told her that I couldn't have done it without their help, I really meant it. I never could have done as well if they had not spent that long afternoon fielding questions at me.

"It went better than well," Jennifer assured me. "Thanks to your interview, *Operation Sally* is off to a great start. All of us at NAL are deeply in your debt for everything you're doing on behalf of the unborn. I'll keep you posted on our next moves. God bless and let's stay in touch."

The following day was so full of excitement that I don't know where to even start. Dad got up early and went to see if the New York newspapers had any stories on my interview. When he got back to our hotel room, we all were just getting up.

"Take a look at this, Louise," he said, handing me a copy of *The New York Times*. I looked at the front page and just couldn't believe my eyes. Right there on the front page was a picture of Bob Jacobs and me sitting around a table. The headline read: "Bob Jacobs No Match for Teen."

As Mom and I sat on the edge of one of the king beds with sunlight pouring through our twentieth floor windows, Dad gave us a rundown of what had been written about the interview.

One of the writers had stated that the pro-choice movement clearly was dealt a major blow by my interview. He even went so far as to say that I had done a masterful job in unmasking the deceptive tactics and words used by the pro-choice camp in support of abortion. Another reporter admitted that she had been on the fence about abortion until last night, but after watching my interview, she was convinced that abortion is clearly wrong.

"Dad, that's incredible," I said.

To hear liberal New York City newspapers giving our movement positive press was nothing short of a miracle. I had expected perhaps a small article buried in the middle of the newspapers but thanks to the general popularity of *The Bob Jacobs Show* I had made the front covers of several New York City newspapers. Never in my wildest dreams had I imagined that, overnight, I would be propelled into this sort of national celebrity.

I guess mom summed it up best when she said that prayer does indeed still work.

Over the next several weeks, the entire nation was blanketed with a massive pro-life advertising campaign the likes of which had never been seen before. Jennifer Poole knew that it would take a lot of work and money to inform America on just what abortion was all about and, thanks to Mr. Moss, she now had it to spend.

Millions of Americans were still unfamiliar with the different types of monstrous abortion techniques. Millions knew very little about fetal development during the first trimester. Millions were shocked when they found out that in many states a minor could get an abortion without parental notification or consent. Millions of Americans were amazed to learn that hundreds of thousands of couples would instantly adopt a newborn baby from a mother who decided to bring her baby to term instead of aborting it. And millions more were outraged to learn that abortion is basically legal in all fifty states right up until birth.

NAL knew that, if people became educated in a fair and honest way to all the truths surrounding abortion, many would change their stance and, as a consequence, they planned to use every means possible to inform our country why every baby conceived in the womb deserves the right to life.

Looking back on my own abortion, I realized that my lack of knowledge concerning what was taking place inside my womb had cost my baby her life. And now I was convinced that people, when given the facts, can and have, in many cases, totally changed the way they view abortion. I did. Nurse Patterson did. Sharon Brolly did. And just last week I learned that our U.S. Congressman, Todd Oliver, had issued a statement saying that after carefully reviewing all sides of the abortion debate that he could no longer support abortion on demand. He felt that he could no longer support a woman's right to choose if it meant taking the life of her developing baby.

If a young teen, a professional nurse, a powerful newspaper reporter and a member of one of our highest elective offices could change, then so could many more Americans. But we would need many more to change the way they looked at abortion if NAL's goal of establishing a new constitutional amendment protecting the life of the unborn ever wanted to become a reality.

Just as that monstrous system of human bondage called slavery could only be defeated through a great civil war and the passage of a constitutional amendment, I also believed that the only way to put an end to abortion was to travel that same path by waging a new war called *Operation Sally* and by passing a new pro-life constitutional amendment.

After we had lunch that day, our limo met us at the hotel to take us back to Palmerville. The past twenty-four hours had been, needless to say, quite an experience for the entire Jordan family. As we drove home, our driver, a man in his fifties with a handlebar mustache, said he wanted to ask me a very important question concerning my interview with Bob Jacobs.

"Before I saw you on *The Bob Jacobs Show,* I knew very little about abortion," he said, as he skillfully negotiated through New York City traffic. "I didn't know the law, I didn't know what was going on inside a mother's womb and I certainly didn't know anything about the horrible methods used to perform abortions. I consider myself a fairly intelligent and basically moral person. Yet, after watching you last night I realized that not only was I uninformed but I was also misinformed. And that's the real tragedy because people who want to do the right thing often are deceived into believing a lie."

"And even worse than that," Mom added, "acting on it."

My mom had really changed a lot since this had all begun. She had always been a wonderful mother, loving and warm, but now she seemed to project a new understanding of the world, and especially the world inside the womb.

By now our driver was becoming animated and I could hear from the tone of his voice that he was pretty upset to discover that he had been sold a bill of goods.

"For abortion clinics to tell us that they are only removing pregnancy tissue when they perform an abortion on a twelve-week-old fetus, just sickens me," he said, swerving to avoid a speeding red Corvette. "I saw what a twelve-week-old fetus looks like and it not only looks like a baby, it *is* a baby. After my wife and I finished watching you, we both became convinced that we could never support abortion. Before last night we really had no strong opinion either way. But once we understood what an actual abortion is designed to accomplish, it became easy to know what position we needed to take."

Now it was Dad's turn to voice his displeasure at the misinformation that was rampantly spread whenever pro-choice people talk about abortion.

"My daughter fell victim to these lies," he said, "and as a result I will never be able to hold our first granddaughter in my arms."

"Do you have any specific examples of what pro-life organizations plan to do in the coming months to combat the pro-choice lies?" our driver asked.

It was wonderful to me to realize that my very first encounter with someone other than my family should prove that my television interview had reached so many ordinary people, so many of them, like our driver, eager to know the truth.

By now, we were just entering Palmerville and it really felt good to be home. The events of the past twenty-four hours, while exciting, had been very draining. As we pulled into our driveway an all too familiar scene greeted us. Several news trucks were again waiting to greet our return. By now I was quite comfortable in dealing with the media and asked dad if I could spend a little time talking with the reporters.

"You've earned the right to do that without asking my permission," he assured me, grinning. "After all, you're a veteran of *The Bob Jacobs Show*. Besides, it's about time that we begin to use the media as an ally and not the opposition."

"Miss Jordan, you were terrific on *The Bob Jacobs Show* last night," a young reporter began as I took my place standing right between our front porch and about ten reporters, each eager to fire more questions my way. "You seemed to have an answer for every question. But do you actually think that you can change enough hearts and minds to influence our legislative leaders to lobby for the passage of a constitutional amendment? As you are probably aware in order to amend our Constitution you need to have two-thirds of Congress and three-quarters of the states vote for any new amendment. You're nowhere near that support level yet."

Over the past few months, I began to learn that in order to alter people's beliefs you have to use the media. I think Adolf Hitler once remarked that if you tell people a lie long enough and hard enough they will come to believe it. The pro-choice forces for over twenty-five years have used this strategy to spread their lies about abortion and the unborn throughout America. And they have skillfully recruited the media as their ministers of propaganda. As a result of this alliance, millions have been seduced into believing that a woman's right to choose must take precedence over a baby's right to live. Trying to reach these many millions who bought the lie, would prove impossible unless we could drive a wedge in between this unholy alliance. I knew that my dad's advice on using the media to help highlight our cause as we continued our campaign would prove critical.

"That's a great question," I replied, smiling. I was glad that Jennifer had helped me choose a new wardrobe for my trip to New York and other public appearances. I was wearing a blue linen suit. I didn't want to look older than I was, but I wanted to look businesslike. "Over the next few weeks we're going to do our best to use every available means to educate and convince people as to why we must put an end to legalized abortion. The only favor I ask of you, the media, is that you cover our activities fairly."

"Can you give us some examples about how you think we should do that?" another reporter asked gruffly. From the tone in his voice it appeared he felt that the media already presented both sides of the issue fairly.

"Well if you think we are distorting the truth, then tell your viewers and readers that we are. If you feel our billboards are in bad taste, don't hold back in letting everyone know about it. If you don't like the tone of our presentations then let us have it. And if you conclude, after seeing and hearing all we have to say, that we are wrong, then write about it and share the reasons why you disagree. But if we make a compelling case on why abortion should be outlawed then please let your readers and viewers know that it may just be time to rethink the way we view life inside the womb. I hope we have a deal."

I didn't sense a lot of enthusiasm to my challenge but there was one reporter that said she would take me up on my offer. Another question from the assembled news media concerned our Constitution.

"Many people have referred to the United States Constitution as one of the greatest documents ever written. In many respects it is a wonderful document that grants Americans tremendous freedoms. Can you tell us why you feel so strongly that it needs to be amended?"

"Well consider this," I told him. "If you were black and lived in America in 1850, this document served to ensure your total bondage by endorsing the institution of slavery. And if you were a woman living in America in 1910 the precious privilege of voting was not yet an option available to her. When rights, which we as Americans consider foundational, are denied to an entire class of people it is not enough to complain or debate the merits of the issue. And it is not even enough to pass laws that attempt to correct these situations. The only appropriate solution is to radically alter the flawed document that created the problem in the first place. And thank God we passed our XIII and XIX amendments abolishing slavery and giving women the right to vote.

"Today an entire class of persons are denied an even more foundational right – the right to live. Abortion kills approximately 1.5 million babies a year. I believe our U.S. Constitution must be amended to guarantee all people from conception to natural death the right to life or else remain a fatally flawed document."

By now I could see that this informal press conference was once again giving me a great opportunity to get free news coverage for the pro-life cause. As I looked to my left, I noticed my old friend from WRRM news, Roger Topaz, standing by my mom. As we made eye contact, we both smiled. He then raised his hand to ask a question.

"Good to see you Mr. Topaz," I said in acknowledgment. Roger Topaz had covered my first TV appearance back in September when my crusade for life first began. He was a favorite of mine and I knew his question would be a sincere one.

"It's good to see you too, Louise," he said, in his gentle but deep baritone voice. "One problem that I have with people who are pro-life is that many of them also support the death penalty. Don't you see an inconsistency in being both pro-life and pro-death penalty?"

"That's a great question, Mr. Topaz. It's interesting to note that there are many people who support abortion but are against the death penalty. And on the other hand there are people who are against abortion but support the death penalty. The real question is which side takes a more consistent position. Pro-lifers who support the death penalty for heinous crimes basically are advocating death for people who obviously have little regard for human life. This position is not at all inconsistent. In essence a pro-life, pro-death penalty position advocates death to vicious, violent and guilty criminals who have murdered innocent life but advocate putting a stop to the vicious, violent and deadly destruction of innocent babies who have committed absolutely no crime. The real inconsistency can be found with pro-choice individuals who oppose the death penalty for violent men who murder women and children in cold blood, yet wholeheartedly support the killing of completely innocent unborn children."

I answered a few more questions before I felt it was time to go inside. I was amazed at how calm and relaxed I felt after holding this impromptu press conference. I felt my answers were right on target and that something like this Q & A was just the confidence builder I needed after a very stressful evening on *The Bob Jacobs Show*. As I walked toward my front door my brother Don came over to me and gave me a big welcome home kiss. He told me that he loved me and that God would one day reward me for all the good work I was doing. But at that moment those words of love and encouragement were reward enough.

15

Operation Sally

Over the next few weeks and months, thanks to the tireless fundraising efforts of Eddie Moss, NAL began to flood our TV and radio airwaves, newspapers, billboards, the internet and the hearts and minds of all Americans with the truth about the unborn and the horrors of abortion.

Some of our most effective communications were handled through the print media. Over one hundred of the largest circulating daily newspapers contained a series of several different ads. Each ad was designed to talk about a different aspect surrounding the entire abortion debate. Four different full-page ads were placed on four consecutive Mondays, each one telling a powerful story.

Our first ad had magnificent full color pictures of three developing babies at twelve, sixteen and twenty week's gestation. Accompanying these pictures was a wonderful description of fetal development from week one through week twenty. And at the bottom of the ad was a written statement signed by over fifty of our world's leading scientists and doctors endorsing their belief that at the moment of conception life begins.

Our second ad, which hit the newspapers the following Monday, focused on the theme – "Why Can't We Love Them Both." This ad was divided into two parts. On the left hand side was a listing of all the services and referrals a crisis pregnancy center provides an

190

expectant mother uncertain as to whether to keep or abort her baby. The long list of services included providing maternity clothes, baby clothes, psychological counseling, free prenatal care, adoption aid and even a place to stay if a hostile home environment threatened her very safety. On the right hand side, there was a "list" of the services provided by a local abortion clinic. Strangely the only word that appeared was "NONE."

On the third Monday, another ad appeared, describing in vivid detail why abortion is such a great threat to our very humanity. It described both graphically and factually some of the most common abortion methods and finally showed in chart format the striking parallels between legalized abortion and what used to be legalized slavery.

Our final fourth ad was aimed at teens and the parents of teens. It taught the three "A s" – Abstinence, Adoption and Abortion. Each "A" was discussed and the ad closed with the following question addressed to teens and unmarried young adults: "Did you know that, when you practice abstinence, it shows you love yourself and your body. But if you get pregnant and decide to put your child up for adoption, it shows you love your baby. However, if you become pregnant and choose to abort your child, just whom are you choosing to love?"

This four-week, four-ad campaign, appearing as it did in one hundred plus newspapers across the country, cost millions of dollars and proved extremely effective. Each one of the ads included the name and address of the National Alliance for Life as the ad sponsor and the number of calls and letters generated was so overwhelming that NAL had to hire a dozen extra temporary staff just to keep up with the avalanche of mail and phone calls. The vast majority of letters and calls were very positive. Many wrote in to tell NAL that, because of the ads, they had changed their stance from pro-choice to pro-life. NAL's one big concern was the same as mine: how would the media view our massive attempt to educate Americans on the evils of abortion?

While there was not a lot of positive coverage, there were several major newspapers and magazines that actually endorsed our ads as being very factual and tasteful. And in an almost unprecedented decision, one of the big four television networks chose to run a one-hour news special describing the recent events surrounding the pro-life movement. I was interviewed and the segment in which I was featured was called *The Louise Phenomenon.*

But what proved to be the most gratifying thing we noticed coming from the media was that they chose not to attack our campaign. Most remained totally silent, which given their usual vocal pro-abortion stand was the equivalent of endorsing our position. Indeed, the tide was turning so quickly that none of us could believe how far we had come in the past seven months. But we also knew we still had a long way to go before we could reach our ultimate goal of placing all human life under the protective wing of an amended U. S. Constitution.

While NAL used TV and radio to air short spots on many of the different aspects surrounding abortion perhaps their most powerful visual presentation was a very professionally produced thirty-minute infomercial on life inside the womb. It aired on just about every major cable network and local media market in the country in early March and was viewed by over twenty million people. Once again, I was privileged to play a major role in the production and implementation of the project.

Usually infomercials are created to sell a product. Ours, however, was designed to educate and sell the concept that life begins at conception and that abortion kills babies. NAL did a masterful job in focusing on one single theme throughout the entire infomercial. In a very unique and powerful way, our organization demonstrated that, from conception until birth, a baby is present and that, in every instance, abortion destroys a living person. That single point was made again and again from every conceivable direction. Portions of several of my interviews were incorporated into the infomercial. And four of the most powerful exhibits from our *Children of the Womb* museum presentation were shown.

Also shown were interviews with former abortion doctors and nurses, newspaper reporters and several U. S. Senators and Congressmen. One interview in particular stands out in my mind. Congressman Todd Oliver, who recently became a pro-lifer, principally through viewing our *Children of the Womb* museum project, shared the following touching comments:

"For years I felt that a woman with an unwanted pregnancy had every right to decide if she wanted to keep or abort her baby. I never thought much about what was going on inside of a woman's body. My focus was on the stress these women must be going through and how they needed to make the final decision. But one day, I was invited to the opening night of the *Children of the Womb* pro-life exhibit in Palmerville, New York. That night, for the first time, I was challenged to consider just what stress the abortion decision puts on the second person involved in an unwanted pregnancy, the child itself. When I was confronted with the clear scientific reality that abortion stops a beating heart, silences measurable brainwaves, severs tiny but perfectly healthy arms and legs and crushes a human skull, I knew I had a major decision to make. I either had to deny the undeniable fact that abortion kills a human being and live with that knowledge or else let my conscience heal by saying no to abortion and yes to life. I thank God that today my conscience is clean and my senses are all back in touch with reality."

Several of the most respected doctors in the world discussed fetal development and presented powerful arguments that so clearly demonstrated the humanity of the unborn that even the staunchest of pro-choice advocates would be hard pressed to combat this avalanche of scientific evidence.

But perhaps the most powerful section of the infomercial came at the end. Working with a team of several doctors and scientists, NAL put together a ninety-second video showing how a baby grows within the womb from conception till six months. I remember watching a film in school on how a plant grows using time lapse photography and being amazed to see how an entire plant grew within thirty seconds as selected pictures were used to speed up plant growth at a phenomenal speed. This same concept was used to film what was going on inside a woman's womb during her first six months of a pregnancy.

Throughout this ninety-second segment the film editor did a wonderful job in blending frame after frame so that what we actually were seeing was the development and growth of a real baby. The only difference was that we were watching six months of growth compacted into ninety-seconds. This fantastic explosion of growth was done so professionally that I just sat spellbound watching life develop right before my eyes.

At the end of this brilliant ninety-second time lapse photographic essay on fetal growth, the narrator made these closing comments, ending with a question aimed at riveting the viewers attention.

"Ladies and gentlemen," he said. "We have come to the end of our journey. Every one of you watching this show is fortunate because your mother allowed you to continue your journey through life. Unfortunately, every year in America approximately 1.5 million of our newest citizens are told, just as their life is being wonderfully mapped out, that it must abruptly come to an end.

"Back in 1776 a very special birth took place. You see on July 4, 1776 the Continental Congress adopted our Declaration of Independence in the city of brotherly love – Philadelphia. On that day the great nation of America was born. For over two hundred years, the following words have stood as the bedrock that we have chosen to build our country on: 'We hold these Truths to be self-evident, that all Men are created equal, that they are endowed by their Creator with certain unalienable Rights, that among these are Life, Liberty, and the Pursuit of Happiness...'[51]

"Looking back on our nation's history it's almost impossible to imagine that the entire black race for almost ninety years were denied two of these three foundational rights. We can thank God that this incredibly ugly period of our history is now just that, history. However, since 1973 another entire class of persons – the unborn – have been denied all three of these foundational rights if they happen to be conceived in the wrong womb. Discrimination based upon place of residence is alive and well today in America.

"The National Alliance for Life asks you to carefully consider the thirty minute presentation you have just watched. Are we just removing 'pregnancy tissue' or 'birth matter' when a woman has an abortion, or are we actually taking the life of a precious new person? At the bottom of your screen we have placed a toll free phone number and our Internet site, www.ISITABABY.com for you to respond to the following question: 'Do you believe that abortion takes the life of a child?'

"Please cast your vote now. Some will tell you that abortion takes only potential life. Others say that abortion may take a life but it's not the life of a human being. Still others contend that abortion may take the life of a human being but not the life of a person. Please don't let semantics influence how you respond. We hope that we have given you enough evidence to cast your vote in favor of personhood. God bless you and good night."

As a young girl one thing I always enjoyed, was traveling by car with my family during vacation, and looking at all the different products that were advertised on those big outdoor billboards that dotted our highways. During *Operation Sally* NAL spent a great deal of money placing several innovative pro-life *Advertisements for Life* ads on over two thousand billboards across America.

One billboard showed a magnificent photograph of a five-month-old baby sucking her thumb, safe and secure, in her amniotic sac with the following words under her picture: "I wonder what she's thinking? She has a wonderful life ahead of her – please don't abort her." But my personal favorite billboard ad had two beautifully photographed four-month-old twins each floating inside their own amniotic sacs. The words beneath these precious twins really touched my heart: "James, plans to become a doctor. Judy wants to practice law. The only thing that can alter their plans is an abortion. Please let their dreams come true – Choose Life."

Over the past few months NAL had also spent a lot of time and money designing a unique website. With just the click of a mouse, you could locate just about every crisis pregnancy center in America. Another click called up extensive adoption information. And still another click would link you to a special gallery of photos. This amazing collection of photos of unborn children at all stages of fetal development was a powerful visual aid designed to document the existence of life at its earliest stages.

On a more disturbing note, another mouse click took you into the death chamber room. Users were cautioned about entering this area since each abortion technique performed today was discussed and graphically shown.

Links to abortion and the law, personal testimonies from former abortionists, listings of support groups for women suffering the damaging aftermath effects of abortion, and lots more useful material made the NAL website an important electronic tool in the fight for life.

As *Operation Sally* continued to blanket America, I was given permission to take the rest of the school year off and travel throughout the country speaking out on the sanctity of life and the evils of abortion. I was privileged to speak at high school assemblies, to debate pro-choice advocates at an Ivy League university, to appear on several major TV news shows and be the keynote speaker at a major pro-life rally to be held in July in Washington, D.C.

Fortunately, whenever I returned home, my mom would be there to help me with my schoolwork. My mom was simply the best. She knew that if I just left school this early during my sophomore year I would lose all credit for the spring term. I'll never forget the conversation we had leading up to Palmerville High's decision to allow me to take the rest of the year off:

"Louise," she said, "Principal Foster wants you to be able to share the pro-life message but he also knows that missing several months of school would make it impossible to give you any credit for the spring term."

"Mom, I really want to do this. Jennifer said she has great plans for me and has hundreds of potential speaking opportunities."

"I agree. These opportunities are too important to pass by, especially with *Operation Sally* moving into high gear."

"Any ideas on how we could get around this dilemma," I asked.

"Well, as a matter of fact I think I have a way for you to both travel and attend school," she told me, as she motioned me to sit with her at our kitchen table. "I talked it over with Principal Foster and he said he was willing to let me home school you during the rest of the year."

"That's great mom but what do you know about home schooling?"

"Not a whole lot, Louise," she said with that shy grin I knew so well, "but I spoke to several women from our church who have been home schooling their children for years. They told me that it's a lot of work but if I was serious they would help me learn the ropes fairly quickly."

"Mom, are you sure you can handle it? More important, are you sure you want to? It would really mean a lot to me. But I'm certain that this will mean a lot more work for you." And of course I was concerned if she could handle something that she had never done before.

"I'm willing to give it a try," she told me, now placing both her hands on my shoulders and smiling right into my eyes. "I think it will be fun and give us an opportunity to spend a lot more time together than we've been able to these past six months."

"Yea, mom it will be great. Studying together, discussing math and science, and while I'm away I can read my English books."

"Before you get too excited remember there are still going to be tests to take," she reminded me mischievously, "just like if you were attending your classes."

"You wouldn't have the heart to fail me - would you, Mom?"

"Don't push it, Louise," she said, laughing.

These were wonderful times in my life. I knew I would be extremely busy trying to balance my speaking engagements and schoolwork; but somehow I knew I would be able to handle it with a little help - well, a lot really - from my parents and NAL.

During the following month NAL instituted a major new volunteer initiative. Eddie Moss was put in charge of all volunteer activities and was given the nickname "General Moss" by Mrs. Gates. NAL flew in over seven hundred key local pro-life activists from all over the country to their D.C. headquarters. Each of these volunteers were put through an intensive one-week training course, similar to the one I had undergone.

As these new troops returned to their hometowns, they immediately began to disseminate literature in massive quantities. Many were able to line up speaking engagements at their local schools and for the first time NAL began to give Planned Parenthood a real run for their money.

Thanks to NAL and General Moss our soldiers were sent out equipped with a powerful arsenal of weapons. And as they marched, they carried with them the banner of truth.

One of their most effective offensive weapons was information. Unlike Planned Parenthood, they truly had a host of options a teen could choose to review if they got pregnant, as well as a wide variety of places they could go to for loving support. And unlike Planned Parenthood, which often encouraged teens to hide their sexual experiences from their parents, these soldiers worked to strengthen family ties by encouraging them to discuss these peer pressures to have sex with their parents.

Another weapon with which these frontline fighters girded themselves was prayer. During the past few months churches and synagogues throughout America began to join together as never before to pray for the unborn. Prayer meetings started popping up all across the country to specifically pray to end legalized abortion.

Armed with the truth, packed with information and backed by prayer the evil forces of Planned Parenthood with their pro-choice faithful were beginning to suffer massive setbacks.

Students by the thousands and by the hundreds of thousands were signing pledges agreeing to abstain from sex until marriage. Abstinence was no longer looked at as a sign of being a wimp but had become a symbol of courage and character.

On the political front, General Moss' ground troops launched an all out push to educate our legislative leaders. NAL firmly believed that, if we were ever going to get a Right to Life Constitutional Amendment passed, we needed to get our elected officials on board. With this in mind, NAL began telling their ever-growing network of volunteers to set up meetings with their local and congressional legislators in order to share their pro-life stories. The reports being sent back to D.C. were extremely encouraging. In little more than a two-month period NAL volunteers conducted personal meetings with over twelve hundred different politicians across America.

Our infomercial question on whether or not the unborn is a child yielded a staggering yes percentage. We received over two hundred fifty thousand phone calls and over three million hits to our website in response to our simple, yet profound question. When we tallied all of the responses ninety-three percent said that abortion does indeed take the life of a child. It now became almost impossible for the pro-choice lobby to deny that abortion kills a person.

Their time-tested strategy of attacking the character of the pro-life community was also now failing miserably. Ever since we launched our "Why Can't We Love Them Both" theme, the love that pro-lifers continued to show mothers facing an unwanted pregnancy became the hallmark of everything we did.

And their once most reliable ally, the media, finally decided, by and large, to stay on the sidelines and watch while this epic struggle for the very soul of a nation was being waged on a level battlefield. Without the heavy support from their main propaganda machine, the pro-abortion forces had no viable strategy to combat the truth that we were now sounding from every venue we could find.

By now we were in the middle of April and Jennifer Poole called me with an exciting idea for a new interview she was trying to set up on *The Jill Morgan Show*. Jill Morgan, like Bob Jacobs, hosted a live one-hour weekly interview show. Her show was based in California and each week she would discuss a hot button issue. And nine times out of ten her opinions would be the opposite of her guest.

"Two days ago Jill Morgan gave me a call and asked if she could do an interview with you," she told me.

I had just finished my dinner when Jennifer called and when she mentioned appearing on *The Jill Morgan Show* my first reaction was to refuse. Jill Morgan was young, articulate, blond, and beautiful but also a national spokesperson for the pro-choice cause. Spending an hour with her would be like throwing me into the water with the sharks and I told Jennifer I didn't think I would be able to handle it.

"I knew you might feel uncomfortable being on her show alone, Louise," she said, "so this time, instead of doing a one on one interview I'd like to invite two other guests to appear with you."

"You mean sort of like a panel discussion?"

"Yes - and I think you're going to enjoy the theme because I told Jill Morgan that I'd like to do a show that focused exclusively on the question of personhood."

Having two other people on the show would certainly take a lot of the pressure off me as well as give our debate on the personhood of the unborn some great national exposure. "But just who are the other two guests," I anxiously asked.

"One gentleman is a seventy-four-year-old former high school science teacher named John Temple who is the great-great grandchild of Jerry Temple, a former slave from Georgia, who worked on a cotton plantation. Jill's other guest will be Max Werner. Max is a retired Jewish doctor, who spent two years in Dachau during World War II."

"You're an absolute genius, Jennifer!" I told her. "I can see how this panel discussion will make for one fascinating night of television."

"I'm glad you're excited about the show," she told me. "Jill really liked the idea too."

We all agreed to a May 6th show date. Needless to say, I was more than just a little curious to meet these two elder gentlemen. And thanks to Jennifer I didn't have to wait long.

16

Personhood

The week before my appearance on *The Jill Morgan Show,* Jennifer arranged to fly John Temple, Max Werner and myself down to Washington, D.C. for two days of informal meetings. I will never forget our first meeting. John Temple and Max Werner were already sitting with Jennifer Poole and Sally Gates in a conference room adjacent to Mrs. Gates' office when my mom and I arrived. This was the first time my mom had visited D.C. and when she asked if I wouldn't mind if she came along for the trip I quickly said yes.

When we arrived at NAL headquarters, Mrs. Gates made the formal introductions. I was really excited to meet Mr. Temple, a tall and imposing gentleman and Mr. Werner, a kind looking elderly man with a moderately heavy German accent. I had so many questions to ask both of them that I didn't know where to start.

In the first place, I couldn't wait to learn more about that dark period in our nation's history called slavery, as well as what it was like to be inside a Nazi concentration camp during World War II. I knew that both of my new friends would be able to share stories and insights that could never be found in my history books at school. After we had chatted for a few minutes, Jennifer Poole began to share what she hoped to accomplish by having all three of us appear on *The Jill Morgan Show.*

"First, I want to thank all of you for taking the time to come down to D.C.," she said. "As you are all aware, during the past six months there has been an amazing change in America in the way people view abortion."

"Thanks in no small part to our young friend Louise," John Temple acknowledged.

"Louise's role has indeed been nothing short of a miracle," Jennifer agreed, smiling and nodding at the same time.

"And without some divine help," Max Werner added, "we could never have come so far in such a short period of time."

"No doubt about that, Mr. Werner, without God's help I could never have done anything."

"Please, Louise call me Max. And I'm sure my friend Big John would rather be called John than Mr. Temple."

"Louise, only my students used to call me Mr. Temple. We're all family here so please call me John."

"Then can I call you Big John, Mr. Temple?"

"It's a deal."

As I smiled at this aged but gentle looking giant of a man, I felt strangely attracted to the inner beauty that Big John seemed to emanate whenever he spoke. His soothing voice made me so relaxed that I was glad he would be right by my side when I entered that California studio next week.

"After talking with many pro-life leaders, we at NAL feel that the climate and time are now just right to actively craft and lobby for the passage of a Right to Life Constitutional Amendment," Jennifer began. She was obviously excited at this prospect and her eyes became alive with anticipation. "Eight months ago, this idea was only a distant dream. But today, thanks to the amazing events of this past year, we believe our dream can finally become a reality."

"Everything has completely changed since Louise shook up our nation back in September," Mrs. Gates added. "Thanks to her a unique door of opportunity has been wonderfully opened to us."

"Yes, but sometimes doors can suddenly close. Therefore, we must act quickly and decisively since the momentum is clearly with us," Jennifer said, now looking totally serious.

"We're all with you as far as the need to move quickly is concerned," Big John concurred.

"Each one of us," Big John continued, "knows the ugly side effects of what can happen when a civilized society throws away their ability to properly define humanity. A great civil war was needed to end discrimination based on skin color. A mighty World War was necessary to put a stop to discrimination based on religion. And today I believe that divine intervention has opened a way for us to see discrimination, based on which womb conception takes place, finally come to an end."

"Well said, John! And that's why I've brought the three of you together," Jennifer exclaimed. "Each of you has a unique perspective on discrimination and how it relates to the issue of personhood. I want all of you to spend the next two days sharing your insights with one another so that on May 6th we can show America the powerful personhood parallels that exist among Negro slaves, German Jews and unborn fetuses."

"I can't wait for the show," my mom added. "I think you've assembled a great team."

I had such a good time just getting to know Max and Big John better that by the end of our two-day "mini" conference I had fallen in love with both of them. Both were strongly pro-life and were personal friends of Jennifer Poole and Mrs. Gates. Their backgrounds, however, were vastly different.

John Temple was a retired high school biology teacher who lived his entire life in the state of Tennessee. He had four children, eleven grandchildren and three great-grandchildren. At six foot four inches tall and two hundred sixty pounds, he was quite a massive figure. But despite his size, John was a humble man who was just full of love and compassion. I felt so comfortable in his presence that, by the time we departed from Washington, I asked if I could call him grandpa. He was the first Temple family member to attend college and he graduated with honors. He loved to read books and travel. But most of all he enjoyed just spending time with his children and grandchildren.

John told us that his great-great grandfather, Jerry Temple, was born in 1839 in Mobile, Alabama. At the age of seven, he was taken from his parents and sold to another slave owner in Georgia. As John Temple continued to share from his past, it became evident to all of us that he was a master storyteller. Just listening to Big John's stories made me feel as though I were living back in the South during the middle of the nineteenth century. I was getting an incredible history lesson about one of our nation's saddest periods without ever having to attend school.

Max Werner, on the other hand, had grown up in Hamburg, Germany. As a teenager, he loved to chase young ladies and play soccer. Max was a brilliant premed student, who even as a junior in college, knew he wanted to become a heart surgeon. Unfortunately all those dreams radically changed when one day Max was awoken from his sleep by two German soldiers and transported to a concentration camp at Dachau. For two years Max had to endure the most inhumane conditions imaginable. But they could never break his spirit. After being set free at the end of the war, Max made his way to America and five years later finished medical school. And during the next thirty years he established himself as one of California's top heart specialists.

Max, like John Temple, was a big man. He may have stood only five feet ten inches tall but he was built like a tree trunk. We hit it off instantly and I knew that my life was going to be that much richer because of these two special people. As Max shared his experiences with John and me, he literally took both of us on a journey to the very center of hell. As he described some of the atrocities that Jews had to endure in these death camps, I felt sick at heart. Max felt that there must have been a strong demonic influence in Germany during the time of the war for such evil to exist.

Well these were my two new friends. It's strange how a common cause has a way of bringing people from totally different backgrounds together. Yet here we were. And somehow I knew that our differences were only going to serve to strengthen the bond among us.

After I returned home to Palmerville, I made a conscious decision to spend the entire week, leading up to our show appearance, just relaxing and spending time with my family and friends. I even got to catch up on a lot of my schoolwork. My batteries were really running low and this week away from the spotlight proved to be just what the doctor ordered. In fact, this was the first entire week that I was able to be at home in months due to my heavy speaking schedule.

Two days before our show Jennifer arranged to fly John, Max and myself out to Los Angeles to settle in and make any last minute preparations. On our first night in LA Jennifer, Mrs. Gates and the three of us met for dinner and unexpectedly, very little of our conversation focused on abortion and personhood. Instead we just swapped personal stories and enjoyed our time together. We really didn't need to discuss the heavy issues that would very shortly take center stage. As we all agreed, if we didn't know what we were going to say by now, then one extra night of preparation wasn't going to make much difference.

The one thing that both Jennifer and Mrs. Gates did spend a few minutes on was to remind us that Jill Morgan was one of the most outspoken pro-choice women in America. Mrs. Gates told us that she didn't expect us to change Jill's mind but hoped we could leave her audience with plenty of things to think about.

On the Friday morning of the show I was up early. I felt like I needed to spend some time by myself in prayer. To my surprise when I met the gang for breakfast Big John and Max told me that they, too, had been up very early to pray. I think that all three of us realized that a little divine help was going to prove essential if we wanted viewpoints to be changed.

Jennifer told us that we needed to be at the studio by three and offered to drive us around the San Fernando Valley to view the magnificent scenery of southern California. After spending a few hours just seeing the sights, Jennifer, always a stickler for being punctual, drove us right up to the entrance of the building where *The Jill Morgan Show* was recorded at precisely three. The studio was located in downtown Burbank, California, which Mrs. Gates told us, was known as the Media Capital of the World.

By now I was pretty familiar with the routine that took place prior to appearing on a major TV talk show. We spent a good twenty minutes talking to the show's producer in the Green Room and met several celebrities that also happened to be in the studio that day. After make-up we all met Jill Morgan and knew immediately that we were going to be in for a real fight for life. She told Big John, Max and myself that while she respected our right to be pro-life she planned to let the laws of our land do the talking tonight.

Jill Morgan was everything that I had pictured her to be. Her long blond hair, deep baby blue eyes and million-dollar smile made her one stunningly attractive young woman. But the dark blue business suit she wore made her look totally businesslike. Like Bob Jacobs, she was a skilled debater, but unlike him, she was tenacious in her ability to present her side of an issue, even if it meant going toe to toe with her guests. And unlike Bob Jacobs, I knew I wouldn't have to spend any of my time trying to figure out where Jill was coming from. She was one lady who wore her views on her sleeve.

At exactly six o'clock Pacific and nine Eastern Standard time the show's theme music began to play and the camera zoomed into the set where we were all sitting at the same round table.

"Good evening," she began, flashing her famous smile. "On tonight's show we have assembled a fascinating panel to discuss one of the most controversial subjects of our time – abortion. And in particular, we plan to explore the central issue surrounding the entire abortion debate, and that is the question of personhood. Is the unborn fetus a person? And here to discuss this emotionally charged topic are Louise Ann Jordan, John Temple and Max Werner."

Following a brief introduction of each of us, she posed an interesting question: Why had each of us wanted to appear on her show to discuss this issue?

"Jill, when my little brother Don took his first breath of fresh air I thought he was the most beautiful and precious thing I had ever seen. If someone back then had told me that my baby brother was not a person, I would have said that they were crazy. And you know I would have been absolutely right. Only the truly blind could deny that Don was not a tiny person."

"OK," Jill smiled, clearly amused. "So far we both agree that a baby is a person, Louise."

"But did you know that though he may have weighed only seven pounds at birth his small size had nothing to do with his being declared a legal person because, according to current U. S. law, just five minutes before my mom's doctor transferred him from her womb to the bright lights of the hospital delivery room she could still have aborted Don."

"I don't believe that's true Louise. Do you mean to tell me that it's legal to perform an abortion in the ninth month of a pregnancy? How is that possible?"

"If you read the *Roe v. Wade* decision, you'll see that our United States Supreme Court ruled that abortion is legal at any time up until birth if a mother and her doctor agree that because of 'health' reasons an abortion is necessary. Sadly the concept of 'health' is defined so broadly that it encompasses anything that might cause physical, psychological, emotional or economic damage to a woman. I grant you that most abortions take place well before the ninth month of a pregnancy but the law still makes it perfectly legal, even at that very late stage. My question to you and to everyone watching your show right now is this: Can anyone honesty look into their heart and say that during that short five minute interval from womb to delivery room that a non-person is magically transformed into a real person?"

"If what you're saying is true," Jill exclaimed, "then what you've just described looks to me like a loophole that unscrupulous physicians can technically use to defend performing very late term abortions."

"That's exactly right," Big John added. "It's a loophole that's part of the law. However, when you refer to these physicians as unscrupulous, aren't we really talking about all abortion doctors?"

Ms. Morgan looked annoyed now and I guessed that Big John's comment had struck a nerve.

"No," our hostess said defiantly. "I believe abortion, though not an optimal solution often is still a necessary one. And thank God we have doctors who are willing to still perform them. To compel a woman to have a child she doesn't want or is prepared to raise can cause her to experience severe emotional and financial distress. And that's why I have fought so hard to keep abortion legal. Max," she continued, regaining her composure, "I'd like to hear what you think about this issue of personhood."

"Jill, the central issue that is foundational to the entire debate on abortion is that of personhood. If we can establish the personhood of the unborn, then according to the Fourteenth Amendment of our U.S. Constitution, they would be entitled to the right to life. Even in *Roe v. Wade*, Justice Blackmun made this admission and I quote, 'If this suggestion of personhood is established, the appellant's case, of course, collapses, for the fetus' right to life would then be guaranteed specifically by the Amendment.'"[52]

Max, now looked right at the show's audience and in a very melodramatic fashion began to explain what the three of us had in common.

"All three of us are here today to contrast our unique experiences in an attempt to demonstrate that the unborn fetus is indeed a person," he said quietly. "Back in the 1840's John Temple's great-great Grandfather, Jerry Temple lived a life of bondage, legally stripped of his personhood by sole virtue of his skin color. I'm sure John will have much to share on this point later. I, on the other hand, was imprisoned against my will by the German government. My crime was that, because I was Jewish, I no longer was on the German's approved list of people groups that they considered to be entitled to full personhood. And Baby Sally's life was taken from her because our Supreme Court ruled, and Louise believed, that she was only 'birth matter' and not a person."

"I can definitely see that our guests are going to try to show all of us that our Supreme Court and Constitution didn't get it right. Our government has, in its wisdom, given women the right to an abortion if they deem it necessary. I think it's important to understand that we live in a country of laws and that what Louise and her friends are going to propose we do is to actually rewrite them and overturn our Constitution. Well, I wish them a lot of luck," Jill said, keeping a close watch on the countdown to commercial. "But we need to take our first break. Stay with us – we've got lots to talk about."

It seemed as if John, Max and myself were three defense attorneys who had just concluded our opening statements in what was, perhaps, the trial of the century. Our job was to convince a jury of perhaps several million viewers that our client, the unborn fetus, deserved to be declared not guilty. It was indeed a daunting task but we were fully prepared to state our case and vindicate our client. And what made it even tougher was the fact that we needed to convince this jury that their very own government had laws that desperately needed to be rewritten.

"I am very interested in your thoughts on what Max and Louise have just shared, John," Jill said as the show resumed. "Do you feel that you can show a legitimate parallel between the personhood issues surrounding slavery and abortion? But before you answer that question, perhaps you can give us a little information on your background and that of your great-great grandfather."

"My biography is not very impressive," John began, "but I like to believe that, during my thirty-five years of teaching high school biology in Nashville, Tennessee, I was able to be a positive influence on the many students who sat in my classroom. As you know, biology is the science of life processes and living organisms. And as a biology teacher, one of the most awesome life processes that I have been privileged to share with my students has been the wonderful development of life from conception until birth. After raising four children and watching my eleven grandchildren and three great-grandchildren grow I can tell you that what we read in Psalm (127:3) is so very true. This wonderful verse from the Bible says, 'Lo, children are an heritage of the LORD: and the fruit of the womb is his reward.'[53]

"My great-great grandfather, Jerry Temple, was born in 1839 in Mobile, Alabama. Jill, the thing that bothers me the most about his slavery was not the fact that he was classified as a non-person, but that he was considered a piece of property. As a result of the laws of the land back in 1839, my great-great grandfather had to spend his first seven years of life living under the illusion that he had a mother and father."

"I'm a little confused when you say that he had to live under the illusion that he had a mother and father," Jill said, frowning. "Even though slavery was a great evil, how can you deny that your great-great grandfather had parents?"

"Because Jill, at the tender age of seven this little boy said goodbye forever to his mother and father when their owner decided to sell him to another slave owner in Georgia," John said and then turned not to face the camera but the audience. "You see as a slave you technically had to have a biological mother but in reality at the moment of birth slave babies became the 'property' of their slave master. Slave families consisting of a mother, father and children were only allowed to stay together when a master felt it would be in his best interest to keep a slave family intact. Sadly, many felt their best interests would be better served by selling off healthy children to other slave owners and pocketing the profits in order to make their lives more comfortable."

There was a long pause during which the stunned silence of the studio audience made its own statement.

"I can just imagine the trauma that young Jerry must have gone through knowing that he probably would never see his mom and dad again," Jill said. "Maybe you can describe what happened to the rest of Jerry's family?"

"Well two years after Jerry was sold, his little sister, Melissa, who was only five, was also sold to a slave owner in Kentucky. These were the only two children Mama Temple, as she was affectionately called, ever had. Just as a horse was the property of its owner, a slave was the property of its master. And just as a horse owner could breed his horses and sell off the offspring, a black female slave often would have to watch her very own children being auctioned off to the highest bidder. In a sense the more unscrupulous slave owners bred them like horses or cattle. And why not, particularly since our government said it was perfectly legal!"

"That's all well and good, John," she began. "I seriously doubt that anyone alive today would condone the practice of slavery. But how can you equate a grown person with an unborn fetus? Do you mean to tell me that you view them both equally?"

"With all due respect," John, politely but forcefully added, "I think you're missing the entire point. Once blacks were legally declared non-persons, under the law, they lost all of their human rights. As a result their new classification became 'chattel property.' As property the only rights that slaves had in America was to submit to their masters. As property they could be bought, sold, beaten and even killed if their owner felt like doing so."

"I understand all of that. I personally view what happened back in the nineteenth century as totally repulsive. But how does this relate to comparing a black slave with an unborn fetus? I just don't see the connection."

"If you can bear with me for a minute I would like to show you how the entire personhood issue between black slave and unborn baby is connected.

"My oldest son Daniel is fifty-two years old. He is a wonderful son who has two of his own sons and a daughter. He lives in Florida and is a successful pediatrician. Back when Daniel was born in the 1940's, had his mother and I decided we didn't want him and tried to have him aborted, we might well have been charged with a crime, since abortion then was illegal in America."

"I don't mean to sound cruel," Jill said, now choosing her words very carefully. "But since abortion wasn't legal back then other couples contemplating one would have been forced to bring an unwanted child into the world. And that's not fair!"

As Max and I looked at each other I think we both realized that our hostess was proving to be quite a formidable adversary.

"I'll tell you what's not fair," John exclaimed, raising his powerful voice for the first time all evening. "If Mrs. Temple and I had been slaves and lived during the 1840's, this same son, Daniel, if born back then could easily have been aborted, no matter how much we protested, if our owner insisted on it, even though abortion was illegal. After all, Daniel was his property and for whatever reason if he didn't want this child, he could have ordered him aborted."

For the first time all evening Jill had to pause before she could respond to one of our arguments. But before she could comment, John once again turned to the audience to make his final point.

"You see," he continued, "back in the 1840's, a white fetus had more rights than a black fetus. In fact, it was against the law to kill an unborn white baby but perfectly legal to kill a black baby, regardless of what stage of gestation it was in. And what gave the slave owner the right to kill this innocent child? Was it just the skin color of the fetus? No! It was the fact that once the black baby was declared a 'non-person' it could then be killed, at the owner's discretion, whether it was living inside or outside the womb."

And now turning from the studio audience to face Jill Morgan, John concluded, "I hope you can now see why slavery, abortion and personhood are so intimately connected."

"So far," Jill said, now talking over the show's theme music, signaling we were going to another break, "the only thing I'm willing to concede is that a black slave should never have been declared a non-person unless he was still a fetus."

It was kind of discouraging to see that despite Big John's powerful logic, Jill Morgan's wall of resistance was still solid and seemingly unshaken. But I had to keep reminding myself that our primary target audience was not our young and vivacious interviewer but her millions of viewers. And based on her in-studio audience reactions so far I could clearly see that many had already been touched. As the show resumed I wondered how she planned to tackle the Jewish issue with Max.

"Max," she began, clasping her hands together and trying to sound compassionate, "I can only imagine the horrors you had to endure while a prisoner in Dachau. But rather than have you describe those conditions perhaps you could take a minute to let us know why you think Germany became so misguided."

"To be honest with you," Max bluntly replied, "the Hitler propaganda machine used the same strategy to rationalize the extermination of Jews that the pro-choice lobby has been using for years to justify aborting innocent children."

"Max," Jill said, as her entire facial expression became one ball of rage, "that's a cheap shot. How dare you compare today's pro-choice crusade with that of the Nazi's? Please, by all means, go right ahead and tell my viewers what strategy the pro-choice movement has in common with the Nazi regime!"

"I'm sorry you're taking this so personal," Max replied in an apologetic tone. "But after talking with many ex-Nazi's during the past forty years most of them have told me that they actually believed that they were performing a service to the German society at large by killing the Jews."

"That doesn't make any sense," Jill said. "How could those German's think they were providing society with a benefit by killing Jews?"

"One of the key Nazi strategies was to change the way the average German citizen perceived its Jewish population. Instead of killing its fellow citizens, the government told its populace that it would merely be 'emptying the ghettos.' And rather than view Jews as useful members of society they needed to be seen for who they really were: nothing more than 'garbage' and 'useless eaters.' Back in 1943, I was stripped of my dignity, robbed of my humanity and viewed as nothing more than a drain on my country's limited resources. As a result of this dehumanizing process all of my legal rights were taken from me. And since the Nazi's believed in the Darwinian evolutionary concept of survival of the fittest, it was an easy leap for them to make in their justification of exterminating our 'subhuman' species."

"I hope you're not going to imply that we who are pro-choice have deliberately attempted to deceive the public into believing something that isn't true?" Jill half laughingly questioned Max.

"I'm not going to say that all people in the pro-choice movement are trying to deliberately lie," Max said, "but I do believe that most have been deceived into believing *the* lie that a fetus is nothing more than 'birth matter,' 'pregnancy tissue,' 'a product of conception' or just some 'feto-placental unit.'"

As soon as Max finished his comment he quickly pulled out and unfolded a giant two by three-foot magnificent full-color photo of a twenty-week-old fetus and asked the cameras to pan in on this precious baby. Max then stood up and looked at Jill, her studio audience and the camera, all in turn, and then asked the question of the hour: "Does this look like a 'feto-placental unit' or a precious gift from God called a baby?"

Jill just sat there quietly waiting for her studio audience to finish clapping. Max had scored a major breakthrough and even Jill Morgan had been put on the run.

But rather than admit we had made a good case for the personhood of the unborn she tried her best to deflect the momentum we had just gained by trying to make our argument seem unfair.

"That's still not a fair comparison," she exclaimed. "How can you equate the killing of a Jew with taking the life of an unborn fetus?"

It was amazing how Max methodically described the alarming connection between the extermination of Jews and the destruction of other German citizens. He began by highlighting how even before the first Jew was led to the gas chamber thousands of Gentile lives were also killed, because like the Jews, they were deemed a burden and an expense to society. The list of people that were put to death included the insane, the elderly in old age homes, retarded individuals, adults and children with deformities, epileptics and in some cases even bed wetters.

"Once many of these so called undesirables were killed," Max began to conclude, now with tears in his eyes, "Hitler then focused on his so called, 'final solution' and when all was said and done six million Jews were killed. It all boiled down to Hitler and the German government making value judgements on who should live and who should die. Depending on what category you fell in would determine if you would live or die."

I felt like this was a good time for me to jump in and make the connection with what is taking place in our present society.

"I believe that America today is traveling on that same wicked road that Nazi Germany took back in the early 1930's," I said. "Value judgements always end up in disaster for the targeted people group. Jerry Temple wound up a slave. Millions of Jews, including Max, were herded like cattle to extermination camps. And today over four thousand babies every day are brutally dismembered through abortion."

"But when Negro slaves and Jews were abused, real lives were involved. In the case of the unborn we have at best potential life," Jill protested. Her face was still very red and I could see she was still taking everything personal. "Again I still have a big problem in treating all three of these groups alike."

"I see you are still hanging on to that old pro-choice propaganda," I said, trying to be as dispassionate as I could although it wasn't easy. "The unborn baby is not potential life. He or she is already life that possesses vast potential. I think this is a good time to bring up another important consideration concerning why certain people groups down through the years are denied personhood."

As we went into another break, I found that I was totally relaxed. Having my two bodyguards with me made quite a difference. Although we came from quite different worlds, not only did we all share the same beliefs but both Big John and Max were doing so much of the talking that I was able to spend time in thinking what I wanted to say when it was my turn to speak. Back in January my allies all had been behind the scenes and I had had little time to think since every question from Bob Jacobs was addressed to me.

"I think it's very interesting to note that Negro slaves, concentration camp Jews and the unwanted inhabitants of the womb have all fallen victim to the classic struggle between the strong and the weak," I said quickly when we were back on the big screen again. I wanted to make sure that Jill didn't use the occasion of the break to take us off focus. "All three groups have been put under subjection because of personal greed and selfishness."

"Well, I guess you'll just have to call me selfish for wanting to help women avoid the agony of being forced to bring an unwanted child into the world," our hostess cynically exclaimed. "Look, Louise," she continued, "let's be serious. A fetus isn't even viable on its own. A black slave and a Jewish person are clearly human beings while a fetus is not."

"Let me give you an example of what I'm talking about," I told her. "I'm sure you'll agree that a two-month-old baby girl if left unattended could never survive on its own. At that young age she is absolutely dependent on her parents for just about everything. But have you ever considered that an eight-month-old female fetus is actually living on autopilot. While this precious child is also totally dependent on her mother for her very survival she is completely safe from any dangers. In fact she really couldn't be left unattended even if her mother wanted to. The only major obstacle she faces is the possibility that her parents might choose to exercise their legal right to abort her. God has a wonderful way of providing a precious baby with all the protection it needs while living inside the womb but He relies on us to provide that protection and love once that child leaves the womb."

"But what does this have to do with the struggle between the strong and the weak?"

"You see the abortion option is the ultimate power play between a government sanctioned, technologically sophisticated doctor of death and a tiny, powerless, unsuspecting baby. Our government has stripped away all legal rights from our most vulnerable citizens. As a result over four thousand of these precious souls every day are doomed to perish through the legal killing process called abortion."

"The Nazi mentality was based on this very concept," Max said excitedly. "Jews were expendable simply because they were an inferior species. They were not wanted and their extermination was a necessary step in the establishment of a pure Aryan Super Race. Since the Nazi's were in control of the government and established the laws that made killing Jews legal, they had the power and the justification necessary to quite frankly, do whatever they wanted to do with their

Jewish population. Void of any weapons to defend themselves and not having any laws to use to defend their right to live, six million Jews found out that they were at the mercy of their captors. Tragically they found no mercy from the powerful Nazi machine and were exterminated from the face of the earth. They were doomed right from the very start because their government lost its way and its humanity."

Max then went on to describe how the weak, sickly, deformed, mentally retarded and the Jew were all considered expendable since none of them had the capability of making a positive contribution to the betterment of society.

"I obviously can't disagree with too much of your analysis, Max," Jill begrudgingly said. "But before I ask Louise to comment on this misguided notion that we should somehow view an unborn fetus on the same level with a live human being, I'd like to hear from you John. Can you give us your thoughts on how the white slave owner was able to justify his right to own another human being?"

John looked really uncomfortable now. I almost felt that he wished he didn't have to answer Jill's question. But his telling commentary was the perfect lead-in to what I was planning to talk about.

"Blacks," Big John began, "became slaves simply because they were the victims of a powerful system of institutionalized evil. They were captured in Africa, brought in chains to America and then legally declared the chattel property of the slave owner who was willing to pay the purchase price. Taken against their will and declared void of any rights the poor black slave had little choice but to remain in bondage. Though many black slaves were physically very strong, legally they were incredibly weak. Since they had no legal rights, they were totally helpless to fight back when physically abused and inhumanely treated. Blacks were doomed to bondage because our American system of government set up laws that excluded this so-called 'inferior' class of people from being able to participate in all the good things our country had to offer its citizens."

As I looked at our interviewer I could see that John's poignant description of slavery in America had finally brought a genuine look of concern to her face. And by the way she asked for my opinion it seemed as if some of the fight had at least temporarily been knocked out of her.

"Thank you John for reminding all of us about this dark period in American history. May we never repeat such a tragic mistake again. Louise, as you know I can't agree with your position on the personhood of the unborn but I respect your right to hold it. So why don't you take a moment to summarize your case."

"Blacks, Jews and the unborn all had the deck stacked against them," I said. "Don't you see, Jill? When their very own governments turned against them by basically declaring them non-persons, all three of these people groups lost all of their legal rights to share in the benefits of the society they lived in. Mr. Temple's great-great grandfather Jerry Temple found out at the young age of seven that without legal rights he was totally helpless to stop his father's master from selling him to another slave owner. Max Werner found out that being Jewish meant that he was no longer entitled to German citizenship. Instead he became a burden to society and a prime candidate for a trip to the gas chamber. Fortunately, Max was one of the lucky ones who avoided that fate. And finally my baby, Sally, while completing her first trimester of life found out that because she was an inconvenience to me, that for a small fee, she could legally be aborted."

We were now almost at the end of the show and I felt that the three of us had done a very good job in presenting our side of the personhood debate. But Jill Morgan clearly had not been persuaded by our arguments and that grieved my heart.

"I just want to really thank the three of you," Jill graciously said, as she smiled right at me, "for taking the time to be on my show. I know we may not agree on this very sensitive issue but I think we have each given our opinions in an open and honest way. In the final analysis the issue of abortion boils down to one of balance. How do we weigh the rights of a fetus verses those of a woman facing the potential for severe financial, emotional and psychological damage if forced to have a child she isn't prepared to have. It's clear to me that our government has made the right choice by making sure that every woman in America is guaranteed the right to a safe and affordable abortion. But as always, my guest gets to make the last comment. So, Louise, please leave us with a final thought."

"Thanks so much for having us on your show tonight Jill. It's been a real privilege to share with you and your audience our love of the unborn. But as we go, I ask you to please consider this. In 1973 our government decided to classify all unborn children as pure property, owned by the mother, instead of being legal entities guaranteed the right to life. Morality was once again placed on trial and it lost. Inconvenience won and life lost. Expert medical testimony about the unique and infinitely complex nature of the unborn was ignored and the selfish cries of women who demanded absolute sexual freedom were embraced. The Hippocratic Oath became the hypocritical Oath. And finally, our medical profession became totally schizophrenic by performing life saving surgery on a six-month-old premature baby in one hospital room and then aborting another six-month-old perfectly healthy unborn baby down the hall."

As the show's theme music played throughout my closing statement I knew that we had reached some of the pro-choice faithful. The only question was how many?

17

Answered Prayer

Our best efforts had done little to persuade Jill Morgan to change her stance but two days after our show aired perhaps our most powerful defection to date took place when Bob Jacobs publicly announced that he could no longer support abortion on demand.

In a brief statement to the press Mr. Jacobs stated that after watching the personhood debate on *The Jill Morgan Show* his conscience could no longer ignore the fact that the unborn child is indeed a person worthy of dignity and the protection of the law. He even went so far as to say that it was pure madness for our society to devote massive amounts of money and our latest medical technology to try to save the life of a six-month-old premature baby on the one hand, and then coldly exterminate a baby of equal age through a government backed legal abortion simply because the latter baby was being carried in the wrong womb.

His defection to the pro-life camp sent immediate shock waves throughout the pro-choice ranks. Bob Jacobs was one of the most popular people in the nation. They knew that if he decided to speak out in defense of the unborn millions of his legion of fans might also choose to rethink their position.

Sure enough, the following day Bob Jacobs was attacked and denounced by every major pro-choice group in America. Fortunately their attacks and attempts to slander the talk show host's character began to backfire almost immediately. Mr. Jacobs over the years had developed a reputation of being a man of principal who based his beliefs on careful research and analysis and not on the latest fads. In short, everyone knew that no amount of money could buy Bob Jacobs' endorsement of a product or a viewpoint. If Bob Jacobs had changed his opinion on abortion, he must have done so by carefully weighing every argument. And the more they attacked him, the more this man of principal and integrity fought to use his show to champion the pro-life cause.

During the next two months the issue of abortion became the most talked about subject in America. Several major cities hosted rallies for life. College campuses held debates on the merits of each position. Talk shows on both TV and radio made the abortion issue a centerpiece of discussion. Almost every nightly newscast had a feature story on some aspect of the abortion controversy. And from New York to California and everywhere in between this life and death issue was now taking center stage.

But what was even more exciting than the discussions that were taking place were the allegiances that were being switched. In the months of May and June alone, NAL was able to confirm that four United States senators and eighteen members of our House of Representatives dropped their support of abortion on demand and embraced the pro-life position. In addition to these important defections, several major Hollywood notables and a host of local politicians publicly stated that they could no longer support a woman's right to choose. And it seemed that every week a different newspaper would feature an editorial describing why it was reversing its pro-choice stance. It was amazing how far we had come since my abortion just ten months ago.

Meanwhile, NAL continued to book me on as many TV shows as possible. During the month of June, I must have appeared on every major talk show in America. As exciting as these speaking opportunities were, they were all just steps on the way to my keynote address at our upcoming pro-life rally on July 26 in Washington, D.C. According to Jennifer Poole, this rally was going to be one of the largest ever held in the history of America. During the last few months NAL had been busy getting everything ready to host this major event, and were now estimating that between five hundred and six hundred thousand people would be attending this unique rally for life.

The mere thought of speaking to a gathering of over a half million people was difficult for me to really believe. NAL purposely didn't schedule any further speaking engagements for me after mid July because they felt I needed some time off to just relax and enjoy at least a part of my summer vacation. In fact, they booked a one-week vacation to Orlando, Florida for our entire family. As you might have expected, it was an all expenses paid vacation. And guess who picked up the tab? Yes, it was Eddie Moss.

Mrs. Gates told me to take the entire week to just relax, have fun and enjoy being a teen. Well, I took her advice to heart and for one solid week I just enjoyed the sights and sounds of Florida and the opportunity to spend time with my family. It was the best family vacation any of us could ever remember taking.

On our second to last day in Orlando I noticed a very familiar face near the entrance of Disney World and realized that it was Mrs. Sterling, my tenth grade English teacher. She had arrived the night before with her husband and three children. I told her that we were here to just relax and get away from all the pressures I had been under this past year.

As we were about to say goodbye, Mrs. Sterling pulled me over to the side and said that, although she knew that I was here to get away from all the business involving abortion, she felt that what she had to share would have special meaning to me.

"You remember Miss Ventura, your science teacher?" she asked me as we stood close together on line waiting to enter the Magic Kingdom.

"How could I ever forget her," I said. "She was the most vocal pro-choice voice at Palmerville High."

Just the mention of her name made me uncomfortable. Ever since I became active in the pro-life movement, she had always made it a point to let everyone in her class know that my views on abortion were in the minority. Her subtle and not so subtle putdowns made attending her class a constant source of anxiety for me.

"Well back in early January I had lunch with her," Mrs. Sterling went on. "She told me that, because of all that had taken place at school since your little show and tell presentation, she felt that it was time for her to move on and was planning to submit her resignation to Principal Foster. Being pro-choice in a school that by now had a faculty that was almost entirely pro-life made her very uncomfortable. She still planned to teach but it won't be at Palmerville High."

I was appalled. Even though she had made my life miserable she was still an excellent science teacher. "I can't believe that because of me she won't be coming back to teach next year," I said.

"Louise, I told her the same thing. She was too good a teacher for our school to lose and I asked her to reconsider."

"Well, did she?"

"She told me that she had made up her mind and that this June would be her last month as part of our faculty."

"I wonder what school she plans to teach at?"

"I had the same question and decided to ask her during another lunch near the end of May. Well, to my surprise, she had some quite unexpected news. It seemed that her favorite television show is *The Bob Jacobs Show*. In fact, she went so far as to tell me that she absolutely idolizes him. When she heard that you were going to be on his show back in January, she felt that he would be able to quickly deflate your pro-life balloon. Well, after watching the entire show, she realized that you had more than held your own defending the pro-life position."

"She said that about me?"

"Yes, but not only that," Mrs. Sterling went on as a group of Japanese tourists started snapping pictures right in front of us. "She told me that she began to search her soul to see if her pro-choice position might just be wrong. Then, when she watched your panel discussion on *The Jill Morgan Show* and learned that Bob Jacobs had become pro-life, she too realized for the first time in her life that abortion was the taking of an innocent life. Apparently no matter how she tried to rationalize a woman's right to choose, she couldn't defend that right any more if it meant that this choice would end the life of an innocent baby."

I just couldn't believe what I was hearing. By now tears were streaming down my face. I had come to believe that Miss Ventura and I were almost mortal enemies, and because of that, to hear that she could no longer defend a woman's right to have an abortion indeed had a special meaning to me.

"But Mrs. Sterling, did she change her mind and decide to stay on at Palmerville High?"

She gave me a big smile and told me that not only would Miss Ventura be teaching science at our school this coming September but that she had already received permission from Principal Foster to devote an entire class period to study the science of fetology!

Having my science teacher change her stance on abortion was quite honestly something I had given up on months ago. But I was finally starting to understand that with God all things are possible. And in my mind God would have to get involved because only a miracle could have changed Miss Ventura's heart.

I hated to say good-bye to Florida but knew that my most important speech was less than a week away. We got back to Palmerville on July 22. As soon as I stepped into our house the phone rang. Don ran to answer it and told me that it was Jennifer Poole.

"Louise," she said, sounding elated and exhausted at the same time. "I've been working non-stop for almost two full months helping to put together the logistics for our rally. We've been working in conjunction with at least a dozen other pro-life organizations to get everything ready. According to our latest estimates we expect to draw at least a half million people."

For a moment I couldn't find the words to reply.

"Where are you going to fit a half million people?" I asked her.

"Don't worry Louise. We've worked everything out," she told me. "I guarantee you, whoever comes out – we'll find a place for them to stand."

"What time am I scheduled to speak, Jennifer?"

"We have you scheduled for three-thirty. Please let me know if there is anything we can do to help you prepare?"

"Don't worry Jennifer, I'll be fine, but thanks for the offer."

"Everyone at NAL can't wait for the rally to start, Louise."

"Neither can I. I only wish it were here already."

"Oh, and before I forget," Jennifer added, just before she hung up, "we plan to have Bob Jacobs speak right before you deliver your keynote address. See you soon."

As soon as I got off the phone, I filled my parents in on some of the details that Jennifer shared with me including who would be speaking right before me. Don't ask me why but the next person I wanted to call and update on the latest happenings with the rally was Jerry Bedford. After we spoke for a few minutes Jerry insisted that we get some of the old gang together to help me with my big speech. I told Jerry that I'd love to have the gang over and we set the time for the next evening at eight.

Asking Jerry to make a few phone calls may not have been one of my brightest ideas. By eight-fifteen the next night, I must have had about thirty of my friends sitting and standing in my living room. But it was great having so many special friends help me prepare for the big rally. Dad had already put Lazzaro's Pizza on alert that he would be placing a major order later that evening. In the meantime, we all talked about the rally and it seemed like everyone had an opinion on what things I should cover in my speech.

"Louise, I think that a great way to gain credibility would be to put together a list of the names of our members of Congress who have turned pro-life during this past year," Sarah said, as she showed me a scrapbook she had put together filled with news clippings detailing many of these conversions.

"That's a great idea," I told her. "I'll give Sally Gates a call and ask her if she can provide me with that list."

"I hope you plan to discuss the latest scientific facts on fetal development," Raymond reminded me.

"And please, Louise, don't forget to bring up that adoption is the one option that all thinking people should be able to agree upon," Jolene Tobin said.

All of these were excellent ideas, and as I looked out of the corner of my eye I could see that Jenny Woods was writing them all down.

As we continued to discuss ideas, the thing that really touched my heart the most was the love that this bunch of teens had for the unborn. And what made it even more special was that these were all my friends!

When it came time for Jerry to offer his advice, everybody knew that we were about to be treated to a mini sermon. The funny thing, however, was that we were all eager to listen to Jerry's simple, yet profound insights. Just as he was about to speak, the doorbell rang and two delivery boys brought ten large pies into the Jordan living room. I told Jerry to hold onto his thoughts while we took a break to enjoy the best pizza in Palmerville. By the time we had finished eating, it was close to eleven. Dad told everyone that, since it was summer, he had no problem with letting us continue our conversation, especially considering what was at stake. It was now time for Gerald Thomas Bedford to deliver his sermon.

"Louise," he said, as he awkwardly stood up and made his way to the center of the room. "I get nervous just giving a presentation in our speech class which only has thirty students. I can't imagine what it will be like for you talking in front of a half million people. Just look at it this way – almost everyone you'll be speaking to will be adults so you won't feel any peer pressure. Also, don't forget we'll all be praying for you. And I believe God will be listening to us when we talk to Him this coming Thursday."

Everyone's undivided attention was now on Jerry. Several of my friends were now also standing while others were either sitting on the sofa or cross-legged on the floor.

"I'm sure that millions of pro-choice supporters will be watching you on TV this Thursday," Jerry went on, now beginning to slowly pace the floor. "Let them know that if they had been successful in making abortion legal back in 1933 instead of 1973, that many of them wouldn't be here to watch you speak at our rally. And please tell America that, even if you made a mistake when you got pregnant, Baby Sally was not a mistake. She was a tiny angel from heaven who God loved just as much as you and me."

Jerry had a way of making you laugh one moment and cry the next. His touching way of putting things was so refreshing that all of us couldn't wait to hear more.

"And, look at Bobby Johnson sitting next to Jolene," he continued. "Bobby and I are very close friends. But he's black and I'm white. I can't believe that if both of us lived during the 1840's, Bobby would have been a slave. I'm so glad that Bobby didn't have to grow up back then. But to tell you the truth, I'd rather Bobby be a slave back in 1840 than to be growing inside the wrong womb today."

We all just sat there stunned over Jerry's last comment until Bobby Johnson walked up to Jerry and the two of them silently embraced. Words did not need to be exchanged at that moment for we all understood that Jerry and Bobby indeed had a special bond between them.

It must have been one in the morning by the time everyone had had a chance to speak about what was in their hearts. By one-thirty our house had become quiet as the last of my friends said their good-byes, leaving me with lots to think about.

As I was getting ready to shut my light off and hit the sack, dad looked in to say good night and tell me how much he had enjoyed listening to our discussion.

"I know you're tired but I just wanted to leave you with one final thought before I let you go to sleep," he said. "I'm sure you know that almost everyone attending the rally will be pro-life. If you really want to motivate them to step up the fight when they return home then why not think about turning the rally into a giant memorial service. But let's not talk about it now. I know how tired you must be. I just wanted you to think about it. Sweetheart, now get some rest and may God bless you."

It was an exciting idea. I went to sleep thinking about it and woke up certain that it was the thing to do. On Tuesday night I placed a call to Jennifer to give her an idea of some of the things I planned to speak on at the rally. "And there's one other thing I want to run by you," I added.

"Shoot, Louise. What's on your mind?"

"I'd really like to use the last few minutes of my speaking time to host a short memorial service dedicated to the millions of babies killed through abortion. Do you think that would be OK?"

I heard her take a deep breath. "I think that's an absolutely beautiful way to end our rally, Louise," she exclaimed. "How did you come up with the idea?"

"Well it really wasn't my idea. I got it from an ex-marine turned hardware storeowner."

"You mean your dad," Jennifer said, as we both laughed.

"Yea. And you won't believe he gave the idea to me at two in the morning."

My dad's continual support of all my pro-life activities was something that by now I had taken for granted. But in addition to being a great sounding board he also had a lot of good ideas, with the memorial service, perhaps, being his best.

As you might expect, our trip to Washington was quite exciting. This time Don came with us and, as soon as we got to our room, he noticed an envelope that had apparently been pushed under the door. It was addressed to me and when I opened it and read the short note inside, I let out a scream that must have been heard throughout the entire hotel.

"Louise, what's wrong? What's wrong?" Dad demanded, dropping our bags.

"Somebody plans to kill me if I speak at the rally," I told him, holding out the note. "This - this is a death threat!"

"If I were you," Dad read aloud, his voice trembling, "I wouldn't speak at Thursday's right to life rally. If you do, you will be dead within a week."

Within fifteen minutes, the police, the hotel manager, Jennifer Poole and Mrs. Gates were all inside our hotel room trying to comfort me and my family and to see if there were any clues as to who might have left such an evil note. During the past year, I had been booed countless times, called every kind of derogatory name you could think of and even had a bottle or two thrown my way. But this was the first time I had ever received an actual death threat.

In the middle of all the commotion, Don came over to me and told me that as long as he was around nobody was going to lay a hand on his big sister. I knew that there was really no way my kid brother could do anything to protect me but I was deeply moved knowing that he meant it with all his heart. From that day forward I never looked at Don as my little brother again but as the second man in the Jordan family.

With our rally less than twenty-four hours away, there was no way, realistically, the police were going to find out who had left that note although they weren't going to take any chances and told us that two officers would be stationed at the hotel overnight. Mrs. Gates asked me if she could speak to my parents alone for a few minutes. After their conversation, Dad seemed much calmer and so did Mom.

"Louise," he began, "Mrs. Gates has told me that she completely understands if you choose not to speak at tomorrow's rally. While she feels this letter is most likely just someone's attempt to scare you off, she certainly realizes that there is always a chance that some sick person might try to make good on their threat."

Jennifer immediately echoed the same sentiments.

"If you prefer to just stay in the background and cheer us on tomorrow that would be perfectly OK with all of us at NAL, Louise," she said. Her hair was still wet and she wasn't wearing any make-up. She had just gotten out of the shower at the gym when she heard the news and immediately ran over to the hotel to find out what was going on.

"Your mom and I are certainly uncomfortable letting you speak in front of such a huge crowd knowing that there might be a madman in it looking to take a shot at you," Dad said, putting his arm around me. "But we both agree that the final decision will be yours and yours alone. You're already a hero to everybody in this room as well as to millions more all across America."

"Whatever decision you make will be the right one," Mom added, taking my hand and pressing it between both of hers. Never had I felt so loved.

Telling them all that I needed to spend a few minutes by myself, I went into the bedroom that Don and I were going to share and quietly sat on the edge of my bed. I closed my eyes and began to ask God for help, begging Him to show me a sign.

Well, it couldn't have been more than two or three minutes after I had finished praying when I had a vision of the largest cemetery I had ever seen. As far as my eyes could see there were empty graves stretching in every direction. A man appeared, someone, who looked like one of the caretakers and I asked him why these graves were still empty. I will never forget his reply.

"These are the graves of the millions of aborted babies who are still waiting to be given a proper burial," he told me. And with that, he pointed to a tiny grave. Its tombstone was already in place and the inscription read:

Sally Jordan
Angel of God
She Died Before Her Time
Aborted By Her Mother

In that moment, my heart broke. After thanking God for His divine guidance I walked into the other room to let everyone know what I planned to do.

"Dad, tomorrow afternoon be prepared to watch your daughter give the speech of her life," I said. "There are just too many lives at stake for me to worry about my own."

"If that's your decision, Louise then your mom and I are with you one hundred percent."

His complete support was what I needed to hear and as the two of us embraced I knew that everything was going to be OK.

"I think for security reasons that it might be a good idea if your family stayed inside the hotel this evening," Mrs. Gates suggested.

"On one condition," my father replied, grinning bravely, "that you and Miss Poole agree to join us for dinner tonight."

We all agreed to dine at seven.

Dad looked like he was now back in full control. It was clear to me that he had no intention of being bullied either. As for Don and my mother, they told me that tomorrow was going to be a day that none of us would ever forget.

I was now so determined to speak that nothing short of an earthquake was going to prevent me from delivering my message tomorrow.

18

<u>The Mother of All Rallies</u>

At ten sharp a limo was waiting outside our hotel to take our family to NAL headquarters. As we drove the fifteen to twenty blocks from the hotel to the building that housed NAL, I couldn't believe my eyes - people were everywhere. As I later found out, buses from up and down the east coast and as far as the Midwest had been arriving in D.C. by the thousands nearly non-stop from shortly after midnight. Unlike past right to life rallies, this time the media was also present everywhere.

People were smiling and talking as we drove by them by the thousands. I had never dreamed of seeing so many people carrying pro-life signs, wearing pro-life shirts and buttons and chanting messages on behalf of the unborn in my entire life. As soon as our limo reached its destination, four D.C. police officers escorted our family into NAL headquarters. I felt like I was a foreign dignitary, but after the threatening letter I had received the day before I welcomed the added security. Mrs. Gates, Jennifer Poole and my old friend Eddie Moss were all on hand to greet us as we got off the elevator.

We all quickly made our way into the NAL boardroom where Mrs. Gates said that she would give us an update on what had already taken place today and what to expect later on at the rally. By the time everyone had filed into the boardroom, there must have been over fifty people, including around a dozen members of the press. With cameras rolling, Mrs. Gates walked up to a small podium at one end of the room and began to address the gathering.

"Where in the world are we going to put all of these people," she said in mock dismay. "I just got a report from D.C. police that as of ten this morning, based on estimates from their overhead helicopters, there are already a million people either assembled around the Washington Monument or making their way toward its vicinity. And as we are speaking, buses are still bringing people in at a rate that has never been seen in our nation's capital.

"We've scheduled our rally kickoff to officially begin at 1:30 PM. Reverend Barry Simmons from Atlanta will open our ceremonies in prayer. Dr. Jason Tepper, one of the world's foremost experts in fetology, will then present the latest scientific findings on fetal development. Next, U.S. Congressman, Todd Oliver from New York will explain why he had to abandon his pro-choice position. Dr. Mary Gibbons, who has personally performed over five thousand abortions, will then tell us why she can no longer do another. And finally, I will give a brief overview on the tremendous strides the pro-life movement has made during this past year. I also plan to touch on where we would like to be one year from now."

As reporters continued to snap pictures and take notes my mind had a hard time wrestling with the inconceivable notion that within a matter of hours I would be addressing a crowd of over a million people.

"Bob Jacobs," Mrs. Gates continued, "has graciously accepted our invitation to speak and will discuss his conversion to pro-life as well as introduce our final and keynote speaker, Louise Ann Jordan. And at approximately 4:00 PM, at the conclusion of Miss Jordan's remarks, Bishop Stephen Hartman of Baltimore will lead everyone in a closing prayer.

"So as you can see, we have planned a very special program, one that we believe will put unprecedented pressure on our political leaders to seriously consider enacting a Human Life Amendment to our United States Constitution. With over a million people present, it will be hard for our Congress to ignore the message they will be hearing loud and clear from each one of our speakers."

Mrs. Gates, Jennifer Poole, Eddie Moss and I ate lunch in a small room at the other end of the floor at eleven-thirty during which we exchanged some last minute thoughts and by noon we made our way into another awaiting limo. By now the latest estimates of this vast sea of humanity that had descended on our nation's capital was put at over 1.2 million people.

I had never seen so many policemen as there were on hand, trying to make sure that the crowd kept orderly, but oddly enough, as we made our way toward the stage I no longer found myself worrying about the threat that had been made on my life less than twenty-four hours ago. By now my entire focus was on making sure that every word of my presentation would be packed with power and conviction.

As I looked out at all the people I silently asked God to make me His instrument and give me the words He wanted me to share today. After all, these millions of aborted babies had all been created in the image of God and no one felt their pain more than He did.

At precisely 1:30 PM Reverend Barry Simmons opened our rally with a prayer that was absolutely heavenly. As soon as he finished invoking God's presence at our meeting, I knew that God was in our midst. As each speaker made their way to the podium and delivered their wonderful messages in support of life, I became more and more confident that when my turn to speak came I would be that vessel that God would use to share His message.

Hearing over one million voices shout words of approval and listening to over two million hands applauding our words of encouragement was a sight I will never forget. By now it was almost a quarter after three, and as Bob Jacobs was introduced as our next speaker, the roar from the crowd was absolutely deafening. As he began to describe his journey from pro-choice to pro-life, and credited his conversion to a very special young lady named Louise Ann Jordan who, he said, had been his chief travel guide along the way, I was filled with pride.

From the day Bob Jacobs told America that he could no longer support abortion on demand, he had been vilified and labeled a traitor by just about every pro-choice group in America. But this man of principle never lashed back in kind at his detractors. Instead he used his energy to promote the sanctity of human life. Just before Bob Jacobs introduced me to the crowd he closed his speech in a most unforgettable way. His words are with me to this very day.

"Ladies and gentlemen," he said, pausing to wipe the sweat from his brow, "for years I supported a woman's right to obtain an abortion. Unfortunately my support was based upon a very flawed line of reasoning. First, to justify abortion I had to accept several false and misleading statements about what was growing inside a woman's womb. As Dr. Tepper has so marvelously demonstrated, by the end of the first trimester a fantastic explosion of human life has burst on the scene. Pro-choice advocates had indoctrinated me into believing that at twelve weeks an abortion is simply the removal of the tissues of a pregnancy. My friends we remove tissues from a Kleenex box not from a twelve-week pregnant woman's womb."

I knew that making a comparison like that must have been a shocking concept to some. But I'm sure that he meant it to be. And I could see, from the expression on my dad's face, as he stood just behind the sound equipment that had been erected to the side of the stage, that he was impressed. As Mr. Jacobs continued to speak I could hear the chant of "End Abortion Now" coming from a group of women who were standing just to my right.

"Next," he went on, "I was able to justify abortion by believing that it was actually an act of compassion, performed to help prevent an unwanted child from being born. After all, this was an unplanned and unwanted pregnancy. To force a woman to bear a child she didn't want would be cruel and almost inhuman. Only recently did I come to realize that this child would at best be unwanted by only one individual, the mother, but wanted by hundreds of thousands of couples who couldn't have children and would do anything to adopt this so-called 'unwanted child.' And the only inhuman act involved in an abortion is the fact that we are taking the life of another human being.

"The final major flaw in the argument of our opposition concerns the entire issue of choice. Once the dark veil was removed from all the other false and misleading pro-choice statements, the question of choice took on a very different meaning to me. It all boils down to this: Allowing a woman to choose abortion means that the child she is carrying is forced to choose death.

"And now it is my distinct and great pleasure to introduce to you a young lady who needs no introduction except to say - God bless you Louise Ann Jordan."

As I walked toward the podium, I prayed a very short prayer asking God to give me the courage to speak words that would make a lasting impression for all of eternity. At that very moment my heart was filled with boldness and a peace that I had never experienced before.

Armed for battle, I took a deep breath and began to address the million plus pro-life faithful.

It was an extraordinary sight looking at this gathering of people over three hundred times the size of the entire population of Palmerville.

"Good afternoon everybody," I began, as I heard my voice echoing over the vast sea of humanity that stood before me, "and thanks so much for taking a day out of your busy lives to spend it here with us as we join our voices to let America know that her practice of legal abortion is just about ready to be declared unconstitutional. As Sally Gates told us earlier, the landscape of America has been radically altered during this past year as millions of Americans have learned the sinister truth - that abortion kills babies."

The rush of adrenaline that I was now experiencing was simply incredible.

"The dark cloak of secrecy that the pro-choice movement has been able to work under these many years has been stripped away from them and they are now in total disarray. And just as God allows the sun to rise each day to take away the darkness, today thanks to your tireless efforts the dark evil secret of abortion has been exposed to the light of the truth. I believe that legalized abortion in America will soon be spoken of in the past tense. But just how soon that will happen depends to a large extent on the actions all of us here do when we return to our communities.

"But before I share with you some specific suggestions on what all of us can do to bring about the day when all human life will be guaranteed the right to life under our constitution, I would like to take a moment to remember all of God's children who have passed on since that infamous day of January 22, 1973.

"That day our high court made history by committing the greatest miscarriage of justice since America became a nation over two hundred years ago.

"Yesterday afternoon when we arrived at our hotel there was a letter waiting for me that contained a death threat on my life if I chose to speak at today's rally. At first I was frightened - just as someone meant me to be - and didn't know if I should speak. Not certain what to do, I began to pray. And during that prayer, something amazing happened."

I told them about my vision then, about the millions of empty graves and the caretaker who had told me that they were the graves of millions of aborted babies.

With that mention of millions of graves a collective gasp could be heard from the crowd. The symbolism of my vision was clearly unmistakable.

"After seeing that vision," I continued, "I knew that death threat or not I was going to speak at today's rally. And at this time I would like to ask all of you to pause for a moment of silence as we remember our thirty million fellow Americans who were sacrificed on the altar of 'inconvenience.' God did everything He could to create a safe and secure environment deep within their mother's womb. He supplied oxygen, nutrition and the child's first home. Sadly misguided judges and doctors decided to 'play' God and call these precious masterpieces of God's creative genius mistakes, and then sentenced them to a horrible death. May we all bow our heads and take a moment to silently remember these children of America's great holocaust."

It was the most remarkable sight I had ever seen. Over one million people standing tall and silently paying their respects to a very special group of kids whose future dreams turned into their worst nightmare. Over to the left, I saw a young man with a little girl on his shoulders waving an American flag. And as I looked to my right several people were holding up signs that read, "God is Pro-Life." For an entire sixty seconds time seemed to be placed in suspended animation as everyone reflected on the grim reality that thirty million members of humanity never had a chance to join the human race.

"Never again can we allow abortionists to use their weapons of mass destruction to destroy innocent life," I went on, my voice loud and clear. "Ladies and gentlemen the abortion chambers in America have served as our killing fields for far too long. It's now time to fix and mend our nation's constitution once again.

235

"Our country was founded on the principles of freedom and equal treatment for all. In order to preserve these ideals, great American heroes have sometimes had to risk everything to speak out against, what they perceived to be, major flaws in the very fabric of our most cherished founding document, the U.S. Constitution.

"It happened well over one hundred years ago when the evil institution of slavery was finally banished with the ratification of our XIII Amendment. On that day back in 1865, the inscription found on one of our nation's most cherished symbols of freedom, the Liberty Bell, for the first time rang true for millions of black Americans. Those precious words read, 'Proclaim liberty throughout all the land unto all the inhabitants thereof.'[54] Today I want to thank those heroes of yesteryear for their role in procuring freedom for millions. But I also want to thank you, the over one million new heroes here today, for taking up the battle cry once again of freedom and justice for all Americans. God bless you all.

"All of us can take great pride as we reflect on just how far we've come during this past year. Our battle cry has gone out from New York to California. It has echoed loud and clear throughout the corridors of Congress. Newspapers, with a pro-choice bias, have in many cases changed their position. And I need not remind you how two of Hollywood's biggest heartthrobs, Randy Roland and Ted Van Bolton, have joined our crusade for life.

"As you are all aware last month Senator Spencer Bonds, democrat from Nebraska, perhaps the most pro-choice member in Congress told Bob Jacobs that he could no longer support abortion on demand.

"And if all this great news were not enough I have one more exciting piece of news to share with all of you. Just this past Monday the National Alliance for Life received this incredible letter which reads:

Dear National Alliance for Life:

We the undersigned have personally performed over three hundred thousand abortions during our professional careers. We have also experienced the great joy in delivering over one hundred thousand healthy and beautiful babies.

As medical doctors we, more than any other human beings, have been given the privilege to explore the wonderful secrets deep within a mother's womb. But each of us, early on in our medical careers, began to realize how our approach to life in the womb had to be radically changed whenever we would move from the delivery room to the abortion chamber.

For example, when delivering a baby, it would sometimes be necessary for us to ask a nurse to hand us forceps so we could gently bring out the baby by its tiny head. But in other cases when we found ourselves inside the abortion chamber, we would ask a nurse to hand us forceps so we could crush the baby's head before removing it from the womb for disposal.

We all knew surgeons who specialized in the very delicate and time consuming surgery of reattaching severed hands. Unfortunately, we became experts in the brutal and deadly surgery of severing hands, arms and legs from over three hundred thousand of our patients. As we continued to rob the cradle of life, nightmares would constantly rob us of sleep. I think it became crystal clear to all of us, after years of taking innocent life, that if there were a literal Hell, then all of us knew we were going to spend eternity there once we died.

After staring at life within a mother's womb in its tiniest form and in its marvelously intricate detail, all of us knew beyond a shadow of a doubt that the only difference between those babies we delivered alive and those we chose to abort was that one mother wanted her child while the other didn't.

And one by one, each of us began to search our souls to find out where we had lost our way. We all, in one way or another, knew that we had become "doctors of death" and desperately needed some great physician to heal our hearts, which had almost become stone cold.

Today we have written this letter to thank God and the National Alliance for Life for helping each one of us abandon our abortion practices. While we can never bring back to life the three hundred thousand babies we aborted, we all have sworn allegiance to fight with all our might to one day make abortion again illegal. We are so grateful for being delivered from this kingdom of darkness and now gladly practice our profession in a world of light.

We would greatly appreciate it if you could read our letter at the July Rally for Life in D.C. God bless you all for the wonderful work you are doing in exposing this great evil called abortion.

> *Humbly yours,*
> *Fifty Abortionists Turned Pro-life*

As soon as I concluded reading this extraordinary letter, there was an explosion of cheers from the crowd that must have lasted for several minutes. I, too, was deeply moved to think that so many people were playing an active role in helping to change the very conscience of our nation.

"So you ask where do we go from here? Well some of you actually need to stay right here in our nation's capital. You see, in order to pass any amendment to our constitution we first need the approval of two-thirds of the House of Representatives and two-thirds of the Senate. But even with that level of support, our battle still doesn't end because we then must get the approval of the state legislators of three-fourths of the states. And that's where all of you come in.

"Today, I leave you with a simple but powerful strategy that, if diligently carried out, will allow us to see the end of this scourge called abortion within two years. First and foremost, we need every one of you to commit to pray daily for the remaining pro-choice legislators both here on the national front in Congress as well as locally in the communities that each of you live and work in. I don't understand much about how prayer works but this one thing I know: the more we storm heaven the more likely God will move in the hearts of those individuals we are asking Him to speak to. So I ask all of you to commit to pray daily for your political leaders who are still pro-choice.

"Second, I need all of you to write your congressman, senators, and local politicians letting them know where you stand on the issue of abortion. Please no form letters or postcards. Good old-fashioned hand written or typed personal letters or personal e-mails are a powerful way to let any politician know what's on the mind of his or her constituents. Letters are one of the most powerful communication tools around and they played a key role in helping

Congressman Todd Oliver from New York change his position on abortion. So please write, and write often.

"In closing I want to sincerely thank all of you for being defenders of the defenseless. I also want to thank you for being the voices for those who are not able to speak for themselves. And finally I want to thank all of you for being part of a very special group of dedicated pro-life individuals that I would like to refer to as 'Team Life.' And our new battle cry from now on will be 'Death to Death.' God bless all of you and please be sure to get home safely."

19

Death to Death

As I concluded my speech, the chant of "Death to Death" began to sound from every corner and every direction. For almost five solid minutes, the only three words that could be heard was the new motto I had just coined. The decibel level was so loud that my ears began to hurt but it was simply awesome. As the rally began to finally breakup, Eddie Moss came up to me and lifted his fist high in the air and shouted, "The beast of abortion has been dealt a death blow. Death to Death. Death to Death."

"Louise, you were incredible," Dad called out as he ran onto the platform to embrace me. Mother and Don were not far behind. We stood, clinging to one another while the electricity of the crowd continued to pulsate in every direction.

At seven o'clock we all made our way back to NAL headquarters and for the next three hours our family was treated like royalty. By ten dinner was ending but not our discussion.

Before Mrs. Gates agreed to let us return to our hotel, she asked my father if we could give her fifteen more minutes to allow her to outline the launch of NAL's exciting letter writing strategy. She told us that NAL believed that a massive letter writing campaign was going to be a key component behind the push to make Congress seriously consider supporting the passage of a constitutional amendment.

"Thanks to today's rally, Mr. Jordan," Mrs. Gates said as she walked over to where I was sitting and placed both her hands on my shoulders, "our elected officials almost certainly will be forced to take a fresh look at the entire abortion issue. And that's where our expanded letter writing initiative comes in."

With an excited look on her face, Jennifer told us that they were planning to kick off NAL's ambitious campaign by placing an open letter in tomorrow's daily editions of over one hundred of our nation's major newspapers. "And Louise," she said as she took out a sheet of paper from a folder in her briefcase, "because you've been such a driving force in making a letter like this possible I just want to read you what you'll be seeing when you pick up your morning newspaper tomorrow."

Dear America:

During this past year we are extremely gratified to know that many of you have taken a serious look at our country's policy of abortion on demand and concluded that it's wrong for our nation. And thankfully many of you have come to understand that the term pro-choice is in reality a code word for anti-life.

We at the National Alliance for Life have dedicated our entire existence to educating every American that abortion is always the wrong choice. Today we are very pleased to report that there has been a great shift in the way we as Americans view the sanctity of life. In fact many of you have decided to get personally involved by volunteering your time in working toward the day when all abortions will once again be outlawed.

In the early years, following the infamous Roe v. Wade U.S. Supreme Court decision that legalized abortion, several attempts were made to pass a constitutional amendment guaranteeing the unborn the right to life. Unfortunately those early attempts were unsuccessful largely because the pro-choice lobby was highly successful in seducing many in our nation into believing their deceptions and lies.

But thanks to a very special young lady named Louise Ann Jordan, who one day decided that principle had to take precedence over consequence, a crusade was launched exposing the dark world of abortion to the light of its own inhumanity. From a small high school classroom in upstate Palmerville, New York to yesterday's massive pro-life rally at our nation's capital, this courageous teen has shown all of us that life is sacred right from the moment of conception.

We believe that now is the right time for people of conscience all across this great land of ours to write their elected officials both in Congress and locally letting them know that the following Constitutional Amendment originally proposed in 1981 must now be passed in order to once and for all put an end to this most deadly form of child abuse – abortion:

"The National Right to Life Committee Unity Human Life Amendment"

Section 1: The right to life is a paramount and most fundamental right of a person.

Section 2: With respect to the right to life guaranteed to persons by the Fifth and Fourteenth Articles of Amendment to the Constitution, the word "person" applies to all human beings, irrespective of age, health, function, or condition of dependency, including their unborn offspring at every state of their biological development including fertilization.

Section 3: No unborn person shall be deprived of life by any person; provided, however, that nothing in this article shall prohibit a law allowing justification to be shown for only those medical procedures required to prevent the death of either the pregnant woman or her unborn offspring as long as such law requires every reasonable effort be made to preserve the life of each.

Section 4: Congress and the several States shall have power to enforce this article by appropriate legislation.[55]

May God richly bless you and please don't forget to write.

Sincerely,
National Alliance for Life

As Jennifer finished reading I became convinced that when this letter hit tomorrow's papers the days of abortion on demand, as the law of our land, would soon be numbered.

"Once tomorrow's papers are out," Jennifer said, now looking all business, "it will be critical that right to life volunteers make as many phone calls as possible encouraging people to write personal letters to their government leaders, at all levels, asking them to support the passage of our proposed amendment."

"And we have to remember that, while NAL and many other pro-life organizations will be working hard to influence Congress through the media, there still can be no substitute for good old-fashion personal letters," Mrs. Gates added.

As our limo drove us back to the hotel, I turned to my dad and said, "What a day. What a week. What a year!"

"And don't forget about tomorrow?" Mom said, as I settled back against her, looking at the moon as it stood high above our nation's capital, wondering at that moment what God must be thinking.

Well, tomorrow came quickly and so did the response that Jennifer and Mrs. Gates were hoping for. Our rally became front-page news in newspaper after newspaper. Some editorials even began to acknowledge that, for the first time since *Roe v. Wade*, there existed the distinct possibility that a constitutional amendment guaranteeing the unborn the right to life might become a reality.

Other editorials, written by pro-choice leaders, were predictably filled with attacks on our character and comments to the effect that any attempt to outlaw abortion would push the women's rights movement back one hundred years. However, several pro-choice newspapers had to quietly admit that a major shift in public opinion toward the pro-life view could no longer be denied.

This combination of our tireless efforts, one of our nation's largest rallies ever, a perfectly timed open letter, and a once openly hostile media now turned unbiased became the combustible fuel that ignited a fire that our pro-choice foes were powerless to extinguish. Over the next six months, the number of pro-choice supporters turning pro-life continued to grow. And the news continued to get even better. For the first time since *Roe v. Wade* became America's blueprint for genocide, abortions dropped significantly by over three hundred thousand during the latest twelve-month period. And this huge drop came about without any major changes to our abortion laws.

However, the avalanche of letters and e-mails that flooded our elected leader's offices since our July rally was something that our country had never experienced before. Numerous news stories were written to document this amazing series of events. But perhaps the best article describing the entire phenomenon was written by an old adversary turned ally - Sharon Brolly. Even though she was handicapped, having only one hand, Sharon Brolly was considered one of the most respected journalists in America.

The following is her article in its entirety. I believe it delightfully depicts our democracy functioning in a way that would have made our founding fathers proud. It is entitled simply, *Letters for Life.*

Last week, Congressman Gary Honeywell from Minnesota told me that he had never seen anything like it before. Congressman Honeywell loves the people in his district and prides himself on always sending every one of his constituents a personal reply to their letters. But over the past six months pride had to give way to reason, and for the first time in his eleven year career as a United States Congressman, Gary Honeywell resigned himself to sending out a form letter in response to the over forty thousand personal correspondences he has received on the issue of abortion.

Congressman Honeywell jokingly remarked to me that, based on the volume of mail he has received, that anyone would think that he was a rock star receiving fan mail. But on a more serious note those forty thousand letters were, in a sense, fan letters written by people pulling for and pleading to spare the lives of the over one million babies scheduled to be aborted in America during the next twelve months.

It's no secret that Gary Honeywell was one of the most ardent proponents of abortion on demand in the Congress. But when his office informed him, three months ago, that they had already received over twenty-five thousand letters asking him to push for the passage of a constitutional amendment banning abortion, he held a press conference announcing that he was taking the matter under serious review. By the time his office had logged in their forty thousandth pro-life letter, just two weeks ago, Congressman Honeywell announced that, after careful examination of all sides of the issue, he could no longer support abortion on demand.

Whether it was the fact that over one quarter of his constituents wrote him letters voicing their displeasure with his current position or whether, during his serious review of the issue, his conscience could no longer hide from the heartbreaking reality that abortion kills a fellow human being, we may never know. But the one thing we clearly know is that the pro-life juggernaut that has been sweeping our country has motivated millions of Americans to take the time and write their elected officials, asking them to help end the practice of abortion on demand.

Louise Ann Jordan, the seventeen-year-old high school student from Palmerville, New York, is regarded by almost everyone as the chief catalyst behind the events that have taken place in the fight to outlaw abortion. When Miss Jordan told the over one million pro-life faithful at last July's massive D.C. pro-life rally to go home and write their elected officials, asking them to support a constitutional amendment banning abortion, she set into motion a chain reaction that's still going on.

Moving stories from all across our land have already touched the hearts of many of us. Take, for example, the heart-warming story of Jerry Bedford. Jerry is a seventeen-year-old high school junior who just happens to attend the same high school that Louise Ann Jordan goes to in upstate New York. If ever there were a classic candidate to have been aborted prenatally, Jerry Bedford would surely have qualified.

Early on in Jerry's mom's pregnancy her doctor told her that if she chose to continue with the pregnancy there was a very high probability her child would be born with a severe handicap. He strongly recommended aborting the fetus. Jerry's parents were just about ready to end his life when at the last minute they had a change of heart. Sure enough when Jerry was delivered he was born with Down's Syndrome.

The life of this young man, who almost didn't make it "out alive," should serve as a testimony to handicapped young people everywhere. Last year Jerry was voted the most popular student at Palmerville High, and according to Louise Ann Jordan, has been one of her most trusted mentors, sharing valuable insights on various abortion issues. In response to Louise's appeal to send letters, Jerry came up with the idea of starting a fan club for unborn children facing potential abortion. One of Jerry and Louise's classmates, Jolene Tobin, decided to run with the idea and today, just six months after its inception, club President Tobin proudly boasts that her wildly popular teen club called "The Children of the Womb Fan Club" has chapters in all fifty states and a membership of just under half a million.

According to Jolene, club members have already written over two million letters, not only to elected government officials but to the editorial pages of just about every single newspaper in America. At club meetings, abstinence and adoption are two key topics. When I asked Jolene what makes this club such a huge hit with young people, she responded:

"When young people find out what abortion is really all about, they can't believe adults legalized the practice. Our club allows teens to take a stand and voice their opinions. And what we're finding out is that many young people have a deep respect for life from conception till death. Our club provides a forum for teens to have good clean fun and at the same time help make our society a better place for all of its citizens to live in."

Another phenomenon that's become quite popular, especially in the Midwest, is patterned after the old Tupperware motif. But this time instead of holding a Tupperware party designed to sell plastic storage containers, parties have been organized to write letters designed to help keep tiny innocent babies from being placed "in containers."

Back in October I was invited to one of these parties hosted by Jackie Taft of Chicago. Jackie's eleven-year-old daughter Tiffany designed the invitations on her computer. The following heart-warming invitation says it all:

You are cordially invited to attend,
"A Letters for Life Birthday Party."
Bring your appetite and we'll supply pen and paper.
Your influence counts!
So let's write our elected officials
Urging them to amend our Constitution to outlaw abortion.
Every child deserves a first birthday party.
Your letters can make that dream come true!

That night over thirty people thoroughly enjoyed themselves as they ate and wrote. By the end of the evening, Tiffany proudly announced that the number of sealed and stamped envelopes containing our letters totaled one hundred seven. I have to say that this was one party I will never forget. But perhaps the most touching letter writing story I've come across while researching this article came from the state of Ohio.

Don Berry is a fifty-seven-year-old corporate lawyer who lives in Cleveland, Ohio. One day, he and a client began to discuss the recent events surrounding the entire abortion controversy over lunch and the idea of "Barristers for Babies" was born.

Don Berry's organization is quite informal and not very large. It consists of about twenty-five Ohio lawyers who decided to pool their talents and launch a very targeted letter writing campaign aimed at just one individual - the very pro-choice senator from Ohio, Eric Faust. Each one of the "Barristers for Babies" lawyers decided to become a defense attorney for an unborn child. In that role each lawyer assisted their unborn clients in writing letters to Ohio Senator Eric Faust explaining why they had a right to live. During a two-month period Senator Faust must have received between twenty to thirty letters from each unborn child. The following are just three of the many actual letters that Senator Faust received.

Dear Senator Faust,

My name is Pamela Davis. I'm twelve weeks old today. I can't tie my shoe yet but I love to suck my thumb. I already go to the bathroom by myself but Aunt Mary told my mom it won't be too long before she will have to potty train me. Uncle John told dad he found the most adorable crib for me but my father told him that a crib wouldn't be necessary since they were planning to abort me next week. Please don't let them end my life. I was so looking forward to spending my first night home from the hospital surrounded by all my Walt Disney friends.

> *Sincerely,*
> *Baby Pamela*

Dear Senator Faust,

My name is Jack Morris. I'm sixteen weeks old today. Someone took a picture of me going for a swim yesterday. The amniotic fluid was just a tad warm but I enjoyed the exercise. I hope to one day try out for the gymnastics team in high school but for now I'm content doing my somersaults inside my very own private training grounds. I heard a rumor that next week my parents were going to withdraw my permit to enter the human race. Please tell me it isn't true. I had dreams of one day going to medical school to become a baby doctor.

> *Sincerely,*
> *Baby Jack*

Dear Senator Faust,

My name is Judy Roberts. I'm twenty weeks old today. My mom just brought me back from my five-month checkup and her doctor told her that I appear to have a physical deformity. Despite the fact that I have a very healthy heart that has already recorded over twenty million beats they are thinking of ending my life. If they could only know that my defect is the same one that award-winning journalist Sharon Brolly was born with - one hand!

> *Sincerely,*
> *Baby Judy*

In a way I'm kind of grateful that when I was born our medical technology wasn't advanced enough to pinpoint birth defects prenatally as accurately as they can today. Because if doctors could and if abortion were legal back then, I might not have had the privilege of writing this article.

Estimates are that over fifty million individual "Letters for Life" have been written since the D.C. pro-life rally this past July. And by the way Senator Eric Faust is reviewing his pro-choice position and plans to let America know if babies like Pamela, Jack and Judy can count on his support.

Sharon Brolly's article not only colorfully described the amazing events of the past six months but also captured the spirit behind the phenomenon. And in early March, just two weeks after Ms. Brolly's article was published, *Barristers for Babies* got the answer they were looking for as Ohio Senator Eric Faust publicly announced that he could no longer support abortion on demand.

If anyone ever doubted that a well-written letter couldn't make a difference then please listen to the closing words from Senator Faust's press conference:

"As I was preparing my remarks last night, a close friend asked me what finally convinced me to change my stance on abortion. Well, I told him that for years I never really listened to what the pro-life side had to say. I had made up my mind that abortion was a necessary fact of life and nobody was going to get me to change my opinion.

"But back in November I started getting hundreds of letters from unborn babies from all across our state. As I read the first few I thought that this must be some kind of silly publicity stunt. However, I noticed that every single letter came typed on the letterheads of some of our most prestigious legal firms in the state. With each day's mail came a batch of about twenty letters sharing some amazing facts and stories from life inside the womb. It was as if these babies had already received their law degrees and were now defending their own right to live by advancing the most thought provoking arguments I had ever heard. Well, by the time I had read about a hundred of these letters I knew that I had to give these babies their day in court.

"After extensive examination of all the issues and some very personal soul searching, I can no longer in good conscience support abortion on demand and I'm now prepared to throw my complete support behind the proposed National Right to Life Committee Unity Human Life Amendment."

It was now just a little over eighteen months since my show and tell presentation at Palmerville High had set into motion the incredible events that literally helped change the conscience of a nation. *Operation Sally* had succeeded in what it had set out to accomplish on every one of its agenda items. Americans now knew beyond a shadow of a doubt that abortion kills babies. And mothers contemplating abortion also knew that pro-life groups were willing to stand by them, helping them in every way to have their babies. Yes these mothers were loved too.

On the adoption front, the news was equally encouraging. And, of course, undergirding everything we did was prayer. During the past year alone an additional twenty thousand American babies were put up for adoption. The only question that remained was did we have enough support to pass our amendment?

The good news was that we had more than enough votes to have the amendment clear Congress. As of last count, Mrs. Gates calculated that three hundred six of the four hundred thirty-five House members were ready to support our amendment. That meant that a full seventy percent of these congressmen were on our side. While, in the Senate, the numbers were even more impressive with a total of seventy-three saying they would back us. With this level of support, we clearly exceeded the two-thirds requirement needed to send the amendment out to the state legislators.

Eric Seaver, NAL's head of Governmental Legislation and Affairs, said that on the state side he was certain that thirty-six states would support the amendment but that he knew that thirty-eight states had to vote in the affirmative for abortion to be declared unconstitutional. Of the remaining fourteen, he felt that seven would still vote to keep abortion legal, four were still on the fence and the other three were leaning toward passing the amendment. Eric felt that, during the next two months, we needed to work extra hard to ensure that the three leaning states of Vermont, Texas and Arizona, when the time for a vote came, would not only lean but fall solidly in the pro-life camp.

During April and May, NAL sponsored pro-life rallies in Vermont, Texas and Arizona. While the turnout was nowhere near the million plus that attended our D.C. rally, we drew fifty thousand in Vermont, one hundred thousand in Arizona and almost two hundred thousand in Texas. I was privileged to speak at the rallies in Vermont and Arizona and the Texas crowd was treated to hearing Jolene Tobin, President of *The Children of the Womb Fan Club* who, in her closing remarks with her usual flair for the dramatic, left her audience spellbound as she described the brave new world that could be ushered in if abortion were to remain legal.

"In closing I would like to leave you with something to think about," she told them. "Have you ever thought about just how valuable the heart of an unborn child is? Well it's priceless. Consider where our medical technology is taking us. I believe that one day in the not too distant future, we may see doctors performing life saving heart transplants between babies scheduled for late term abortions and newborns born with severely defective hearts. After all, the aborted baby's heart will be of no use to him once he is killed. Why not take his perfectly functioning heart and use it to save the life of a newborn whose heart is badly failing.

"This procedure may be unethical today, but before 1973, it was also considered highly unethical to abort a baby; as well as illegal in most states. And if surgery is successful, one can only conclude that doctors have performed a human heart transplant between two tiny persons. But the shocking reality is that we had to kill one person to save the life of the other."

Volunteers continued to write letters and share literature in Texas, Vermont and Arizona expressing such deep compassion and conviction that leaning hearts became touched hearts. By the beginning of July, Eric Seaver announced, that based on his contacts in these three states, we could now safely put them in the solid support column, bringing the number of states willing to support our proposed amendment to thirty-nine.

In early June, Congress proposed adopting the National Right to Life Committee Unity Human Life Amendment as our nation's twenty-eighth Amendment to our U.S. Constitution. By the time the vote was taken three hundred twelve House members and seventy-four U.S. Senators voted to adopt the amendment. We now had only one hurdle to go - state ratification.

By now almost two full years had passed since I got involved in the right to life movement. During that time I've learned many valuable lessons and met a lot of wonderful people. One lesson that's proved of great help, not only in our fight to ban abortion, but in many personal areas of my own life, is the power of prayer.

Just how does prayer work? Well, that's still a mystery to me. But the one thing I'm certain about is that without God working behind the scenes we could never have come so far.

And as I continued to talk to God, He impressed upon me that the time for traveling around the country was over. Now was the time for prayer.

During the next two months, millions of the other pro-life faithful did likewise and prayer became the silent talk of the land. I believe as a result of this special season of prayer, on September 5, 2000, just eighty-eight days after Congress proposed the National Right to Life Committee Unity Human Life Amendment, state ratification became a reality and abortion on demand was ruled unconstitutional. God even allowed the date of ratification to prove significant. For it was exactly two years earlier, on September 5, 1998, that I aborted Baby Sally.

Back in 1776, fifty-six men placed their signatures on our nation's founding document, the Declaration of Independence. Today it gives me great pleasure to let children of the womb in all fifty states know that they too are now part of the dream those courageous men staked their lives on. Finally, those magnificent words penned over two hundred years ago can now ring true for all Americans:

"We hold these Truths to be self-evident, that all Men are created equal, that they are endowed by their Creator with certain unalienable Rights, that among these are Life, Liberty, and the Pursuit of Happiness..."[56]

And since creation clearly occurs at conception, equality must begin there too. And thank God our United States Constitution now affirms this self-evident truth.

SOURCE NOTES

Chapter 1

1. Joe S. McIlhaney Jr., M.D., Why Condoms Aren't Safe (Colorado Springs: Focus on the Family, 1993), p. 6.

Chapter 2

2. John C. Willke & Barbara H. Willke, Why Can't We Love Them Both (Cincinnati: Hayes Publishing, 1997), p. 76.

3. Milestones of Early Life (Snowflake, Arizona: Heritage House '76).

4. John C. Willke & Barbara H. Willke, Why Can't We Love Them Both (Cincinnati: Hayes Publishing, 1997), p. 80.

Chapter 3

5. John C. Willke & Barbara H. Willke, Why Can't We Love Them Both (Cincinnati: Hayes Publishing, 1997).

6. Ibid., Pictures in the back of book.

7. Ibid., p. 76.

8. Ibid., p. 77.

9. Ibid., p. 76.

10. Milestones of Early Life (Snowflake, Arizona: Heritage House '76).

11. John C. Willke & Barbara H. Willke, Why Can't We Love Them Both (Cincinnati: Hayes Publishing, 1997), p. 80.

12. Ibid., p. 80.

Chapter 4

13. Randy Alcorn, Pro Life Answers to Pro Choice Arguments (Portland, Oregon: Multnomah Publishers, 1994), p. 93.

Chapter 5

14. Randy Alcorn, Pro Life Answers to Pro Choice Arguments (Portland, Oregon: Multnomah Publishers, 1994), p. 173.

Chapter 6

15. John C. Willke & Barbara H. Willke, Why Can't We Love Them Both (Cincinnati: Hayes Publishing, 1997), p. 116.

16. Ibid., p. 116.

Chapter 7

17. Curt Blattman, The Challenge (Shippensburg, PA: Companion Press, 1991), p. 95.

18. Randy Alcorn, Pro Life Answers to Pro Choice Arguments (Portland, Oregon: Multnomah Publishers, 1994), pp. 172-173.

19. Ibid., p. 171.

Chapter 9

20. Curt Blattman, The Challenge (Shippensburg, PA: Companion Press, 1991), p. 42.

21. John C. Willke & Barbara H. Willke, Why Can't We Love Them Both (Cincinnati: Hayes Publishing, 1997), pp. 112-113.

Chapter 10

22. Psalm 139:14 (KJV).

Chapter 11

23. Roe v. Wade, 410 U.S. 113 (1973).

24. Milestones of Early Life (Snowflake, Arizona: Heritage House '76).

25. Gary Bergel, When You Were Formed In Secret (Intercessors for America, 1998), pp. I-7 & I-8. Reprinted by permission of Intercessors for America. For additional prayer helps, visit http://www.ifapray.org, www.yifa.org, or call 1-800-USA-PRAY (872-7729).

26. Milestones of Early Life (Snowflake, Arizona: Heritage House '76).

27. Ibid.

28. John C. Willke & Barbara H. Willke, Why Can't We Love Them Both (Cincinnati: Hayes Publishing, 1997), p. 79.

29. Gary Bergel, When You Were Formed In Secret (Intercessors for America, 1998), pp. I-8 & I-9. Reprinted by permission of Intercessors for America. For additional prayer helps, visit

http://www.ifapray.org, www.yifa.org, or call 1-800-USA-PRAY (872-7729).

30. Milestones of Early Life (Snowflake, Arizona: Heritage House '76).

31. The First Nine Months (Colorado Springs: Focus on the Family, 1993), p. 5.

32. Milestones of Early Life (Snowflake, Arizona: Heritage House '76).

33. Ibid.

34. Ibid.

35. Ibid.

36. Gary Bergel, When You Were Formed In Secret (Intercessors for America, 1998), p. I-8. Reprinted by permission of Intercessors for America. For additional prayer helps, visit http://www.ifapray.org, www.yifa.org, or call 1-800-USA-PRAY (872-7729).

37. John C. Willke & Barbara H. Willke, Why Can't We Love Them Both (Cincinnati: Hayes Publishing, 1997), p. 81.

38. Ibid., p. 79.

39. Ibid., pp. 82-83.

Chapter 12

40. Matthew 1:18 (KJV).

41. Matthew 1:20-21 (KJV).

Chapter 13

42. Roe v. Wade, 410 U.S. 113 (1973).

43. Roe v. Wade, 410 U.S. 113 (1973).

44. Dred Scott, Plaintiff In Error, v. John F. A. Sandford, 60 U.S. 393, 19 How. 393, 15 L.Ed. 691

45. The First Nine Months (Colorado Springs: Focus on the Family, 1993), p. 5.

46. John C. Willke & Barbara H. Willke, Why Can't We Love Them Both (Cincinnati: Hayes Publishing, 1997), p. 76.

47. Milestones of Early Life (Snowflake, Arizona: Heritage House '76).

48. Ibid.

49. Gary Bergel, When You Were Formed In Secret (Intercessors for America, 1998), p. I-7. Reprinted by permission of Intercessors for America. For additional prayer helps, visit http://www.ifapray.org, www.yifa.org, or call 1-800-USA-PRAY (872-7729).

50. Milestones of Early Life (Snowflake, Arizona: Heritage House '76).

Chapter 15

51. Declaration of Independence.

Chapter 16

52. Roe v. Wade, 410 U.S. 113 (1973).

53. Psalm 127:3 (KJV).

Chapter 18

54. Leviticus 25:10 (KJV).

Chapter 19

55. John C. Willke & Barbara H. Willke, Why Can't We Love Them Both (Cincinnati: Hayes Publishing, 1997), p. 37.

56. Declaration of Independence.

About The Author

Curt Blattman is a graduate of Princeton University and New York University Graduate School of Business. A successful New York City banker, his passion is to be an advocate for those millions of unborn children unable to defend their right to life.

Printed in the United States
15701LVS00004B/205-354